MY FRIENDS THE MACLEANS

Published by
MACMILLAN & CO LTD
Little Essex Street London W C 2
and also at Bombay Calcutta and Madras

Macmillan South Africa (Publishers) Pty Ltd Johannesburg

The Macmillan Company of Australia Pty Ltd Melbourne

The Macmillan Company of Canada Ltd Toronto

PRINTED IN GREAT BRITAIN

MY
FRIENDS
THE MACLEANS

JANE DUNCAN

MACMILLAN
London · Melbourne · Toronto
1967

FOR ALAN AND ROBIN AND
ANOTHER OF THE ILK

PART ONE

'But these are all lies.'

I FIRST met Rob and Marion Maclean in December of 1949 when my husband and I visited for the first time the West Indian island of St. Jago and from the moment of that first meeting I had a liking for Marion. There was a great deal in our backgrounds to bring the Macleans, my husband and me together for we were all Scots — a notoriously clannish race — met together four thousand miles from home on the hard, sun-baked earth of a tropical island. Apart from this wide common ground of race, Rob Maclean, like my husband, was an engineer by profession and Marion, like myself, came of farming stock although her people had been wealthier than mine, farming some of the lush land of Lowland Scotland instead of the hard rock of a hill in Ross-shire that my family tried to cultivate. Marion and Rob were some ten years older than we were. At this time, my husband and I were thirty-nine and Marion, I think, was about fifty while Rob was probably a little more.

Being a Scottish Highlander, I have the characteristic long memory of my race so that, mentally, I trail behind me a complex tangled web of association and near-superstition. I try very hard to be realistic but, in spite of this, I am easily led away into enchantment and it is obvious to me now that, in those early days, I saw Marion Maclean in an enchanted light.

In the part of Ross where I was brought up, on a little croft called Reachfar near the small fishing port of Achcraggan, the figure 7 had a superstitious significance. The fishing people said that every seventh wave of the incoming tide was bigger than the six that preceded it; the people in general said that the seventh child of a seventh child was endowed with Second Sight. My own grandmother had been such a seventh child of a seventh child and was locally reputed to be a witch. And the people believed too in Shakespeare's seven ages of man, that in every seventh year people underwent a major physical change. One of the first things that I learned about Marion Maclean was that she had seven sons.

It is difficult to describe the aura that this fact cast about her in my mind; this fact together with the fact that, although she and I had race and a country upbringing in common, the remainder of the main outline of her life was as different from mine as it could possibly be. She had married before she was twenty and I had never thought seriously about marriage until I was thirty-five; she had seven sons and I, following an accident during my first pregnancy, had lost my child and was incapable of having another. It seemed to me that Marion Maclean was exactly the woman I should have liked to be had not the ebb and flow of life decreed differently.

In December of 1949, I thought that we were paying an ephemeral visit to St. Jago and that, after January of 1950, we might probably never again see the Macleans but sometimes I think that the phrase 'we live our lives' is entirely erroneous and that it should read instead 'our lives live us'. It seems sometimes that we are not actively living our time here on earth but passively existing, merely, as channels through which the life force makes its mysterious way out of the past and on into the future, sometimes sweeping us along over part of its course, sometimes beaching us on a shoal at the side of the main stream like so many withered leaves. Instead of leaving St. Jago for good in January of 1950, the stream of life carried my husband and me back there in June of that year and in July of 1952 we were still there.

4

From the moment of that first landing in the island the social initiative in our lives seemed to be taken away from us in the pleasantest possible way. Travelling on the same aeroplane from London with us were Sir Ian Dulac and Sandy Maclean, the seventh son of Rob and Marion, who was only eight at the time. Aeronautics have made gigantic strides since 1949. Those were the days of aircraft names like 'Star Tiger' and 'Star Panther' which had an unromantic habit of disintegrating in mid-air and disappearing without trace and Sir Ian and Sandy were travelling by air without sanction and, indeed, contrary to the orders of Madame Dulac, Sir Ian's redoubtable mother and Marion and Rob, Sandy's parents. At St. Jago Bay airport, my husband and I were co-opted by our new friends Sir Ian and Sandy to help them take the shock of the parental wrath and in this simple way the whole course of our lives was changed.

Over a drink at the hotel, Madame Dulac discovered that we were Scots, that I had known as a child a man with whom she had danced in Edinburgh some sixty years before whereupon she turned to the hotel-owner, a Portuguese known as 'Ike' and said: 'Mr. and Mrs. Alexander won't be staying in this gin palace of yours. They are coming to Paradise.'

At that time Madame Dulac's age was always referred to as 'somewhere around the eighties' while her son Sir Ian's age was 'somewhere in his sixties' but I have never known the accurate age of either. Madame had come to the island some sixty years before, from Scotland, as a young bride and throughout those sixty years she seemed to have concentrated all her powers on getting her own way in everything so that, by the time I met her as a widow 'somewhere around the eighties', she was a tight round little bundle of personal force that rolled, albeit in a helpful, hospitable well-intentioned way, over everything and everybody and she laid down the social law for the entire white population of the island.

5

By July of 1950, my husband and I were installed in Guinea Corner, a small Georgian house that was part of the Dulacs' vast estate of Paradise and which lay about a mile from the house of Olympus where the Macleans lived. Rob Maclean, who had come to the island in, I think, 1919 as a young engineer to work in the Paradise sugar factory, had risen in the course of some thirty years to become manager of the whole vast enterprise of the estate and it was not long before we became aware that Madame, from a business aspect, was no more than a figure-head while Sir Ian, a retired soldier and colonial administrator, made no bones about the facts that sugar-milling was a sticky mess and rum-distilling a stinking process with neither of which he chose to concern himself. From a business point of view, Rob Maclean was Paradise.

While Sir Ian rode about the estate, dabbled in local politics, sat on the magistrate's bench and aired his views at meetings of the Chamber of Commerce and meetings of the Yacht Club Committee, Madame sat in the Great House of Paradise interfering in the affairs of everybody and everything from the new tuberculosis ward at the hospital to the reason why her cook's grand-daughter had had an illegitimate child and with all this benevolent interference she required a certain amount of help. Before my arrival, Marion Maclean had been her lady-in-waiting for, although there were some six other European women on the estate — wives of chemists and agronomists — Madame had her own peculiar views as to the qualifications required in her attendants and these views rendered Mrs. Murphy from Ireland and Mrs. Grey and Mrs. Cranston from England unsuitable. It is the fact that I was straight away deemed suitably qualified to send out circulars asking for contributions to the tuberculosis fund that makes me think that Madame was guided by her choice of her ladies-in-waiting by racialistic bias but, however that may be, by the end of 1950, Marion and I were sister attendants on Madame,

6

co-operating closely to keep her eccentricities of all kinds within near-reasonable bounds.

While Marion and I co-operated over Madame, Rob Maclean and my husband — Alexander Alexander, familiarly known as 'Twice' — co-operated over the sugar-milling and rum-distilling plant and the four of us swam happily along, presenting a united front to the wilder eccentricities of Madame and Sir Ian and to the periodic uproars of disagreement among the white staff in the bungalows of the Estate Compound.

For two years, I saw more of Rob and Marion Maclean and especially of Marion than I did of any other people on the estate or in St. Jago. If anyone had asked me who I knew best in the island at this time, I should certainly have named the Macleans. It was only later that I realised that, either because of a casual unstudied acceptance of what seemed to be the familiar or because of my almost enchanted admiration for Marion, I knew nothing of the Macleans at all.

During my first eighteen months at Paradise, I had met none of the Maclean boys except Sandy, the youngest, for all the others were in Scotland. According to Sir Ian, they were all clever boys. Donald, the eldest of them, was a veterinary surgeon in Edinburgh, I knew and the second son was an engineer while the others were in various stages of their education at school and university and mostly training as engineers, following in the footsteps of their father. Not having met the boys, I did not see them clearly as personalities and the mist that hung around them in my mind was intensified by Sandy's habit of referring to them not by name but as 'my topmost brother' or 'our Number Four'. For me, six of the seven sons did not exist as people. With the exception of Sandy, the boys were no more than a vague nimbus, six segments of the magic circle of seven that surrounded Marion and, strangely, this nimbus did not encircle Rob, their father. Rob, if I thought of him as a

7

person at all which I doubt, was in my mind 'another Scots engineer, like Twice and all the rest of them', for most Scots engineers have a way of being engineers first with all other characteristics such as being fond of food, women or music coming a very poor second.

At the end of 1951, however, I made the acquaintance of the Macleans' third son, Roderick — Roddy for short or, in the parlance of Sandy 'our Number Three' and, as at the turn of a kaleidoscope, the whole cosy pattern of the Maclean family in my mind disintegrated. Roddy was a strikingly handsome young man of twenty-three who did not resemble either of his parents but who, when I first met him without knowing him to be their son, had had about him an air vaguely familiar. Rob Maclean, his father, was a big man, well over six feet in height, very heavily built, with a big squarish head covered with rough sandy-grey hair and round eyes in a squarish face that was not tanned but covered all over with freckles joined together. More than anything, he looked like an outsize teddy-bear. Marion was, like myself, very typical of her race and many people said that there was a resemblance between us but this resemblance was purely racial, I think. Marion was sparely built, not as tall as my five feet nine inches, with dark brown hair that showed none of the grey that mine showed and blue-grey eyes. Roddy had the sturdy build of his father but in him the rough sandy-grey hair was jet black and springy and, instead of the round hazel eyes of his father, he had eyes larger, less round in shape and of a rich gleaming brown. Roddy always made me think of some reckless adventurer of a sea-going kind, a pirate or a buccaneer, a rover in wild free places. I thought of him in this way before I knew anything about him because the daring roving spirit seemed to emanate from him, from his very flesh, every time I saw him. It may be that I have inherited something of my grandmother's Second Sight but I do not think so, for my picture of Roddy as a buccaneer with a

8

dagger in his hat was a tidy sentimental affair compared
with the trail of carnage that he blazed across our smug
little lives in the Paradise valley, in seven short months,
between December of 1951 and July of 1952.

He arrived in the island ostensibly a qualified engineer,
after five years at Glasgow University and in workshops on
the Clyde but, at the end of seven months, it was discovered
that, while in Glasgow, he had not studied engineering at
all, but had read English and arts subjects generally instead, while sending faked reports of his studies home to
St. Jago. In the course of his seven months in the island,
before this discovery was made, he caused much anxiety of
various kinds, in the main by getting a negro girl called
Lucy Freeman pregnant while at the same time getting
himself engaged to marry Dee Andrews, an English girl
who was staying with Twice and me for a holiday. Indeed,
at the end of seven months, Roddy had made St. Jago too
hot to hold him and this is the point where he impinged on
my personal life for, when he was finally on the run, a
fugitive from the combined wrath of his father and Sir
Ian, it was to me at Guinea Corner that he came for temporary sanctuary.

That he came to me may seem, at first glance, to be
curious for, socially speaking, I was the last person to whom
Roddy should have come after behaving so badly to my
young guest Dee Andrews but there are reasons that lie
deeper than social reasons. When Roddy came to me that
July day, he knew that the society of Paradise was em-
battled against him and he made his appeal to me on a
deeper level.

Another thing that Roddy had done during his mis-spent
— from his parents' point of view — years in Glasgow was
to write a book, a novel entitled *But Not For Love*, which
had been very well received by the more knowledgeable
critics. It was written under a pen-name and I bought and
read it, unaware of Roddy's authorship of it and chanced

to speak in praise of it in his hearing. At that time, he did not tell me that he had written the book but when the hunt was up and he was about to ship as a hand on a lumber-boat leaving the island, it was to Guinea Corner that he came to wait for his brother Sandy to bring him his passport and some manuscripts from his room at Olympus.

In the heat of the afternoon, I was lying on the sofa in the drawing-room, re-reading *But Not For Love* because of my interest in the discovery that it had been written by Roddy when he himself suddenly appeared at the open french window.

'Why, hello,' I said.

'Quietly does it,' he told me, coming into the room and sitting in a chair on the other side of the window from my sofa. 'You see before you a fugitive on the run.'

Out of the shaded dimness, his teeth flashed a smile, his eyes gleamed under the ruffled shock of black hair and his brown skin shone with sweat above the soiled white shirt that stuck to his chest. This was a bold, reckless young man, a creature with only the barest veneer of so-called civilisation, maybe, but vitality, courage and gaiety sparkled all about him, seeming to light with a bright glow the dim corner where he had sat down, seeming to make the humid inert air vibrate with energy.

'So well you might be on the run,' I said but I could not help smiling at him. 'What are you doing here?' My attempt at severity was not a success. 'How did you *get* here, anyway?'

'Got a lift on a truck and then walked in through the cane. I didn't want to risk coming in by car.'

'Why come here at all? Especially here?'

'This is the last place they'll look for me,' he told me with an impudent grin. 'Where's Dee?'

'Upstairs. It's all right,' I reassured him. 'She is in bed with a cold.'

'Good.'

'What have you come for?'

'To meet the kid — Sandy. He hasn't been here?'

'No.'

'He is bringing me a suitcase from the house.'

'What made you choose to meet him here?'

He reached a long arm across to my sofa and picked up *But Not For Love.* 'This. I suppose you know it's mine?'

'Yes. Dee told me last night.'

He looked down at the book. 'I came because of this and because you gave me the keenest pleasure I have ever known when I saw you reading it on the ship and you said it was good. You said it was good in the right way and for the right reasons — I mean my way and my reasons. That made me think you wouldn't sell me down the river today.'

'I won't sell you down the river, Roddy. What are your plans?'

'There's a lumber-boat sailing for the Gulf tonight— I've shipped on her as a hand. I've sailed that way before. It's cheap and I like it.'

'You are making for the States?'

'Yes.'

'Your passport?'

'It's in order, visa and all. It's among the stuff the kid is bringing.'

'Money, Roddy? Dollars?'

'I'm all right. That first slim volume — ' he nodded with a smile at the book ' — has hit the best-selling lists in the States as well as in England.'

He looked so gaily on top of his world that I felt I must bring its reality and intractability to his notice. 'I suppose I ought to raise a general alarm about your being here.'

'All you have to do is call your yard boy,' he said laughing and I suddenly began to wonder why someone as bold and reckless as he was should be running away like this.

'How did you know that today was the day to clear out?' I asked.

'The kid 'phoned me at the office that Sir Ian was at the house talking about me and Lucy Freeman and horse whips so I told him to meet me here with the locked suitcase from under my bed.'

'Roddy,' I said, holding the book between my hands, 'with this book to your credit, why don't you stand your ground and face things out? You are not the first man to get a girl into trouble as it is called and you won't be the last and —'

'Just to clear the ground,' he interrupted me, 'I am not responsible for Lucy's trouble. That is the result of an encounter she had with a seaman in Victoria Court. Paradise office doesn't know that Lucy spends most of her nights in Victoria Court.'

'But you *could* have been responsible?'

He grinned at me. 'As my Glasgow landlady says: "If you go among the crows you must be ready to be shot at." Yes, the infant could have been mine, I suppose.'

'Anyway, she has had a miscarriage.'

'I knew she was doing her best about that.'

'Roddy, why are you running away like this?' I asked point blank, for I felt that he was trying to lead me away from this question and I was very much more wary of Roddy now than I had been formerly.

'Because I am a coward,' he said.

'Look here,' I said angrily, 'the least you can do is be honest with me!'

His face changed, became naked, vulnerable, as if he had allowed a protective mask to drop from it. 'It is true,' he said. 'I am a coward — not a coward-and-a-bounder-by-gad-God-dammit—' he parodied the voice of Sir Ian '— perhaps, but I am cowardly about a scene with my father. I don't want it to happen. If my father and Sir Ian came at me in a horse-whipping frame of mind, somebody might get hurt. I am younger and more agile than they are. And that would be a pity.' As he spoke, his jaw tightened, cording the muscles in his neck and I knew that Roddy, with his temper out of control, would be a formidable adversary.

'It's better to get out and let everybody cool down,' he ended.

'But this?' I held up the book. 'If you tell them about this?'

'The damage would be done before I could get round to it.'

Another change came over him. He seemed to withdraw into himself, even to lose physical colour, as if his vivid eyes and brilliant hair were merging away into the dim shadow, where he sat. 'I have been trying to tell my people about that book ever since I came home in December. I've never got round to it. I've missed my chance now.' He stared at me, frowning, as if he were trying to come to a decision. 'Have you a cigarette to spare?' he said then.

I gave him the cigarette and, as he struck the match, he seemed to make up his mind. 'All this is difficult to explain, Missis Janet. You see, when I wanted to read English at the university, I was asked at home if I wanted to be a bloody schoolmaster. I didn't. I wanted to be a bloody poet but I had enough sense not to say that. I went to university and read English at the parental expense for five years. I reckoned that if they had the money for me to do what *they* wanted, which was engineering, the same money would do for what *I* wanted. The chances are that I shall have to go on living with me for a long time and with all due respect to Twice, I find engineers pretty boring.'

He gave me his impudent grin again and I felt that, very subtly, he was beginning to lead me away from the main issue once more and it irritated me that this six feet of vibrant blood, bone and muscle should be as elusive as a brown trout in a Scottish stream. I am not quick of wit but I think I have a certain tenacity.

'I still think' I said in the voice that Twice calls 'hammering' and in which I myself could hear the beat of persistence, 'that if you told your people about this book—'

He expelled a long sigh, as if giving up. 'In the light of all that has happened,' he said, 'you probably think that I have got cheek for anything. I haven't. Not about my writing.' He pulled his shoulders forward, tucked his elbows close to his sides and he made me think of myself scribbling at the writing-table when Twice came in unexpectedly and I hid the papers under the blotter, screening them, protecting them while, physically, I seemed to feel myself shrivel and grow smaller as I shrank towards the core of myself. 'My writing makes a coward out of me, a real coward,' Roddy went on, talking more to himself now than to me. 'It is the fear that they will laugh or the look of non-comprehension on their faces or with that—' he pointed to the book I held '—the fear of how they will try to value it, ask how much money I got for it and when I am going to get on and write another one. I—I get *craven* at the thought of talking to them about it, of seeing them pick it over as if it were some doubtful fish lying on a slab!' His voice shook as he spoke the last words but with a physical jerk he broke away from the thoughts he had spoken aloud and said: 'God, I wish that kid would come!'

'When does your boat sail?'

'Six.'

'There's time yet.'

I passed my cigarettes to him, noticed that his hand trembled as he took one and now I felt ashamed that I had forced him into this exposure of himself and I also felt embarrassed, as we tend to feel when someone steps outside of the mental image we have held of him. It was easier for me to sit opposite and talk to the devil-may-care Roddy I had always known and to wait until I was alone before

14

trying to encompass this new image that had emerged.

'What in the world made you propose to Dee Andrews?' I asked him after a short silence.

'I didn't.'

'Didn't?'

'No. It was her idea. She suggested it and I was brought up to be a little gentleman after all but please believe me when I say that it was a marriage that I never intended to take place.'

His strong white teeth showed in a mischievous grin and the Roddy I had thought I knew was before me again but after a second he became grave. 'That poor brat is in the hell's own muddle, Missis Janet. I've meant to tell you this before but it's a bit difficult and I hadn't the guts to tell you but I'll tell you now. If you throw me out, it doesn't matter. I'm on my way anyhow.' He grinned again, became grave again. 'That girl is a-sexual, Missis Janet — maybe a Lesbian like that Denholm bean-pole down at the Peak — but a-sexual anyway.'

'I know,' I said, hoping to astonish him and succeeding.

'You know?'

My satisfaction was only momentary. 'Yes, now. But I didn't know until Cousin Emmie drew a diagram for me last night,' I confessed. 'I think she drew a diagram for Dee too — a diagram of Dee for Dee.'

'That was what was needed but I hadn't the guts to do it,' Roddy said.

'Anyway, Dee is now going in with Isobel Denholm on the Mount Melody project.'

'Dear Heaven! What goings-on here in Paradise!' said Roddy and began to laugh uproariously.

'Hush! She is upstairs, remember.'

'Think of that old Cousin Emmie —' Roddy began.

'Yes, just think of her. It was she who blew the gaff about you and the Freeman girl, by the way.'

'Damn it, I might have known it! One couldn't have a

15

tumble anywhere without her happening along. She makes me think of the chorus in a Greek play.'

I laughed, thinking that this was as apt a description of Cousin Emmie as I had yet heard. At that moment, I saw from the window a suitcase being pushed on to the garden wall from the cane-piece beyond.

'There's Sandy,' I said and Roddy sprang up. 'Wait here. I'll go.'

I could see only Sandy's red head on the other side of the wall and the head of Samson, his pony, as he asked: 'Is Number Three here, Missis Janet? Will you give him this case? And tell him good luck. I gotta go back. Mother's only at the Great House.'

'All right, Sandy.'

There was a rustle among the sugar-cane, Sandy and the pony became invisible, the afternoon sun blazed down and, feeling that I was caught up in some absurd melodrama, I lugged the heavy suitcase across the lawn and into the house.

'I feel a perfect fool,' I told Roddy.

'As long as that's all, it's all right,' he said, kneeling down by the case, taking some keys from his pocket and checking what it contained.

'And now what?' I asked as he relocked the case and stood up. 'How do you propose to get from here to the Bay carrying that?' I pointed to the case and glanced at my watch. 'It's twenty past four.'

'I'll manage all right.'

'Take these,' I said and gave him a packet of cigarettes and a box of matches. I held out my hand. 'Good luck!'

'Thanks.' He shook my hand and jerked his head at the book that lay on the sofa. 'I'll send you a copy of the next one for free.'

I picked up the book and held it between my hands again. 'Shall I tell Paradise that you wrote this one?'

16

'Tell them if you like. What's one more sin among so many?'

Suitcase in hand, he stepped out of the french window. In the sunlight, he turned to smile at me, the bold reckless smile that comes only to those who have the world before them and no old debts to the past and no old doubts from the past trailing behind them.

At that moment, Miss Morrison, Sir Ian's Cousin Emmie, who was staying at the Great House walked in through the door at the other end of the room. Roddy disappeared into the garden and, the next thing I knew, he was rolling down the drive in the Daimler car that belonged to Dee Andrews who was in bed upstairs, nursing a feverish cold.

FOR most of the time, life looks to me like a deep slow-flowing river whose black waters are obscured by a heavy surface scum of trivialities. That afternoon, while I had been talking to Roddy, the scum had been swept aside, the deep black water had been momentarily visible and I had had an awareness that life was more than the day-to-day triviality of Paradise affairs but with the disappearance of Roddy and the entrance of Miss Morrison, the scum closed over the surface again and it was not until after I had given her tea, Twice had arrived home and our cat Charlie, in spite of its masculine name, had had kittens in the laundry roof, that I had the opportunity to consider that my action of the afternoon in helping Roddy to evade his angry father might have a significance that would lead to unpleasant consequences.

When Miss Morrison had gone away and Twice and I were having a drink before dinner, I said nervously: 'Twice, a thing happened this afternoon. Roddy Maclean came here.'

Twice frowned at me sharply and I became more nervous not because I was afraid of him but because I am a slow thinker who tends to act by instinct and rationalise my actions later on and, on this day, I had not had time to rationalise what I had done before having to tell Twice about it. In the closely knit little world of Paradise, it was essential that he should know at once that I had helped Roddy to outwit his father.

'Here?' he asked. 'But Rob and Sir Ian have been scouring every dive in the Bay for him! Where is he now?'

'Out in the Caribbean on the way to the States, I hope.'

Twice has very blue eyes which the tropical tan of his skin seems to make more blue and they glared at me very fiercely now as he said: 'Janet, what do you mean? What has been going on between you and that bloody boy?'

'Twice Alexander, if you take that line, we are not going to get anywhere!'

'What I am interested in is where we are at the moment? Why did he come here? Why did you —'

'Shut up! Stop the ham drama.'

'Drama?' Twice visibly grabbed at his temper, clenched his big fists between his bare brown knees and said: 'You didn't even let Marion know he was here?'

'No.'

He expelled an exasperated breath. 'Look here, start at the beginning and tell me what happened. When did he get here?'

I told him of Roddy's arrival, of what had been said, of Miss Morrison's appearance and of Roddy disappearing into the garden and then I added: 'And the next thing I knew he was rolling down the drive in Dee's car. She must have left the keys in it in her hysteria last night.'

Twice glared at me, aghast and when he began to speak he was stammering with rage. 'He took the car? After how he treated her? After you had helped him? And you sit there as if all this were decent and reasonable?'

'Decent and reasonable!' I almost shouted. 'There is no decency or reason in this thing anywhere with Rob Maclean and Sir Ian chasing that boy with horse whips because he wanted to be a writer and not an engineer. You are all mad, I tell you, mad!'

There was so much more that I wanted to say in order to make Twice understand why I had acted as I had but I was not as yet certain enough about my motivation to find words and consequently broke down into a misery of tears. The title of Roddy's book *But Not For Love* came into my mind and, in the associative way that the mind works, I remembered the last few lines of Rosalind's speech from which the words of the title derived. 'You go on about reason and decency but these are all lies, these things, all *lies*!' I babbled incoherently. 'The only true thing in all this is that if Roddy Maclean wants to write, they have no right to try to stop him!'

'For God's sake stop crying and pull yourself together,' Twice said angrily. 'I don't give a damn about what Roddy Maclean does. What I do give a damn about is what *you* have done and what we are going to say to Rob Maclean.'

Because I could not explain coherently why I had done what I had and because his anger with me showed no sign of abating, I brushed the tears from my eyes and gave myself up to rage.

'*You* don't have to say anything to Rob Maclean,' I said. 'If you are ashamed of what I have done, you don't have to take any responsibility for it. *I* can say anything that has to be said to Rob Maclean. Neither he nor anybody else in this bloody island is going to dictate what I do and don't do. They have dictated for far too long already.'

'Janet,' Twice said coldly, 'control yourself for pity's sake. And you are being damned unpleasant, incidentally. Of course it is *we* who have to cope with Rob. You know that. As far as Rob or anybody else here is concerned, your actions are also mine.' His voice grew warmer. 'In this case, I don't know as yet why we did what we did this afternoon but we have done it now and we have got to stand by it.' His tone became exasperated again as he added: 'Stop *crying*, damn it! You are forty-two, not nineteen!' But with his hard, factual logical mind, he could not let well enough alone. 'Janet, why didn't you tell that chap to clear out of here and take no part in this?'

'I don't know,' I wailed, trying to stop crying. 'It is something to do with this ghastly place and all its shibboleths and everybody making a drama about things that don't matter and nobody seeing the things that do matter.' Anger rose in me again, drying my tears. 'This place — Paradise, forsooth — is one great big lie, a big white lie in the middle of a black island. Everything connected with this Roddy affair is lies, except the book that he was afraid to tell his parents about. Madame went on as if this Lucy Freeman he was larking about with was a bush innocent that Roddy has victimised when the little trollop has a room in one of the brothels in Victoria Court. He is supposed to have jilted Dee when *she* asked him to marry her in the first place. The whole thing is one tissue of lies and falsity, I am telling you, except the book. The book is a reality and he preferred to run away rather than face his parents about it. What sort of parents are they. If Jock or I had written a book, my father would have been so pleased that —'

'I can think of no two men' Twice broke in coldly on my tirade, 'more different from one another than your father and Rob Maclean.' He went on to speak in a cold level tone and I knew that he was talking what the world calls 'sense' but I found myself clinging rebelliously and desperately to some obscure truth in myself that lay deeper than the level of worldly sense. 'You have to think of this from the point of view of Rob and Marion,' Twice was saying. 'They are strict disciplinarians in their family — a thing you have always admired in them, by the way.'

'But —'

He disregarded me. 'Rob Maclean will tell you himself that he is not a bookish man. These are the words he would use. Rob and Marion value things like security and stability and Roddy has shown little sign of either up till now, but what he has done is to swindle them for five years, then come out here, create mayhem and involve them in social disgrace. All this is bound to get out and the whole island will know about it.'

21

'The island! As for knowing about it, there will never be any *real* knowing. Even *you* don't understand why I did what I did today.'

'If you yourself knew and could tell me why, it would be a help,' he said. 'But I am old enough to know that there is a hell of a lot of what you do that one has to take on trust. Only, I do wish in this case that you had thought before you did the thing instead of finding out why you did it some time next year, probably.'

'I am sorry, Twice. It was just because of all the falseness and horse whips and drama and nonsense. God, I wish it were eighteen months hence and we were back in Britain where we belong. I am so sick of this place and all the carry-on that —'

I stopped as Twice got up and, going close to the mosquito screen, stared out into the darkness, his head cocked as he listened. I got up too and saw the headlights spraying the grass on either side of the approach to our gate.

'We are going to be sicker of this island in a minute,' he said. This is the Rolls. Stand by for sound.'

'They can't kill us,' I said as the car stopped, secure in the feeling that Twice and I were united again, but as Rob Maclean sprang out of the car and on to the veranda, this statement seemed to be in some doubt. Like a charging ox he came at me and, instinctively, I retreated until the backs of my knees were caught by a chair in a corner, causing me to sit down with a bump. He bent over me, his eyes like sharp lights in his fleshy face which was suffused purple with rage. He looked more like an angry beast than a man in that moment and I felt the saliva of disgust flood about my lower back teeth.

'Where is he?' he shouted.

'Who?' I asked.

'You know bloody well, you bitch!'

I heard the voice of Twice: 'Now, look here, Rob!' and the voice of Sir Ian: 'Good God, Rob —'

I stood up and my eyes were level with the downbent, thrust-forward face.

'If you mean Roddy,' I said, 'he is well out on the high seas on his way to the States by now.'

Rob's big hands jerked forward, the fingers crooked and, for a second, I thought he was going to seize me by the throat. The man was literally beside himself, so enraged that his mind was outside of him and all control of his body abandoned. I stood staring and rigid with fright, while there came a muddle of questions and ejaculations from Sir Ian, until Rob drew one hand over his face from left to right as if to wipe away a mask. Then the madness seemed to leave him; he spoke more normally but with deep enmity.

'He was here? You saw him?'

'Yes, he was and I saw him.'

'You — you helped him to get away?'

'Yes, I did.'

'You knew what he had done?'

'Yes, better than you did, I think.'

'You should be bloody well shot!' he told me, stamped down the steps, got into the car and was driven away rapidly into the darkness.

'Look here, Sir Ian,' Twice said angrily, 'what has happened hardly justifies all this drama.'

'Rob is goin' on a bit right enough,' Sir Ian said as he sat down. 'All the same, I hardly blame him. I've never seen such a perishin' carry-on in me life.' He stared at me with his brows drawn down. 'That young scoundrel came here today? Here to this house after all his carry-on with little Miss Dee an' everythin'?'

'Yes.'

'And you helped him to get away?'

'Yes.'

Sir Ian looked at Twice who was sitting with his hands loosely clasped between his knees, his eyelids heavy as his

23

eyes looked down at the hands. In a puzzled way, Sir Ian looked back at me.

'Why?' he asked. 'Why did you help him?'

I was still looking at Twice and he now looked up, straight into my face, his eyes very blue under his sun-tanned forehead and a faint smile tilted one corner of his mouth.

'I helped him because I didn't want you and Rob and your horse whips to catch up with him,' I told Sir Ian.

'But dammit, Missis Janet, I don't understand you! You helped that young scoundrel to get away after — after Miss Dee an' everythin'? What *for*, dammit?'

While Sir Ian spoke, Twice went along the veranda and came back with the copy of *But Not for Love*.

'Sometimes, sir, Janet has difficulty in tracing her own motives but she helped Roddy partly because of this, I think,' he said and handed the volume to Sir Ian.

Sir Ian took it as if it were a bomb that might explode in his face, held it at arm's length long-sightedly and read from its spine, separating each word as if they were words he had never seen before: 'BUT NOT FOR LOVE S T BENNETT' He then looked up at me. 'What's this got to do with it?' he barked in his military voice.

'Roddy Maclean is S. T. Bennett.'

'Roddy — Maclean — is — S. T. Bennett? Roddy Maclean is — You mean that young scoundrel wrote this book?'

'Yes.'

'Well I'm damned!' He now opened the book and read a line or two before he closed it with an angry snap. 'I still don't see what this has to do with this afternoon's carry-on. Now, why did you help that young devil to get away? Tell me that!'

'Look, sir,' Twice said, 'this affair is far more complicated than Roddy getting a coloured girl into trouble and making a fool of Dee Andrews and all that. Roddy has made a fool of more than Dee Andrews. The five years he was

24

supposed to be doing engineering at Glasgow, he wasn't.'

'Wasn't? Then what the hell *was* he doin'?'

'Studying English and Classics and writing poetry and that book,' Twice said.

'Good God!' Sir Ian gave a jump. 'Does Rob know about this?'

'Not yet,' I told him.

'Then how do *you* know?'

At tedious length, I explained to him how, the night before, Dee Andrews had come home in a hysterical state, announcing that her engagement to Roddy was broken and how, later, when she had calmed down, she had told me of Roddy's Glasgow past and his authorship of the book.

'But the fellah can't have any conscience!' Sir Ian exploded.

'Not much,' I agreed.

'And yet you helped him to get away?'

Having failed to make Twice understand my motives, I had the sense to know that I could never make Sir Ian understand. 'Look, Sir Ian,' I said, 'I would help the man who wrote that book even if he had murdered his poor old grandma. I don't expect you to understand that but that is how I am. After all, what terrible sins did Roddy commit? When he was going up to the university, he asked his father for permission to read in the faculty of arts. Rob would not allow him to do it. Rob considers that there are only three professions, engineering, veterinary science and medicine with engineering away ahead of the others. Roddy was told he was to be an engineer. People like you and Rob talk a great deal and with great approval about courage. Do you realise that, at the age of eighteen, Roddy made up his mind to get the sort of education he wanted and be-damned to his father? Do you realise how he has strung Rob along all these five years with the steady risk of being found out? Doesn't that take courage?'

Sir Ian was very fair-minded but he was unwilling to make any concessions. 'But what about this business about makin' a fool out o' little Miss Dee? Gettin' engaged to her an' carryin' on at the same time with a coloured girl? How d'ye intend to put a shine on that?'

'I am not intending to put a shine on anything,' I said, 'but as far as Dee is concerned, it is my belief that you cannot make a fool of anybody who hasn't already got the potential for being a fool. Dee is a muddle-headed little ass.'

'But good gad, she is a woman and —'

'Come to that,' Twice interrupted in a low voice, 'we are not at all sure about it.'

'Sure? Sure about what, dammit?'

'It seems to us,' Twice said, 'that Dee is what is called a Lesbian.'

'A Les —' Sir Ian began to shout.

'Shut up!' I said. 'She and Isobel Denholm are up there in the back bedroom!'

'She an' Iso — Good God!' Sir Ian pulled out his handkerchief and mopped his forehead. 'Look here, I'm damned if I know what this perishin' place is comin' to.'

Twice poured a drink and handed it to him and I went on with my explanation. Sir Ian and I had been very good friends ever since we met at London airport; this was the first time that I had ever done anything of which he strongly disapproved and since he had arrived with Rob that evening, I had discovered that I did not care whether or not Rob ever forgave me for helping Roddy but that I cared very much that Sir Ian should understand and forgive me.

Twice's intervention with his remark about Dee Andrews was helpful for the old man temporarily forgot about Roddy, thus relieving the strain, while he pursued this new development.

'How did you come to this notion about Miss Dee?' he asked me in an undertone.

'It is just something that has gradually seeped through. I don't think the girl herself knew she had a homosexual tendency until this upheaval with Roddy. And then there was Isobel Denholm. She has been seeing a lot of Isobel lately.'

'There's somethin' queer about the Denholm girl all right,' he agreed, 'but all the Denholms were a queer lot, come to think o' it.'

'Then Miss Morrison helped to bring it into the open too,' I said.

'Cousin Emmie? Ye-es. Her an' that old camel Fanny Murgatroyd livin' together all those years. But good gad, you heard the latest? Now that old Fanny's dead, Emmie's goin' to marry her brother — old Fanny's brother, I mean. Emmie told Mother this mornin' an' she's fit to be tied — Mother, I mean. No wonder. Have you heard anythin' like it? Emmie's damn' near eighty!'

'Actually I had heard,' I told him. 'Miss Morrison was round here this afternoon and told me herself that she intended to get married when she went back to England.'

'Old fool!'

'That's hardly accurate, sir,' Twice said. 'Miss Morrison is no fool. She knew more about Roddy than any of us, if you think of it.'

'Huh, a fine mess it is too!'

'I don't see that it is all that of a mess,' I said. 'This coloured paramour of Roddy's is not the innocent little piece that you all imagined. Roddy told me she has a room in one of the brothels in Victoria Court and I believe him. As for Dee, it is a God's blessing that she and Roddy quarrelled for if they had married it would have been a disaster. In fact, I don't see that much harm has been done except that we all know a bit more about ourselves and each other and Rob Maclean's third son is a novelist instead of an engineer as Rob wanted him to be.'

'He's a novelist and an unscrupulous young shyster and he's probably a good many other things as well and you helped him to get off this island before Rob caught up with him,' he told me, but I knew that he was less angry than he had been.

'That's right. So I did,' I said. 'So what?'

He looked at me, looked down into his drink and then up at me again, his shaggy white eyebrows drawn down over his eyes. 'Rob Maclean is never going to like you for it,' he said.

'Does that matter? I don't know at this moment that I particularly like Rob Maclean, He seems to me a little bit of a bully and I have never liked bullies.'

'Still, that young devil is Rob's son, Missis Janet. It is for Rob to deal with him, not you.'

Determinedly I took my stand while Twice watched tensely from the chair across from me. 'Sir Ian, that young devil is twenty-three years old. He is a man first and Rob Maclean's son second. He has a right to his own way of life and I, as one of his friends, have a right to help him make his way if I want to.'

'Dammit,' he said to Twice, 'I always had a liking for the Highland regiments.' He turned to me. 'You — you like the fellah, me dear? You — you believe in him?'

'Yes, I like him although I agree with you that he doesn't fit in very well as a social person — he certainly doesn't fit into the society here at Paradise. I think he was wise to get out. And I certainly believe that he has talent — a literary talent, I mean.'

Sir Ian nodded. 'You would know more about that than I would, me dear.' He sighed. 'I suppose it is as well he got away as he did. I'd begun to think that Rob would murder him out o' hand. In fact he will, if he ever catches up with him now.'

'Won't this make any difference when Rob hears about it?' Twice asked, holding up the book.

Sir Ian shook his head. 'I doubt it, me boy. That young rascal made rings round Rob Maclean every way ye look at it an' made a bloody fool o' him. Rob ain't the sort to forget that.'

'Even although the boy is his own son?' Twice asked.

'Rob ain't much of what I would call a family man,' Sir Ian said quietly.

When he had gone home and Twice and I were having our belated dinner, I said: 'That was an odd remark Sir Ian made just before he left. If a man who has co-operated in the production of seven sons is not what you would call a family man, it seems to me that there is some loose thinking and some looser copulation going on around here.'

'I take your point,' Twice said, 'but what Sir Ian said is true enough. Rob isn't what one means by the expression "a family man". His establishment — his wife and family — are just part of his position, like his big car and so on. They are what I believe are coming to be known in the U.S.A. as status symbols.'

'What can you mean?'

'I am putting it as clearly as I can. Rob Maclean is first, last and all the time manager of Paradise Estate, the big shot, the Caribbean expert on all matters pertaining to the production of sugar and rum. It is only in so far as things — all things, including wives and children — contribute to that position that they exist for him. If they don't contribute to the fame and dignity, they don't matter one damn and compared with Paradise Estate, sugar and rum, which are the main props of his position, they don't matter much anyway.'

'Twice, how long have you been aware of this?' I asked.

'I don't quite know — a fairish time, I suppose. It is going on for four years since we met him, isn't it?'

'And you never said anything?'

'Why? I mean you met him the same minute that I did.'

Twice ran a hand through his hair. 'You — you didn't know?' he asked.

'No. I didn't know.'

'It is a queer thing,' he told me, 'how most of the time you notice every finicking little thing about people and yet how, now and again, you miss something enormous that everybody else can see at a glance. You were like this about that woman Muriel. You thought she was a poor pathetic down-trodden soul when it always seemed to me that her eye was always very much on the main chance.'

We went to bed shortly after that and I thought about Rob Maclean for a long time before I fell asleep but all that I discovered was that I knew nothing about the man at all except that he used to make me think of a teddy-bear and a few facts of a social nature such as that he had been born in Scotland, was married to Marion by whom he had seven sons and that he was manager of Paradise Estate, St. Jago.

I have a friend who, when she tries to explain something that she has said or done, invariably prefaces her explanation with the phrase: 'I am a person like this — ' and it was savagely frightening now to discover that, although I had what we call 'known' Rob Maclean for nearly four years, I had no idea what he was 'a person like'.

THE next day was a Sunday. The year on Paradise Estate pivoted round the sugar crop and divided itself into two periods of six months each, the first from January to June, known as the In-Crop season when the sugar cane was harvested and the factory and distillery were processing and the period from July to December, known as the Out-of-Crop season when the sugar cane grew to maturity in the fields again and the factory and distillery were overhauled and prepared for the next spell of sugar and rum production.

The time of which I write was near the end of July, when the weather was at its hottest but there was always a relaxing of tension in the Out-of-Crop and the days had a less rigorous routine. There was no work done on Saturdays or Sundays but, as a rule, Sir Ian, Rob and Twice would foregather during the forenoons at the factory office, make a few plans for the coming week and then come either to our house or to the Macleans' at Olympus for a drink before lunch.

On this morning, Twice and I had no more than finished breakfast when Sir Ian arrived on our veranda again.

'Good mornin',' he announced sternly, 'look here, what is goin' on in this place? The watchman down at Paradise Wharf has just been on the 'phone to me. He has got little Miss Dee's car down there.'

I have never been given to crying over spilt milk and have always believed that to be in for a pound is no worse than being in for a penny. In the bright morning, I saw that my action in helping Roddy was the equivalent at

Paradise of an entire dairy entirely spilt and in the darkness of the night it had come to me that in being on Roddy's side, I was in for my entire intellectual and emotional capital. In the light of this, it seemed to me the best course to maintain an unruffled front.

'Oh, good,' I said. 'Twice, when you go up to the office, will you give Don Candlesham a ring and ask him to run the car up here?'

Sir Ian made a jerky movement, then became rigid and glared at me like a bull frustrated in some dire design by sudden total paralysis. 'Now, look here, Missis Janet,' he spluttered, 'if I am right in thinking that you lent that young bounder that little girl's car, you had no damn' business to!'

'You are not,' I said.

'Not what?'

'Not right in thinking I lent him her car. He took it. I didn't know he had it till it drove out of that gate down there.'

'Googorralmighty!' He collapsed on to a chair and began to mop his face. 'He came here, you helped him and then he pinched that car?'

'Yes.'

'But lord above us, don't you care?'

'Care? Not particularly. Why? I am not like Rob Maclean. I don't mind being made a fool of, if that's what you mean. I can't afford to mind. I am always being made a fool of. Anyway, he hasn't done the car any harm, has he?'

'No. At least it seems not,' he conceded unwillingly. 'It seems he drove in there, gave the keys to the watchman and told him to ring me this mornin'.'

'Well, what are you beefing about?' I asked.

He looked at me for a long moment, then looked at Twice and then back at me again. 'I'm damned if I know whether I am on me head or me heels. Mother's round

32

there at the house goin' on like a ptarmigan an' Rob's in the factory office lookin' like thunder —'

Sir Ian frequently used the word 'ptarmigan' to describe Madame in a temper but none of us had ever informed him that the word he should use, if any, was 'termagant' and Twice never failed to be amused at the mistake so that, now, he gave a chuckle of laughter.

'This ain't a laughin' matter,' Sir Ian said sternly.

'Isn't it?' I asked. 'With all that is going on in the world, it seems to me out of proportion to make all this fuss about Rob Maclean's son making an ass of Rob Maclean. Speaking for myself, I am sick of the whole affair. I am going upstairs to see Dee and Isobel.'

'How is she this mornin'?' Sir Ian asked.

'Better. She will be getting up later on. She and Isobel are going up to Mount Melody tomorrow.'

'So they really are going into this hotel business together?'

'Oh yes, sir,' Twice told him.

He gave his forehead another rub with his handkerchief. 'I just don't know what's goin' on,' he said sadly, 'what with young women livin' together an' startin' hotels for tourists an' young men writin' books an' stealin' cars.' He drew his eyebrows down and glared at me. 'Nothin' like this used to go on before!' he told me accusingly.

'But Sir Ian *I* didn't make Dee and Isobel decide to run a hotel together or turn Roddy into a writer,' I protested.

'Maybe not but nothin' like this happened before.'

'But times are changing, sir,' Twice said. 'Young people are different from what we were.'

The bright old eyes were still fixed on me. 'It seems to me that some people are just different anyway,' he said then but he smiled as he added: 'not that I am blamin' you really, me dear. I sort o' see why you helped the boy an' all about his book an' that an' when you brought Miss Dee here you weren't to know that she'd go in for hotel-keepin' an' Isobel Denholm but has it ever struck you that you are almost everlastin' in trouble?'

'Me? I am not in any trouble. It is a fine Sunday morning, Crop's over, Dee and Isobel are leaving tomorrow and I am looking forward to a nice peaceful time with the house to myself and Twice at home instead of flapping round Barbados and Jamaica.'

'It is next Friday that Rob and Marion and the kid fly home, isn't it?' Twice asked now.

'If they go at all,' Sir Ian said lugubriously.

Twice frowned sharply. 'What d'you mean, sir? Why shouldn't they go?'

'No reason except that Rob's gone cussed. He said this mornin' that he wasn't goin' — that Marion could go over with the boy an' put him to school herself like she's done with the others.'

'But Rob hasn't had home leave since we have been here — that's over three years,' Twice said.

'Ye think I don't know that?' Sir Ian snapped in a brittle way that was very unlike his usual splutter and bluster and then he added more calmly: 'Rob's in a real temper, me boy an' when Rob's like this he'll do any damn' thing just to upset as many damn' people as he damn' well can.'

'That is just childish,' I said 'and somebody should give him a good smacked behind.'

'Now, look, Missis Janet —'

'Oh, I am not going to do it,' I assured him. 'Even if I could, I wouldn't. This is none of my business.'

'Was helpin' that young devil Roddy your business?'

'Yes,' I said shortly, 'it was. That was a human issue where my ideas of what was right differed from Rob Maclean's but whether Rob Maclean goes on leave to Scotland or sulks in the factory office is a Paradise social or political affair and I am not a bit interested or concerned.'

'The trouble is that all the human affairs as ye call them

34

an' the social an' political affairs get all mixed up in a place like this an' Rob's makin' an upheaval about goin' on leave because he didn't get a chance to give that son o' his the thrashin' he deserved.'

'Then Rob Maclean is a muddle-headed ass,' I said angrily. 'And another thing — it seems to me that Roddy and I didn't make a fool of him as he seems to think. If he asks you, you can tell him from me that he was a fool long before Roddy and I started in on him.'

'Now, hold it, Janet,' Twice told me. 'There is no use in making a bad mess worse.'

I looked from one of them to the other and was at once sorry for my flash of temper. In spite of Sir Ian's remark about my being in 'everlastin' trouble', the fact remained that, until now, Twice and I had fitted very smoothly into the rigid little world that was the European community at Paradise. In spite of the quarrels which periodically ripped the social fabric to rags, quarrels mainly among the wives of the European staff, living dull lives in the humid heat, I had never been involved and Guinea Corner had always been a popular house.

By 'everlastin' trouble' Sir Ian meant various incidents in which I had been involved, when I had aired my views with considerable force and these incidents had always arisen out of situations similar to this one with Roddy Maclean. It had always seemed to me that there was something in the air of the island, something in the rigid framework of Paradise that exerted a pressure upon people which caused a distortion of their minds so that, sometimes, things that were of little intrinsic importance swelled monstrously while, at other times, the people around me seemed to be blind to what I felt was some heinous injustice. There was no doubt in my mind that I myself was affected by the island and by the physical and social climate of Paradise to the degree where I had to take a very firm grip on my nerves, my temper and even my standards of behaviour and thought. The humid heat, the glaring light, the harsh colours all battered at a body and eyes that belonged to a more temperate zone and, since I have never believed that I am so unique as to have nothing in common with other people, I was certain that the other whites at Paradise felt strains similar to those that I felt. Nothing was easier than to give way to blind rage as an outlet for these strains and tensions and I felt that this is what Rob Maclean was doing now, blowing up a teacup storm into a hurricane for the relief of the pressure that had built up in himself.

'I think we are all letting this thing get out of proportion,' I said now with an assumption of nonchalance. 'I did what I did and Rob Maclean says I should be shot for it, but he won't shoot me because he would swing for it. He is therefore feeling a little frustrated but I don't see anything we can do about that. Would it help if I went to him and apologised? Is that what he wants? That I should say I am sorry?'

'But, are you sorry?' Twice asked.

'Good lord no! But I could easily say I was if it would please Rob.'

'There are times when I think you don't have any morals at all an' that's a fact,' Sir Ian told me.

'But I am truly sorry that you are all so upset about this. I think you are silly to be so upset but I am still sorry about it.'

'*I'm* not upset, as ye call it,' Sir Ian said. 'It's Rob. The more I think o' that young rascal writin' tellin' Rob he had passed his Physics exam while he was writin' books all the time, the more I feel like laughin'. An' then, yesterday, Rob an' I huntin' for him round all the bars in the Bay while he was walkin' in here through me own perishin' cane — that's comical too, when ye think o' it. Only, Rob don't see it that way.'

'Did you tell Rob about the book yet?' Twice asked.

'Yes, right off when I first saw him this morning'. He only got so red in the face I thought he'd burst an' I wished I'd kept me damn' mouth shut.'

'Is he quite right in his head?' I asked.

'Janet,' said Twice, 'shut up.'

I did what Twice told me and a prolonged silence descended upon us until Sir Ian slapped his knee and said: 'Dammit! With one thing an' another, I've never told ye me big news! It's Edward. When I got back last night there was a cable. He's comin' home for a holiday.'

'Sir Ian, how splendid!' I said. 'Isn't Madame thrilled? When is he coming?'

'Next week — not this next week that this is Sunday of but the next. 'Smatter o' fact, if it wasn't for Edward comin', Mother would be more of a ptarmigan than she is already about this thing o' Roddy.'

Edward was Sir Ian's only child, Madame's only grandchild and the heir to Paradise but he did not like the island or its climate and in the time that Twice and I had been in St. Jago, he had been home only once, for a short time at Christmas of 1950. It seemed to me that Edward did not regard St. Jago or Paradise as his home. He had been born in England while Sir Ian was in the army and after Sir Ian's wife died when the boy was quite young, he had spent most of his school holidays with relations of both parents in Great Britain or with Sir Ian if he was serving in not too distant parts.

I tried now to remember Edward as he had been when I saw him that Christmas time but I could not visualise him clearly. I had an impression that he was tall, more slightly built than the burly Sir Ian and good-looking in an in not-too-distant parts.

'Remember last time he was here?' Sir Ian asked now. 'Remember that play we did? The Varlets? By jove, that was a *proper* night!'

The night thus described by Sir Ian had ended in attempted murder and I marvelled that the human race, having evolved the supreme grace of language, should so commonly put it to such erroneous use.

'It's funny how things get different,' Sir Ian said next in a thoughtful voice. 'They get different and ye can't put your finger on how it happened. We never do plays at Christmas now. We're gettin' older. I suppose that's what it is.'

He seemed downcast momentarily and to cheer him up, I said: 'Is Edward still as keen on pictures as ever, Sir Ian?'

Edward, I had heard at various times, was a keen amateur of painting and on his travels about Europe on sugar and rum business for Paradise, he lost no opportunity of going to exhibitions and adding to his considerable collection.

'Keener than ever, it seems to me,' Sir Ian replied. 'As well as travellin' for sugar an' rum business, he's travellin' for pictures now too — doin' it in a commercial way, I mean. He always spent more time in galleries than in rum-shippers' offices anyhow but now he has joined up with some gallery fellah in London an' arranges for pictures by Frenchmen and Italians an' that to be sent over to England for exhibitions.' He slapped his knee suddenly in a characteristic gesture. 'Dammit, that's somethin' that never struck me before!'

'What, sir?' Twice asked as the old man frowned out across the garden.

'Edward's always been keener on pictures than he was on sugar an' rum an' Paradise here or the Army. I've always known that an' it's never worried me. Look here — ' he frowned hideously at us both ' — *why* is Rob Maclean so damn' mad because one o' his sons has taken to writin' books?'

'Yes. Precisely. Why?' I asked while Twice glanced at me warningly.

'It's on account o' not gettin' his own way, I suppose,' Sir Ian answered himself, taking no notice of me. 'Rob likes to get his own way.' He stood up and said to Twice: 'Well, boy, comin' up to the office for a little? See how Rob is feelin' now, eh?'

I HAD no opportunity to speak further to Twice about the Maclean affair until after dinner that evening when our guests, Dee and Isobel, had retired upstairs to their bedroom, but the thought of the upheaval lay at the back of my mind all day. And I became more and more oppressed by the knowledge that not myself but Twice was going to have to bear the consequences of an action that had been wholly mine. It was Twice and not I who had to work in close co-operation with Rob Maclean.

As soon as the girls had gone upstairs, I said: 'How was Rob when you saw him this morning?'

'Very surly.'

Twice sat staring at the floor, frowning, preoccupied, distant and, as I looked at him, I had a desolate sense that even two people as well attuned as he and I were could never be completely together, that the moment of isolation was always lying in wait. He had not understood and would never understand why I had done what I had because I could never communicate to him in terms he could understand the reason for my action. For this communication to be made, Twice and I would have to be persons even more like one another than we were already. He would have to set as much store by books and writing as I did and this was not in his character any more than it was in my character to derive the satisfaction that could be derived by Twice from a complicated mechanism in smooth operation. It seemed ironical that life had found so surely the chink in the armour of our relationship.

Twice, a practical person, completely the engineer, had never understood my passion for imaginative literature and, quite frequently, had displayed little patience with it, incapable of understanding that, when he had so many books on social history on our shelves, I preferred to read poetry or fiction. He would, it seemed to me, have understood better any other motive for action than the motive which had actuated me in this situation into which I had, inadvertently, been led.

'Twice,' I asked into the silence at last, 'are you really furious with me about all this? You know, don't you, that I wasn't being in any way malicious in what I did? That Rob *did* seem to me to be in the wrong?'

'Good heavens, darling, I know that. And now that the heat and panic have died down, I agree with you that Rob was going a bit far in dictating the boy's life.'

'Then why are you so sort of faraway?'

He smiled. 'I am not faraway — not from you anyway but I am away out of my depth about Rob Maclean.'

'Why?'

'That man isn't just angry in an ordinary way because you helped his erring son to slip through his vengeful fingers. There is more to this fit of rage than that. Do you know what I think? I am almost afraid to say it because it sounds so damned far-fetched. This thing about not going on leave isn't just a tantrum because of last night's carry-on, as Sir Ian thinks. In fact, last night's carry-on wasn't basically about Roddy at all. Rob Maclean is furious because Edward Dulac is coming out here. Roddy was a fine focal point for his wrath about *that*. Rob hates Edward Dulac's guts.'

'But Twice why for goodness sake?'

'This is what sounds far-fetched but I think it is because Edward is heir to Paradise.'

'Twice, you're dotty!' I said but even as I spoke the words I knew they were a protest against some truth so unreasonable by my own standards that I did not want to believe it.

Twice, on the whole, did not interest himself in people and their peculiarities as much as I did but it was now borne in on me, in the light of what I had learned during the past twenty-four hours about Rob Maclean, that these nearly four years at Paradise had been, on the part of Twice, a minor masterpiece of diplomacy. Originally, Twice had come to the island as the representative of his British firm Allied Plant Limited because, in the years following the war, many existing enterprises in the Caribbean undertook expansion programmes and much new capital and many new enterprises were coming into the area. We had become established at Paradise through the hospitality of the Dulacs, as I have explained, and this suited Twice as a centre because Paradise itself had undertaken an expansion programme which demanded much of his attention. In 1952, this programme was in its final stages and at the end of August, when we returned from our local leave in the hills, the last of the new installations would be made before the start of the 1953 crop. After that, Twice's tour of duty would keep us in the island for another year or so but when that tour ended, we had asked the firm for a post that would domicile us in Britain. It was not that we were homesick. It was merely that we — and particularly I — were tired of the lush whites-in-the-tropics way of life to which neither of us had been born and had entered too late in life so that, deep down, we had never ceased to feel disoriented.

It came to me as a shock now that these years that Twice had spent here at Paradise must have contained some fairly rough sailing if Rob Maclean was even a quarter of what Sir Ian, Roddy and Twice himself had now led me to believe he was. This Rob Maclean who was rising out of the ashes of last night's scene about his son was not the 'ordinary engineering colleague' of my loose imagination but

42

someone who was becoming more sinister with every new fact I learned about him and every new opinion I heard of him.

'Maybe I am dotty,' Twice said now, 'but I don't think so. You see, power is heady wine to Rob and he is a drunkard for it. He loves the taste of it, the smell of it and he loves the applause after his speeches at sugar federation meetings as if they were the music of ice tinkling in another bumper glass of power.'

'You would be quite lyrical to listen to if your subject wasn't so damn' silly. Power! What power has Rob Maclean got? Big frog in sugar in the little pond of the British Caribbean? Power in *sugar*! Heavens, all the sugar in the British Caribbean would go into one Cuban or Peruvian *centrale*!'

'Not everybody takes your cosmic view of things,' Twice told me a little coldly. 'You always think in terms of infinity — I think it must be because of being born on that hill at Reachfar and seeing the four corners of the earth from the first moment you could see at all. To be the big sugar frog of the British Caribbean spells power to Rob Maclean and he wallows in it and loves it and I think he feels that, one day, Edward might come home here and decide to manage this place himself which would put Rob out of power and on to a pension or that if anything happened to Madame, Sir Ian and Edward may decide to sell this place and retire home to England and the picture galleries.'

'I see,' I said, which meant, of course, that I did not 'see' at all but was trying to understand something that was utterly foreign to me.

'As things are, I think Rob almost deludes himself that Paradise is his and that Madame and Sir Ian are pensioners and hangers-on. You see, he was here for years after Sir Ian's father died, managing the place for Madame while Sir Ian was at sundry foreign wars and Edward was at school. Sir Ian only came back about a year before we came out here, you know and you also know that Sir Ian never sets foot in the factory or the distillery if he can help it. To most people, Rob Maclean is Paradise and to Rob, Paradise is his and if it isn't it should be because he has given his life to it.'

'Twice,' I said, 'you are aware that what you are saying is tantamount to saying that the man is megalomaniac or, not to be fancy, not quite right in his head?'

'I am aware of that. On the subject of this place and his position in it, Rob is not quite on balance. After all, did he look truly sane to *you* on this veranda last night?'

I shivered. 'No, he didn't. This is all very frightening. Twice, have you seen him like that before?'

'Once or twice.'

'What about? What caused it?'

'The time I remember best was — you remember that time last year before we went home on leave when Sir Ian suddenly said that if I was fed-up with Allied Plant I would always be welcome as engineer at the factory here? Well, a day or two after that, Rob came out of Sir Ian's office and he came straight at me and his face was a bit like it was last night. I thought he was going to try to throttle me although I could not think of anything I had done to make him feel that way but it was as if he suddenly changed his mind and he walked straight past me. He avoided me for two days and then, on the third day, he said: "Sir Ian's been telling me you might be joining the staff here?" I said something about it being a bit unlikely because the climate didn't suit *you* too well and I could feel the relief oozing out of him but I knew I was right about him not wanting me on the Paradise staff when he said: "In that case, you are right not to consider it. It would be a mistake to risk Janet's health."' Twice laughed. 'It is funny how often the bit of fancy trimming gives a man's real thoughts away. If Rob Maclean had wanted me here, he would have let you die a thousand deaths from malaria or anything else, hating you the way he does.'

I stared at Twice and knew even while I stared that my mouth was gaping open. 'Hating me? But that was a year ago,' I said. 'It is only last night that I made him angry.'

'Oh, he has always hated the sight of you,' Twice said airily. 'I thought you knew.'

It was only after he had stated this fact so familiar to him that he came round to thinking of its impact on myself. His wide blue eyes stared at me, his expression wavering between amusement and chagrin. 'You didn't know?'

'No.'

'Queer. You are usually pretty quick on the trigger about things like that.'

'I have never paid much attention to Rob,' I said thoughtfully. 'I have always been more interested in Marion. In fact, I have seen very little of Rob except at parties and things where there were a lot of people. He has always disliked me, you say?'

'You are hurt, of course?'

'Well, nobody likes to be told that somebody hates her. But, no, I am not hurt. The more I learn of Rob, the less I would like to be liked by him. I am not hurt but I am interested. I wonder why he should dislike me? Last night is the first time I have crossed his path in any real sense.'

'I think the key to it lies in what you said a moment ago — that you never paid much attention to Rob and have always been more interested in Marion. That is not at all Rob's idea of the fitness of things. And then, of course, you made your mark with Madame and Sir Ian right from the first jump when you wrote that play about the varlets.' Twice gave a roar of laughter. 'There is no doubt that literature is destined to come between you and Rob Maclean!'

'Literature!'

This play, *Varlets in Paradise* was an instance of what,

45

for want of a more accurate term, I must call 'life' gathering momentum and taking the initiative out of my hands. It had begun as a small affair to amuse Sir Ian and Sandy Maclean, who both fancied themselves as amateur actors, at Christmas of 1950 and in the end developed into a full-scale melodrama presented in the garden of Paradise Great House before an audience of hundreds.

'He took part in the play himself in the end,' I pointed out.

'Yes and he still believes that, but for him, it would have been a colossal flop.'

'To be fair,' I said, 'that is something that we shall never know but if it pleases Rob to think that he saved the day, there is no harm.'

'It pleases him no end. He often talks about it in his more relaxed moments as if he had written it, produced it and acted all the parts himself.'

'All this is very astonishing. Can you tell me out of this horde of secret knowledge of yours just when Rob first started to dislike me?'

'Right from the first jump at the airport, I should think. You did all the wrong things. You hit it off with Madame and Sir Ian, you didn't seem to be impressed by Rob and, anyway, you simply are not Rob's type. He will tell you himself that he doesn't like brainy women.'

'Would you seriously describe me as brainy, Twice?'

'I wouldn't describe anybody as brainy — it is one of those words that seem to me to have no meaning but that is how Rob would describe you. But I don't want you to get the impression that Rob's dislike of you makes you in some way unique. It doesn't. Rob doesn't like anybody particularly, except Rob Maclean, of course. The rest of humanity is just something he has to put up with, something sent to try him.'

'I wonder if he *will* get into that aeroplane next Friday?' I said after a little.

'Your guess is as good as mine. Quite apart from Edward coming, he doesn't like leaving *me* here in engineering charge.'

'Does he think you might blow up his beloved factory?'

'No, it isn't like that.' Twice's voice was impatient. 'You simply don't understand about Rob, Janet. It's just that —'

'It's not a question of not understanding so much,' I broke in, 'as that the man you are describing doesn't seem to me to be real. I mean all this rubbish about power and being boss of Paradise, it's not *real*. It's a pipe dream!'

'It may have started as a pipe dream. I suppose most manias do. Mania is a sort of solidified pipe dream, isn't it? This is like a cloud that has solidified round Rob's mind. I suppose it is difficult for you to understand because power is a thing that has no appeal for you yourself but it is a failing to which men are subject — think of the Napoleons and the Hitlers. A thing you have often said to me is that one always expects people to behave as one would behave oneself in any given situation and one is always astonished when they don't. The reason why Rob doesn't like to go away and leave me in charge here, especially now that Edward is coming home, is that he is afraid that I will do what *he* would do if he were in my place.'

'Which would be?'

'Grab Paradise for *myself*, you ass.'

'But you don't *want* to be manager of Paradise!'

Twice expelled a hard breath and glared at me before saying very slowly with a pause between each word : 'Rob Maclean thinks that Paradise is literally Paradise and that everybody wants it the way he does.'

'Why don't you tell him you wouldn't have it with a packet of rice thrown in for free?'

'If I did, he wouldn't believe me. He would think I was making some fearfully sharp political gambit.'

When recapitulating a chain of events like this, there

is a danger of giving the impression that, at this time at Paradise, Twice and I spoke of nothing other than the Maclean affair. This, of course, is false. Life contained the usual amount of other trivia and it is only from the vantage point of many years later that one can select what, at that time, was in reality trivial and what was significant. During the week after the débâcle on our veranda, for instance, Twice and I drove Sir Ian's Cousin Emmie to the airport on her way home to London and, there, I met for the first time Mrs. Miller of Hope, a plantation owner whom Twice had met previously. This was an event which proved significant for me, but that is another story and, this being the story of the Macleans, I am trying to select only the incidents that are relevant to them, although many of these incidents passed for trivia at the time and my meeting with Mrs. Miller seemed much more important.

As the week following the scene on the veranda unfolded, no certainty emerged as to whether Rob would board the aeroplane on the Friday or not. I found it extremely difficult to take this new Rob Maclean seriously and all the discussions between Twice and myself were imperilled by my tendency to laugh, whereupon Twice would become exasperated. In a way that was obtuse, although not intentionally so, I could not see this new Rob with his dream of power as the head of Paradise as a real person at all. He took on in my mind the quality of a creature in fable, like the frog that blew itself up until it burst, so that I no longer thought of him as a man or as an engineering colleague of Twice or as the husband of Marion but as a creature that had no real human existence or potential.

'It is getting to the point,' I told Twice, 'when I am beginning to wonder if I ever knew a man called Rob Maclean at all. It is as if his too solid flesh had melted.'

'Well, it hasn't,' Twice said shortly. 'He is still around as

48

large as life and very ugly and myths and pipe dreams apart, there is a silly situation developing. The whole Compound is seething with the row between us and the Macleans and I feel a bloody fool up there at the factory. And one knows that they haven't got anything like the right version of what happened but I can't call the chemists and shift engineers together and explain it to them.'

'I suppose they think we have quarrelled about the broken engagement.'

'Whatever they think, it is cheap and nasty and bloody undignified,' he said angrily.

'I have already said I am sorry,' I told him, on the verge of tears. 'What more can I do?'

'When did you last see Marion?' he asked.

'Over a week ago.'

'That has never happened before. I bet all the female eyes in the staff bungalows are glued to the windows, gloating because her car never comes over here.'

'Twice, I think you are letting this whole thing get utterly out of proportion,' I said, growing angry. 'What if they are gloating? They are always gloating about something. They have nothing better to do. Look, send your car down for me tomorrow forenoon and I'll go over and see Marion.'

'No. Don't do that. I don't want a chauffeur to see you being turned away from the door of Olympus.'

'You are crazy!'

'I don't think so. I am closer to this thing than you are. I tell you what to do. Tomorrow forenoon, send Caleb over with a note inviting Marion to tea and see what happens. We must get this absurd nonsense cleared up somehow. It is worrying Sir Ian and Madame.'

'All right. I'll send Caleb over first thing in the morning.'

'No. Wait until Rob's car has come down to the factory.'

'All right,' I said again.

Twice left me and went through to his study and I stayed

49

on the veranda, looking across the dark park to the lights of Olympus on its high hill. To my left, on the level ground, shone the lights of the staff bungalows and away to my right the tall black smoke-stack of the factory was visible against the sky with the lights of the Great House behind it. I felt that this saucer-shaped valley that enclosed me was a prison where the walls were made of distorting mirror glass, where all the shapes were bent, exaggerated, where even my relationship with Twice was being twisted out of true.

THE next morning, when I had seen Rob's car turn into the approach to the factory, I sent Caleb, our yard boy, off to Olympus with my note to Marion and when he had gone, I went tensely upstairs to the veranda outside my bedroom so that I could watch him go across the parkland, dotted here and there with coconut palms, round which the houses of the white staff lay. Olympus was something like a mile from Guinea Corner and was perched, like so many of the older St. Jagoan houses, on one of the high rocky pinnacles which are a feature of that volcanic landscape. I watched Caleb leave the parkland on the opposite side, cross the metalled road and disappear among the shrubs and trees of the drive up to Olympus, an approach more like a spiral staircase than a road, for it was not more than a shelf cut into the hillside, going up and round to the summit. It would be a little time now before Caleb would reappear on his homeward way and I imagined his sure black feet padding along and up and around that drive which I had climbed on foot only once, in my early days at Paradise.

Instead of thinking about Marion, my real anxiety, I stood on the veranda picturing Caleb going up the road, picturing the road itself and visualising the wide view of Paradise from the gravel square at the front of the house where visiting cars were parked. Suddenly, the analogy of the gods upon Olympus struck me. They too must have had a wide view of their vast domain. Had this analogy, perhaps, contributed to those dreams which, Twice said, enthralled Rob Maclean? As soon as the thought came into my mind, I smiled, imagining what Twice would say of such an idea and, at the same time, I thought it possible that Rob Maclean had probably never heard of the Olympus of the Greek gods or, if he had heard of it, he would not have remembered it nor have realised that this old St. Jagoan house had been, rather fancifully, called after it. This was part of the large area of human knowledge which Rob Maclean referred to as 'all that rot.'

Memory works in a peculiar way. When I first came to the island, a facet of it that interested me very much was these fanciful place-names from mythology and from the Bible and the other names which were hostages to the future, like Retreat or Content or those that were nostalgic, which caused a little settlement of a few shacks and a rum shop to be called Edinburgh. I remembered now that, in those early days, I had once asked Rob if there was any record of why this settlement had been named Edinburgh and he had replied: 'I don't know. I have never been interested in all that rot.'

I had never thought of that remark from then until now but, in the instinctive way that one does, I think that I had decided that Rob would describe most of the things that interested me as 'rot' and I had thereafter taken my questions about the island to other people, chiefly to Sir Ian. I had pushed the thought of Rob Maclean aside, I now saw, for I seem to have an automatic reflex in my mind that pushes into a corner thoughts that do not please me. Probably most people are equipped with a similar reflex. But Rob Maclean had not stayed in the corner where I had pushed him or, rather, this flux that we call life, working through our two personalities had brought him and me into collision.

At last, I saw Caleb emerge from the driveway, cross the road on to the grass of the parkland and I went downstairs and out to the gate to meet him. When he gave me the envelope with my name on it in Marion's handwriting, my hands were trembling so much that I had to wait for him to go away round to the back garden before I opened it. 'Dear Janet, Thank you. I shall come over about three o'clock. Marion.' Everything is all right, I thought. If she were angry, she would not have written 'Thank you' like that. Twice must be having delusions. He is over-tired and needs a break from this place. Everybody has always known that Rob is difficult to work with and Twice has probably had a bit too much of him and sees him in a distorted light. But then I remembered the suffused face of Rob that night when he said: 'You should be bloody well shot!' Maybe Marion was as angry as Rob was but was determined for political reasons to put a social face on things. More lies, I thought. It would be worse than anything to have Marion arrive, politely drink a cup of tea and go away without having mentioned Roddy at all.

The more I thought of this, the more probable it seemed that it could happen. I had always known that Marion was a woman of strong reserves and, as far as I knew, she never talked intimately to anyone. Certainly she had never talked so to me although she had always made me feel that she liked me and trusted me. I felt that I had had her confidence, as it were, without her ever confiding in me about herself, although she had frequently confided in me her views of Mrs. Cranston or Mrs. Murphy in the course of the periodic social upheavals in the Compound. The nearest Marion had ever come to making a confidence in me, I now remembered, was a month or two ago when I mentioned to her that Dee Andrews had come to loggerheads with her family.

'Family loggerheads are the hardest ones to put right,' Marion had said then and I had thought that there was a deep shadow behind her calm grey eyes but, in a moment, she had broken away from the subject and turned to something else. Perhaps, I now thought, she had an inkling at that time that Roddy was heading for trouble while all the rest of us were utterly unsuspecting.

By the time three o'clock came, I had worked myself into such a nervous state that I could not keep still and my hands were cold in the blazing heat of the afternoon. I do not mean that I was afraid of Marion's anger, if she was angry. In a quarrel, I think I can give as ill-tempered an account of myself as most people but I was nervous because I did not want Marion to be angry with me or quarrel with me. It was only now that I realised how very attached to her I was and if she was going to quarrel with me over what I had done for her son, it meant that I had made a wrong estimate of her and had become attached to someone who existed only in my own imagination. If Marion was coming to Guinea Corner to quarrel with me, it meant that she was 'a person like Rob' instead of the woman I thought she was and I did not want to face this sort of disillusionment.

When she drove up to the house, I went to the door to meet her. She came on to the veranda and sat down, as if the events of Saturday had never happened and while the maid brought in the tea and we spoke of Paradise affairs, I began to wonder if Rob had never told her that Roddy had made his escape through my connivance. If, as Sir Ian said, Rob felt that we had 'made a fool of him', it might be that he was trying to conceal this from his wife. The best part of an hour went past, Roddy was never mentioned and I came to the conclusion that Marion did not really know of my part in the affair so, when Clorinda had removed the tea tray, I said: 'I am afraid that Rob is very angry with me, Marion.'

'Yes,' she said. 'He is.'

I looked hard at her, to try to discover whether she were angry too but it was impossible to tell what she felt or thought. She sat there, looking back at me, her face expressionless, her grey eyes placid, her hands still in her lap, looking as composed as she always looked, even in the midst of the most uproarious Compound quarrel. This was another of the things in her which I had admired but now I was less sure that I found it admirable. I was feeling that, instead of being reserved and controlled as I had thought, she was in actual fact utterly detached, so detached from me and my feelings that she had no need of reserve or control. Rob was angry with me but she did not care. She did not care if all the world were angry with me. She had the detachment from me and my feelings not of the friendly gods who live on Olympus, but the detachment of the Fates or the Furies who go their way with utter unconcern for human life.

The mind works very quickly and the adumbration of this detachment of hers which I have tried to describe formed in the few seconds that it took her to speak the words: 'Yes. He is.' But, in those few seconds of discovery, my own attitude to Marion changed for, although relationships are the most important factor in human life, they are also the most fluid and in the climate of this cold detachment, I saw a relationship that had been of value to me wither away before my eyes. Resentment of Marion began to smoulder in me. My mind does not work in a very orderly way. When I am faced with an unexpected situation such as this was, I do not deploy my thoughts in orderly logical sequence. Instead, I suffer something like a mental explosion which makes me angry and I then tend to vent this anger on the person who created the unexpected situation, thus causing the mental explosion.

'I suppose you are angry too?' I said sharply.

'No. There is no point. Roderick is gone now,' she said calmly but the cold in her voice as she pronounced her son's full name made me shiver.

'If that is how you feel I am glad that I helped him to get away.'

'If what is how I feel?' she asked.

'Good God, don't you feel anything at all?'

'That is hardly your affair, Janet,' she told me in a tone that was mildly remonstrative, 'any more than it was your affair to interfere in the discipline of my family.'

She was so calm and superior that it was a blessing that the tea tray was no longer in front of me for I think I should have thrown every article it contained at her but, making a wild grab at the reins of my temper, I seized *But Not For Love* from the table and held it in front of her in a shaking hand.

'Did Rob tell you about this?'

'He mentioned some book or another, yes,' she said.

She made no attempt to take the book from me so that, in an anti-climatic way, I had to put it back on the table which made me angrier still.

'Aren't you interested at all in what Roddy has achieved?'

'I should be more interested to hear of him settling down to a reasonable way of life.'

'I don't understand you,' I told her. 'I just don't understand. If I had written a book like that, my father would be so pleased that —'

'It is not in the least necessary that you should understand me, Janet, and a little silly of you to suppose that I should resemble your father.'

Suddenly I knew that I was going to cry. 'Go away,' I said. 'Please go away.'

'Janet, I do wish you would control yourself,' she said with slight impatience. 'To fly off the handle like this is absurd and ridiculous. You are always doing it. You seem to have no judgment as to where your province begins and ends. It was extremely ill-judged of you to do what you did last Saturday but there is no point in making a scene about it now. Roderick will be dealt with in due course. He will not be allowed to pursue this fantastic way of life.'

'*You* can't stop him!' I said like a defiant child.

She rose to her feet, seeming to tower monstrously above me so I sprang up too, to overtop her with my extra two inches.

'I don't wish to discuss this ridiculous business any further,' she said. 'The trouble that Roderick caused has been detrimental enough to us all at Paradise without you and I, the senior women on the place, having a public quarrel.' She smoothed her silk dress over her hips. 'Now, about the Great House. Madame wishes the annual appeal for the Tuberculosis Fund to go out as soon as possible. I am leaving for Scotland on Friday, as you know. I take it that you will help her with it?'

'Of course I shall!' I told her angrily.

'Very well. We shall consider that arranged. Good-bye for the present, Janet,' she said coolly, went down the steps into her car and drove away.

I ran upstairs to my bedroom, sat down on my bed and began to cry, to cry because I had been so wrong about what Marion Maclean was 'a person like' and after a while the sheer silly uselessness of this was borne in on me so that I stopped crying and became angry again.

When, very shortly, Twice came in from the factory, I was still angry and when he looked round the drawing-room where I was now sitting, obviously expecting Marion still to be with me, I became angrier still.

'She's gone.'

'Oh-oh! Did you throw her out?'

'No.'

'Did she flounce out in a rage then?'

'No.'

'Then did she melt down and dribble away through the floor-boards?'

I glared at him. 'No. She gave me my instructions about the Great House while she is away in Scotland, then said good-bye-for-the-present and sailed out like a duchess. For the present! I'll present her! By golly, the next time I see her I'll—I'll—You know what? That woman's got no feelings. She said Rob told her something about some book or another. Some book or another! And d'you know what she said? She said I was *always* flying off the handle!'

I had to stop for breath and Twice said: 'People tend to exaggerate, use words like always when they mean with moderate frequency.'

I turned my back on him and glared out of the window. 'I take it you had what Sir Ian would call a bit o' an up-an'-down?' he now enquired.

'No, we didn't,' I said, still with my back to him. '*She* was neither up nor down but dead level.'

'And *you* threw the teapot at her?'

'No. Clorinda had taken it away by then.'

When Twice began to laugh at my literal answer to his question, my wrath began to subside and the social significance of what had happened between Marion and me struck me for the first time.

'I wish I had never asked her here today,' I said, on the verge of tears again. 'I have only made everything a lot worse, Twice. But she was so distant and detached and awful and wouldn't even take Roddy's book out of my hand when I tried to give it to her, wouldn't even look at it—'

'Listen, I'll get us a drink and we'll sit down and chew this over calmly, if that is a word that can be applied to any situation in which you are involved. Now, sit down over there and don't move until I come back.'

When I had told him as coherently as I could of what had passed, he said: 'It is this confounded book of Roddy's that is blinding you to all reason, Janet.'

'Confounded book! Twice Alexander, you are as bad as that damned—'

'Shut up!' We glared at one another. 'Now then,' he went on, 'look at it this way. You helped Marion's son to do something his father didn't want him to do. If Marion had helped someone to do something I didn't want, would you have fallen on her neck with gratitude?'

'But you wouldn't want your son not to write books if he wanted to! If we had a son, that is.'

'Janet, do try to be reasonable. You know that if anybody did anything I didn't like, you would spring on them like a tigress. Can't you see that Marion might feel like that about Rob?'

'But Marion isn't like me. That's the whole point, don't you see? She didn't care a damn that Roddy had written —'

'Janet, the point I am trying to make is that Marion wants to preserve her solidarity with Rob just as you would preserve yours with me. She is married to the man and naturally she takes his side against anybody else, just as you would do.'

'She is *not* like me. She is not a person like me at all. It wasn't like that. She wasn't taking Rob's side.'

'You told me that she said you had no right to interfere with the discipline of their family,' Twice said.

'She didn't say *their* or *our* family — she said *my* family.'

'Don't quibble!'

'I am not quibbling. This is the whole point. Rob didn't come into it at all. Neither did Roddy. It was all cold and detached and horrible and nobody really mattering to anybody and nothing mattering except quarrelling being ridiculous and detrimental!'

'This is a lot of irrational nonsense!'

'Oh, all you rational reasonable logical people just make me sick! Marion Maclean is rational and reasonable enough and if that is what you want, go up to Olympus!' I was crying again now. 'Oh, Twice, I'm sorry. I am just in a temper because Marion Maclean isn't the person I thought she was, that's all. It's not her fault. I had made up my mind that she was a person like — like —'

'Like your father who would be proud that his child had written a book—'

'Yes and she isn't like that at all. She is — she is — oh, I don't know.' I dried my eyes, pulled myself together firmly and said: 'Twice, being rational and reasonable is all very well but you have to remember that there are certain fundamental things that are neither rational nor reasonable by the standard of the human brain. Two of these things — or are they only opposite sides of a single thing? — are what we call good and evil. Now, no matter how you reason with me or try to rationalise for me this thing of Marion's and Rob's attitude about Roddy's book and his right to live his life in his own way, you will never make me see it as other than evil and born out of evil.'

'I see,' Twice said quietly.

'I am telling you this because I want this to be the last scene between us about this Roddy affair. I will do what you, Marion and everybody else wants me to do around this place. I will carry on here at Paradise as if nothing has happened but only on the condition that you accept the fact that I am living a lie.'

'Living a lie? Aren't you being a bit melodramatic?'

'No. I am not. I think it is time that everybody around here recognised the fact that this entire Paradise set-up is one big sham and lie but there is nothing I can do to make them recognise it because they don't want to recognise it. And it doesn't matter. We'll be out of it in a year's time or so. But it is essential to me to know my own truth or where I stand and I would like you to recognise that truth too. I know it is almost bad taste nowadays to speak the words right or wrong, good or evil. Everything is relative and comparative, people will tell you. But bad taste or not, I still think that the attitude of Rob and Marion Maclean to their son is born out of evil and is itself evil and that is that. And now that we know where we stand, we will get on with this lie. Can you send a car round tomorrow forenoon to take me round to the Great House? The sooner we start on this charitable appeal nonsense for the TB ward, the sooner we will be finished.'

'Do you know what you look like at this moment?' Twice asked. 'That great big boulder of Reachfar rock that sticks up at the corner of the Little Parkie.'

'I am sorry, Twice. I suppose I am laying down the law a bit. But it is partly this confounded place. I have to lay down my own law now and then or I'll go demented.'

He smiled at me. 'I know. And I am a little like your father about that big boulder. Every time he passes it, he swears at it but he has an affection for it all the same. I offered to blast it out for him but he made a million excuses and so the boulder is still there.'

PART TWO

'— but not for love.'

For twenty-four hours the Maclean affair was not mentioned by Twice and myself and, naturally, we were both conscious of this area of silence that lay between us. He and I had had a number of disagreements down the years, as most couples do, but never any of this fundamental nature and there was nothing I could do to resolve the situation. Twice, although he could recognise the false nature of the Paradise social structure and had once likened it, aptly in my opinion, to a blown ostrich egg which decorated a table in Madame's drawing-room, did not seem to be affected by this falseness as I was and did not feel my urge to fight against it, probably because his energies had an outlet in the creative nature of his work while I spent my days either alone or with Madame and her charitable projects or in the uneasy company of the Compound wives, among whom a violent quarrel was always simmering just under the surface.

Twice, too, had been hurt by my harshness during our quarrel after Marion's visit and, although I was sorry about this, I was not prepared to soften my attitude. All I was prepared to do was to say no more on the subject and hope that time would soften the hard edges of this gulf that had opened between us.

When he came back from the factory on the Friday evening, however, twenty-four hours after our quarrel and we were sitting at tea, he said: 'Well, Marion and the boy are off to Britain but Rob is up at Olympus.'

If I had made the comment that rose immediately to my mind, Twice and I would have been plunged into another quarrel, I felt sure, so I merely said: 'And what sort of a mood is he in now?'

'As smooth as silk and he apologised to me today for the row on the veranda last Saturday night.'

'He did?'

'Yes, in front of Sir Ian. I got the impression that he was acting under orders. It was all very formal. It made me feel like saying: Oh, not at all, old boy. Come around and call my wife a bitch any old time — Good God,' Twice burst forth suddenly, 'Rob Maclean's got brains! He must know that there are some things that a few apologetic words will never wipe out!'

'Give him the credit for saying the words anyway. He probably hated saying them. Besides, he probably quite honestly regards me as a bitch, doesn't he? It was you yourself who told me he had always disliked me.'

'His attitude to you is different now, though. Before, he regarded you as silly and ineffectual like all women, especially what he calls brainy ones but now he seems to see you as somebody — and a woman at that — who is actively intriguing against Rob Maclean.'

'Intriguing? Me? He really is mad, Twice. It must be obvious to everybody that I couldn't intrigue a herring off a plate. I am no good at hiding from my left hand what my right hand is doing. I need both my hands and my feet as well for everything I undertake.'

'It is this thing of people always seeing other people in terms of themselves. Sir Ian has come right round over the Roddy affair, not because of anything you have said or done but because Sir Ian is the type to come round in the end anyway. He is an old man and not a fool and he is the first to admit now that he had a rush of blood to the head when he grabbed his riding stick and went off after Roddy last Saturday. But Rob thinks that you have won Sir Ian over to your side and against Rob by diplomatic means and low cunning. And the silly thing is that I don't think Rob really cares a damn whether one of his sons writes books or not. He has five more potential shift engineers for Paradise in the making, not counting Roddy.'

'Are you telling me that that man had a family of children in order to provide engineers for Paradise?'

'It is not as simple as that. Nothing in life is that simple. But when Marion started producing sons, I think Rob visualised the day when Paradise factory would run on three Maclean shift engineers and Paradise cattle would have a Maclean vet. and the whole issue would be governed by Papa Maclean.'

'You are mad too, Twice!'

'Am I? When Roddy came home last year, supposed to be a newly qualified engineer, what happened? He was out into the power house at the factory, wasn't he? Donald, the eldest boy is a vet., isn't he and coming out here when Davidson retires? Hugh, the second one, is specialising in sugar mill construction at Greenock, isn't he?' I had to admit that all this was true. 'There is nothing wrong in it,' Twice went on. 'Most men use their influence to get jobs for their sons and Mackie, Vickers and Christie, the three shift men here now, will soon be on their way. They won't get any further here. Every shift sugar engineer has the ambition to be chief of his own factory, very much like fifth engineers in ships wanting to be chiefs eventually. Paradise doesn't carry a chief. Chief engineers tend to be blokes with a deal of character, not to say bloody-mindedness, who might argue now and again with Rob Maclean. Is this diagram clear to you?'

'Quite clear as a diagram but hardly comprehensible as a picture of human character, Twice.'

'The silly thing is that in spite of everything, I have a lot of use for Rob. I like him, in spite of certain things about him that seem to me to be queer. After all, there are a lot of things about me that Rob thinks are queer.'

'Such as?'

c* 67

'Well, I read books on social history and I spend hours listening to music on the record-player —'

'Yes, all that rot,' I said, 'I see what you mean.'

'You are quite right. That is what he would say. All that rot. And then, there's you.'

'Me?'

'If Rob had his way, he and I would be up around that factory from six in the morning until eleven at night and he simply didn't seem to be able to take in the idea, in spite of lots of hints, that I wanted to see *you* occasionally so one evening I lost my temper a bit and told him point-blank that, on the whole, I found you more interesting than the factory, especially at the end of an eight-hour day in the said factory. Since then, every time I tell him I am going home, he looks at me as if he were sorry for me. He regards my weakness for you as a sort of minor tragedy, as if I had been born with a humped back or something.'

'Does he indeed?'

'Yes. I believe he thinks that if it wasn't for the way I waste my time with you, I could go nearly as far in my profession as he has.'

'Is that so?'

'If it wasn't for you, I believe he would even give me a helping hand on my way up, but with you hanging on to me, antagonising all the big shots like Rob Maclean, I would never get anywhere in the end so it isn't worth his while.'

'And you say you like this man who has this opinion of you?'

Twice grinned. 'Yes, I like him.' The grin disappeared and he said gravely: 'I like him mostly because I am sorry for him. It seems to me that Rob has got up a hopeless blind alley out of sheer devotion to his job. That is how it all began. He came out here as a youngster and threw himself body and soul into this place and now it is as if the place had devoured him. It is the great passion of his life and it doesn't really care a damn for him and he knows it but he can never admit it. I can't help liking him, Janet, in spite of everything. You see, there is something in human nature that makes one tend to look kindly upon someone who is weaker than oneself. This sounds smug and conceited and I wouldn't say it to anyone but you but that is how I see Rob. I am no man of iron but I am not quite so weak as Rob.'

I think I was jealous of a generosity in Twice which I could not find in myself and this made me say obtusely: 'So now he is a weakling? A couple of nights ago, he was the sugar power of the British Caribbean.'

'Don't *try* to sound stupid,' Twice told me. 'You know as well as I do and better that it is possible to be a power in sugar or steel, finance or fornication and still be a spiritual weakling. And now let's shut up about this and play some records.'

While the music played, I felt that Twice and I had come nearer to one another again. My mind played around the phrase 'the place has devoured him' for this had real kinship with my own view of what this island could do and it was possible that Rob might be a victim.

The days settled down into the Out-of-Crop routine and although, at first, I missed Sandy Maclean, who used to visit me frequently, I had plenty of other interests and very soon the time which I described in my mind in the words of my childhood as 'the week that the Macleans got different' was absorbed into the past and I found that life at Paradise with Rob 'different' was very much like life at Paradise as it had always been for, with Marion away, Madame's affairs took up much of my spare time.

The Monday after Marion left the island, Edward Dulac arrived and Madame, who still lived in a spacious Victorian way, had spacious ideas of entertainment which she used to still carry through in the spacious Great House with its retinue of servants.

'We must give a little dinner-party for Edward, dear,' she informed me on the day that Marion left. 'Perhaps you will be good enough to write the cards for me. I have made the list. Here it is.' She handed me a list of twenty-four names. 'And, of course, you and Twice and Rob must come too and then with Ian and Edward and me, we shall be thirty. Just a nice number. For a week today, dear.'

I wrote the cards and envelopes as she had asked me to do and thanked her a little insincerely for her invitation to Twice and myself, which it was impossible to refuse and when the evening came I bathed and dressed with some misgiving.

I had not set eyes on Rob since the evening when we had the scene on the veranda but in the interval I had thought about him a great deal so that I now felt as if we were going to meet for the first time some strange charac-ter about whom I had heard much and who, although I had not met him before, already disliked me.

'You don't look so much like a well-dressed peasant in that blue thing tonight,' Twice told me. 'You look more like Boadicea in a slightly tetchy frame of mind.'

'You needn't be funny. I have seen the seating plan for this table tonight. Rob is right across from me, over the middle épergne of orchids.'

'All I ask is that the two of you don't start heaving the Coalport. Where am I placed, by the way?'

'One down from Rob between Mrs. Buckley and Miss Sue Beaton. Their combined weight is about thirty-five stones and if you give me one wrong look I'll will them to grind you to powder.'

'Between those two busts, I won't be able to look at any-body. Are you ready? Let's go down and have a quick one before we start.'

The dinner-party was very much like any one of the many I had attended at the Great House and Rob Maclean looked very much as he had always looked. He did not speak to me over the sherry beforehand, during dinner nor afterwards but there was nothing unusual in that, when I considered it. Rob Maclean had never spoken to me at these affairs, nor did he speak to any of the other women more than to bid them good evening. At parties, Rob spent his time, except when he was at table, with a group of men, the most eminent men present, as a rule, and had the scene on the veranda never taken place, so that I was watching him specifically, I would never have remarked the fact that he did not speak to me.

In the drawing-room, after dinner, he attached himself to Edward, who was circulating from group to group about the big room in a rather self-consciously dutiful way and when I saw the two of them heading for the corner where I sat with Madame and a few women, I had a momentary urge to lift my long blue skirts above my knees and run like a hunted stag, but much of my life had been given to the suppression of urges of this kind and it was not impossible to suppress one more.

'I am glad to see you again, Mrs. Alexander,' Edward told me. 'I hardly saw you and Twice at all that Christmas I was here with all the fuss that was going on.'

He had a pleasant face and shiny, well-barbered dark hair. He was taller than I had remembered — as tall as Rob Maclean — but very slightly built and very elegantly tailored. He was not yet thirty, I thought, but in the backwater atmosphere of Paradise, he had a cosmopolitan air that made one feel that he was older. Beside him, Rob looked chunky, bulky and curiously menacing but this last was probably a figment of my over-tense imagination. Madame rose from her chair. 'Sit down here for a little, Edward. I must go over and have a word with Maud about the TB ward. Come, Sue.'

Madame and Miss Beaton moved away across the room, Edward sat down beside me and Rob took the chair that Miss Beaton had vacated. Feeling a movement behind me,

71

I looked up and backwards to see Twice standing there, his hand on the back of my chair. With a determination to steer clear of all Paradise politics, I plunged in: 'Sir Ian tells me that your collection of pictures is growing larger than ever, Mr. Edward.'

'It is not so very large really. Dad and Granny go on as if I had a gallery-full of Picassos in London but I haven't, unfortunately. You are interested in painting, Mrs. Alexander?'

'I get pleasure from pictures but I wish I knew more about them.'

The conversation about painting went on, Rob saying nothing, Edward doing most of the talking, until Twice put in: 'An odd thing happened when we were home on leave last year. Janet and I bought a painting of the Firth below Janet's home from an old dame in a little town near Glasgow and it has turned out to be something quite good. On a small scale, it is a bit like those things you read sometimes about Holbeins being found in stable lofts in Ireland.'

'What a thrill that must have been!' Edward's eyes sparkled with pleasure. 'Have you brought it out here?'

'Yes,' I said.

'May I come round and see it?'

I do not know whether it was my imagination that saw a stiffening of Rob's shoulders under his black coat but I did not imagine the tightening of Twice's grip on the back of my chair. The carved mahogany behind my right ear gave a distinct creak.

'Of course,' it was Twice who answered, 'but it is nothing important, you know. But we bought it as a picture postcard of a view near Janet's home and it turns out to be more than that.'

'Who is the painter?'

'A man called Stubb who was drowned in the sinking of the *Rawalpindi* during the war, we are told.'

72

'Who identified it for you?'

'Egbert Fitzhugh,' I said. 'He has a gallery in Bond Street and he makes something of a hobby of these Stubbs.'

'I know he does.' Edward smiled at me, very amused. 'I know who *you* are now too, Mrs. Alexander. I mean I know in a second way who you are. You are, in old Egbert's words, that Scots friend of Monica's who's got the twelfth Stubb!'

'You know Fitzhugh?' Twice asked.

'I've known him for years. Everybody who is interested in modern painting — or any painting, probably — knows Egbert. Actually, he and I are colleagues in a mild way. I sometimes help him to arrange London exhibitions of Continental pictures. I say, how interesting all this is!' He leaned forward. 'Did you by any chance see the Serafini and St. Hubert exhibition at his gallery when you were at home last year?'

Twice and I had indeed seen the exhibition. We had been to the private view and to Egbert Fitzhugh's dinner-party which followed it. Edward was delighted.

'Did you notice that Head of a Girl by Serafini? Wasn't it a lovely thing?'

'Lovely,' I agreed. 'My friend Monica Daviot bought it at the private view. Egbert Fitzhugh was far from pleased.'

'He is still displeased about that,' Edward said and laughed. 'He had his eye on it for his own collection.'

'Have you met Monica?' Twice asked.

'No. I only know her from Egbert as his brat of a cousin who got away with Serafini's Head of a Girl. Egbert's word portraits of people are drawn in a single line and the only people he can remember and draw at all are those who own pictures that he covets.'

'Yes,' Twice said. 'We noticed that he was a very single-minded sort of bloke.'

Rob Maclean had turned his head round and upwards a little to look up at Twice when he spoke and the light from a wall-sconce behind him threw one side of his face into relief, the other into shadow. In his eyes, I saw a look of animal wariness and on the lighted temple there was standing out a little squiggle of vein that seemed to be too full of blood. He had not spoken a word since he sat down.

'I think, perhaps,' I said, 'I had better join Madame in the tuberculosis corner and find out the latest plans for relieving the wealthier people of their money.'

Edward smiled and stood up. 'When may I come round to see your painting?'

Over his shoulder, I could see the face of Rob Maclean who was also standing.

'Oh, some time when you are free,' I said, 'but I am round here with Madame a lot these days. It hangs in the drawing-room. If I am out, Mr. Edward, just go in.'

'I won't do that,' he said. 'I shall come round tomorrow morning when you are at home, if that won't be a nuisance.'

'We were going to discuss that cooperage contract tomorrow forenoon, Edward,' Rob said, speaking for the first time.

'That can wait, Rob. We'll see to it in the afternoon. A quarter of an hour will settle that,' he said impatiently and turned to me.

'About eleven o'clock, Mrs. Alexander?'

'All right. Come and have a morning cup of coffee, Mr. Edward,' I said.

When Twice and I were home at Guinea Corner and undressing for bed, I said: 'That was one of the less enjoyable evenings I have spent. There is something very frustrating in having to be almost rude to a man that you like in order to placate one that you don't like.'

'In particular when you don't succeed in placating the one you don't like anyway,' Twice told me. 'The way Rob looks at things, he will always remember tonight as the night when you went all out to seduce Edward away from

74

him and cooperage contracts with your picture of Poynt-
dale Bay and cups of coffee.'

'Don't be so silly!'

'I am not being silly. People remember events and people
from the aspect that touches them most deeply, like
Monica's cousin Egbert calling you the woman that has
the twelfth Stubb. But no matter what Rob thinks or re-
members, I think you tried very hard tonight and I give
you full marks.'

'Thank ye kindly but I don't say I am going to be able
to keep up this diplomatic attitude for ever. I am simply
not the sort, Twice, and you know it and it is a great strain.'

'You won't be required to keep it up for ever. In a little
more than a year from now, we shall be on the high seas
and leaving this island for good.'

'That's true. And every day of this coming year that I
don't lay eyes on Rob Maclean I shall consider well spent.'

Edward arrived at Guinea Corner the next day punctu-
ally at eleven and stayed until he had to go back to the
Great House for lunch at one o'clock. I found him the most
pleasant sort of guest and would have enjoyed his visit
greatly had I not, throughout the first hour, been haunted
by the guilty fear that Twice, at the factory, was having
to deal with Rob in a tantrum. It is difficult to describe the
complexity of my feelings that morning.

Basically, I was full of resentment that Rob, a man in
whom I had no interest, was, for a reason that seemed to
me monstrously unreasonable, conditioning my behaviour
to this man for whom I felt liking and who interested me
more than anyone I had talked to for a long time. I have
never been clever at complex relationships where some
things must not be said, where there are restraints and
diplomatic diversions to be made round dangerous ground
so that, for the first hour Edward was with me, I was unable to behave in my natural way. I felt on my guard and,
at this point, personal vanity came in and I feared that

75

Edward would find me guilty of some sort of affectation or, even worse, that he might think that I was wary he might make an attack on my matronly virtue. And, behind everything, there was my childhood training that social upheavals were extremely undesirable, that it was the duty of a woman in my position to 'get on' with all her husband's colleagues, business acquaintances and employers but there was nothing in that training that indicated how I should 'get on' with someone who was firmly determined not to 'get on' with *me*.

It is strange that a mind distorted as Rob's seemed to me to be acting like a lens that distorted my own mind so that, although in a factual way I knew that Sir Ian and Madame knew as much of the Roddy affair as I did, I did not develop from my knowledge of these facts the probability that they had told Edward about it. The Roddy affair had culminated for me in the enraged face of Rob on the veranda that night, followed by the queer revelations that Twice had made about him, revelations to me so dire that they must be kept secret, hidden, discussed only between Twice and me when we were alone.

I was amazed, therefore, that Edward, when he had examined our one picture of any importance and had looked at some of our books and gramophone records, turned to me and said: 'I gather from Dad that you had a bit of a comic upheaval over young Roddy Maclean?'

The amazement was followed by something like a surge of relief that the affair had been mentioned, so that my hand jerked as I stubbed out a cigarette.

'One of our typical Paradise teacup storms,' I said.

'A little more than that surely? This book that Dad tells me about is not what I would call typical of a Paradise situation. I would never have believed that the Macleans could produce a son who could write. Dad told me you have a copy of the book. May I borrow it?'

'Yes. It is up in my bedroom. I'll get it.'

Thankfully, I left him and went upstairs and, standing in the bedroom with the book in my hand, I was reluctant to go downstairs again, reluctant to perform the simple action of passing the book from my hands into Edward's. Since the meeting with Edward the night before and the conversation between us in Rob's presence, an eerie tenseness had taken a grip on my mind, so that my action in lending Edward a book which had been written by Rob's son seemed to be fraught with significance, as if this action were a link in some fateful chain. Over the years, I heard the voice of an eccentric old fortune-teller wailing: 'We are all links in a chain, links in a chain!' and at this I shook myself impatiently and stamped away down the mahogany stairs, making an unnecessary amount of noise, as I tried to assure myself that the ground was firm beneath my feet, the stairs and the house.

Edward looked very urbane, standing in the middle of the floor and as I handed the book to him, he said: 'Is it any good?'

'I think it is quite a remarkable first novel and the reviewers were madly enthusiastic. And the boy is only twenty-three. He really did take all of us here for a twopenny joy-ride, you know. He seemed simply to be a rather brash reckless young man, gambling at Sloppy Dick's bar and making passes at the girls and so on. That he was a writer would have been the last thought. Why do people have to be so complex?' I asked, thinking not of Roddy but his parents.

'I think a father like Rob Maclean would make any son complex,' Edward said, startling me. If I were inhibited, caught up in a conspiracy of silence about Rob Maclean, this man was not, as he went on to demonstrate. 'Rob is a queer character,' he said. 'I know he has been the backbone of this place all these years and I don't want to seem ungrateful for all he has done for us but —' he paused and gave me a strangely intimate glance '— it is terribly difficult to like somebody who one feels doesn't like *one*, don't you find?'

I caught my lower lip between my teeth for a second before I said: 'Yes. That is true.'

He smiled at me before he continued: 'You are more fortunate than I am in a way. Dad tells me that Rob told you openly that he would like to shoot you. I think that must be more comfortable than knowing that he would like to shoot one but does not say so for political reasons.'

This turn in the conversation was so strange and un-expected that I felt that the ground was shifting beneath my feet as the whole picture of Paradise social relationships broke up and changed perspective before my eyes. Hitherto, the key of the design had been the solidarity between the Macleans at Olympus and the Dulacs at the Great House with Twice and myself as a minor bulwark to this solidarity but, now, not only was this design shifting but Twice and I, inevitably, were being shifted along with it. I was certain that Edward Dulac was speaking to me of Rob Maclean as he had never spoken of him to anyone else and I was not sure that I wanted to be drawn into this intimacy so I tried to take significance from our exchange by saying: 'In the words of my friend Sashie de Marnay, you and I are cosy little hatees together, then?'

He seemed to recognise that I wanted to withdraw and he said, smiling: 'That is roughly the position but one does not have to worry about it overmuch.' Then, pausing, he frowned before he continued: 'So far, I have not had to see too much of Rob but I may have to see more of him in the future. Granny is showing her age,' he ended.

I felt that I had come through a jungle swamp into firm open territory. I liked Madame, not so much as a person-ality but as one likes a period piece of furniture, with a little tenderness, and I liked to talk of her, especially to this grandson of whom she was so fond and proud. 'Your coming home has given her a tremendous lift,' I told him. 'She was more upset about the Roddy Maclean affair than I have ever seen her about anything, not the book part but his love life, if that is what one calls it.'

Edward smiled. 'It must be quite difficult to live as long as Granny has and keep up with all the changes, especially changes in things like love lives.'

'I think she has kept pace in a remarkable way,' I said but I did not add that Madame had used her power as mistress of Paradise to slow the pace of life to meet her own demands. It was as if she had built around herself a protective citadel, an edifice which had no windows looking in the directions which she did not wish to see and if someone like myself was invited within this citadel to chat with her and exchange a few opinions, it was tacitly understood that one left certain mental baggage, such as the colour problem, outside as, on the physical plane, one might leave an unpleasantly wet umbrella on the doorstep.

'Do you like living in this island?' Edward asked me next. 'Don't you find it something of a wilderness? No theatres? No concerts? Parochial?'

'I do find it parochial and something of a wilderness although I have no right to be so patronising for my young life was spent in the main on top of a rocky hill in the Highlands of Scotland. But I don't mind the lack of metropolitan things like theatres and concerts here in St. Jago so much as I mind the volcanic nature of the atmosphere — the undertow of the colour question and the feeling of social and political uncertainty, you know. And there is something in the air that makes me distrust my own judgment. It is difficult to explain. I feel that I am not the same person here as I am at home in my own climate and that the home me is the real me and this makes me distrust the island me. And I don't think I am unique. I think that all people from temperate zones undergo some distortion of personality when they live in places like this — a sort of sea change. In some cases, the change may be of the rich and strange sort but not in mine. The change in my case is strange but not enriching. The sun bleaches and dehydrates me and distorts my vision.'

'For myself,' Edward said, 'I loathe the place. I wish Granny could be persuaded to come back to England or Scotland but she won't.'

I tried to imagine Madame extracted from the setting of the Great House and all its appurtenances and settled in a flat or a house or a hotel-suite in London or Edinburgh where she would be Mrs. Dulac, one rich old woman among a lot of other rich old women, with all the trappings of power stripped away from her, but my mind shied away from this vision of nonentity and pathos and I said: 'I don't think you could uproot Madame now. It would kill her.'

'I suppose so.' He sighed. 'If only Dad and I didn't hate this place so much —'

'But I have always thought Sir Ian loved Paradise!'

Edward shook his head, smiling ruefully. 'No. Dad always hoped to retire to London, potter along to his club in the forenoons and go up to Scotland for a bit of fishing and shooting in the season. It is not Paradise Dad loves but Granny.' He looked down at the book he was holding and smiled again. 'Dad is living at Paradise but not for love.'

'He is living here for love of Madame,' I said. 'I don't think one ever does anything of importance unless one wants to do it because of something in oneself. Sir Ian may not like it here but would like London and Scotland, with Madame on his conscience, even less.'

'Astringent, aren't you? And what particular love keeps *you* here when you dislike it so much?'

'I distrust the island more than I dislike it,' I told him, 'and, obviously, I am here because Twice is here.'

From the glance he bent on me, I became aware that

this reason had not occurred to him and, in a sudden flash, I discovered that Edward Dulac was a young man of intellect rather than emotion, a man with little to give except intellectual exchange, a man who would do things but not for love, except of himself. He was the only grandson of Madame, the only son of Sir Ian, both of whom adored him but he seldom troubled to write to them and this was his first visit to them in eighteen months. He was a fairly self-centred person, I began to think — cold, reserved, analytical and, like many people of this kind, his calmly balanced way of thinking and expressing himself made him seem much older than his years. Now that I remembered it, Madame had told me on the occasion of his last visit that he was twenty-five which meant that he could be no more than twenty-seven now but he seemed to me to have all the poised assurance of a man of forty who felt himself to be successful.

'And when Twice leaves here,' I continued, 'I shall leave too, at the end of next year or early in 1954, that will be. But I don't want to give the impression that I have been miserable all the time we have been here or that I don't appreciate all the kindness that has been shown us here at Paradise.'

Edward rose to his feet. 'Don't forget that our manager would like to shoot you,' he said.

'That is part of the volcanic nature of the atmosphere, I suppose,' I said lightly as we went towards the door.

Standing on the steps outside, he looked away across the valley as he said: 'Thank you for a pleasant forenoon, Mrs. Alexander. Or may I call you Janet? I cannot bring myself to the Missis-Janet idiom that Dad uses, I am afraid. And my name is Edward.'

I did not reply at once but waited until he turned his head to look at me. 'Janet will do very well, Edward,' I said then and he at once looked away across the park again. He reminded me a little of the father of Delia

Andrews, a man who found intimacy of any kind extremely difficult.

'I see Rob's car leaving the factory,' he said now. 'I shall meet him in the park. He will be very displeased with me *and* with you. Good-bye for the present, Janet.'

As I watched him drive away, I thought how contrary it was that the one subject which Edward cared to discuss with me on an intimate level, the subject of Rob Maclean, was the one subject that I did not wish to discuss with him at all.

The cars of the various factory executives on their way home to lunch were now radiating across the park towards the various staff bungalows and I waited on the doorstep until Twice drove up.

'What sort of morning?' I asked.

'Tempers in my department were very short but that was to be expected. Has Edward been here from eleven o'clock until now?'

'Yes.'

We came into the house. 'What did you find to talk about?'

'Plenty but some of it wasn't much to my liking.'

Twice frowned sharply. 'In what way?'

'He insisted on talking about Rob Maclean. It appears that the main thing that Edward and I have in common is that Rob hates us both. Yes. You were right. Rob hates Edward's guts but he may not be aware that Edward knows it.'

'How did the subject of Rob come up?' Twice asked, still frowning.

'How do you think? *I* didn't raise it but I couldn't keep it down either.'

While Twice drank his pre-lunch glass of beer, I told him all that had passed and when I had finished he said: 'I am glad that you told him we are going home next year and that you didn't like the life here and all that. I don't think

I am getting swelled head and I certainly hope I am not having pipe-dreams for there are too many of them around here already but I have an idea that Edward has it in mind that it is time Rob retired and I took his place.'

'Heaven preserve us! Twice, you wouldn't consider—'

'No. Don't panic. This morning, just after Edward had spoken to me in an oblique way that gave me this notion, Rob joined us—he never leaves me alone with Edward or Sir Ian if he can help it—I made a point of telling Edward right then, in Rob's hearing, that I didn't see this island as a place to grow old in. Edward caught on at once. He is pretty acute.'

'Acute,' I agreed, 'but a cold sort of fish. I don't think he likes anybody much except Edward Dulac. I may be wrong. He doesn't hate violently like Rob. He goes in for a cold, nose-curling fastidious dislike. In a way, I would rather have Rob.'

'Why for pete's sake?'

'If you can hate some people as violently as Rob seems to do, it argues that you can also love some people fairly violently, doesn't it? I mean the potential is there, isn't it?'

'Rob may have a love-potential,' Twice said, 'but I have never noticed it in use. No. Rob doesn't love any of us. With an effort, he can be civil to us, even smile at us now and then but it's not for love, except of Rob Maclean.'

EARLY in August, Edward went back to London and Rob travelled along with him, in the same aeroplane.

'Your theory about his not wanting to leave you alone here with Edward seems to be right,' I said to Twice.

'Yes, but I think he is convinced now that I am not competing with him for Paradise,' Twice replied. 'Anyhow, whatever the reason for his going, I am glad that he is gone. I'll get on faster with the installation of that new stuff up there without Rob in my hair but, all the same darling, I am not going to take my local leave. There simply isn't time.'

'But Twice!' I was so disappointed that I wanted to burst into tears. We had rented a cottage in the hills for the last two weeks of August and the first two of September, the period when Paradise was at its hottest and for weeks now I had been looking forward to going to bed and waking up in the cool air of the Sierra Grande.

'I know, darling,' Twice said, 'but I just can't avoid this. If I don't get this programme completed by December, there will be a delay in our getting home to Britain for one thing. And I have got to get over to that project in Trinidad too before the end of this year. What I think you should do is tell the Yates they can have the cottage. They haven't found a place yet and you could go to Mrs. Miller at Hope for a month.'

'I am not going anywhere, leaving you here slaving and working,' I said flatly. 'If you can't go, neither of us goes.'

'Janet don't make things more trying than they are already.'

84

'Darling, I am not saying this to be difficult or to try to blackmail you. It is quite simply that if you can't have a holiday, I am not going on my own — not to Hope or anywhere else. I am going to stay here and see that you are properly looked after. That is my job and I am going to do it. Apart from what I feel, what sort of a rocket would I get from Dad if I wrote and told him I was at Hope larking about while you were sweating it out down here?'

'Oh, you and your Dad and your Calvinistic Reachfar consciences! You are as thin as a rake. You look hellish. Dad doesn't *have* to know you are at Hope!'

'Twice Alexander, what a thing to say to a person! I look hellish, indeed. I ought to clout you over the ear and, another thing, to cheat Dad would be just plain immoral. And another thing—'

'Forbye and besides,' Twice interpolated in the idiom of my friend Tom.

'You shut up. I may be as thin as a rake and look hellish but I don't go getting bronchitis every time the wind changes.'

'Don't exaggerate. I haven't had bronchitis for months.'

'You are the one who needs the leave, not me and I am not going and that's the end of it.'

'Not quite. You will go to Mrs. Miller at Hope when I go to Trinidad.'

'All right. That's different. Yes, I'll go then.'

Having made this stand, I did not feel that I had any right to utter a word of complaint about the hurricane weather at Paradise during that August and September and this was very difficult for me. The unpleasant is always more bearable if I can be vocal about it. One hurricane after another passed by out at sea, off the north coast of the island and although, as the vulture flew, Paradise was ten miles inland, the eye of a hurricane passing eighty miles away is near enough to cause days of oppressive low pressure, filled with torrential rain. The rain caused land-slips, the roads became dangerous, people stopped moving about unless it was absolutely necessary so that I had few visitors. Twice was at the factory from daylight till dark and sometimes much later and, day after day, I sat stickily in shirt and shorts, mopping the sweat from my face while I wrote letters to people in the temperate climate of Britain, succeeding in this way, sometimes, by an effort of imagination in cooling myself down while I talked on paper to my father, George and Tom at Reachfar or Edward in his London flat which I had never seen.

The correspondence with Edward began over a parcel of books which he sent me as soon as he landed in London, some for me to keep, some to be read and then placed on the shelves in his suite at the Great House. In the letter that accompanied them, he told me that he would be grateful if I would report to him occasionally about Madame because Sir Ian, as a letter-writer, was strictly in the field-postcard category of 'I am well. I hope you are too.' This had the effect of making me remember that, while Edward was in the island, I had accused him mentally of not caring about his father and grandmother and never writing to them and that I seemed to have made a false accusation made what Twice calls my Calvinistic conscience rise in arms so that I wrote a much longer and warmer letter of thanks for the books than I might otherwise have done. This long letter caused him to write again and, by the end of September, the correspondence was firmly established and I was writing to Edward every ten days or so.

Early in October, Sir Ian discovered that Madame was going blind and had the best eye specialist in the island to see her, only to discover that nothing could be done. The old lady was very gallant about this affliction and would not, even, publicly admit the nature of the trial that had overtaken her. She decided that, instead of going blind, she was troubled with neuritis in her knees and elbows

86

which became worse when she rode in her car to go visiting and also if she poured out tea from her heavy silver
teapot.

'So I shall stay in my own house, Janet,' she informed
me. 'If people wish to see me, they must come here and
perhaps you will be good enough to come round and pour
tea for me.'

In her own house, every floorboard and corner of which
she had come to know down the long years, anyone who
was not fairly familiar with her — there were not many
who were familiar with this grande dame — would never
have known that her sight was impaired at all.

'The worst thing is that my right elbow is extremely
troublesome, my dear,' she went on. 'To write is extremely
painful. Not that I have a large private correspondence any
more. I have outlived most of my contemporaries at home,'
she said with pride. 'But there is Edward. I have never
been a great letter-writer but I flatter myself that I am
better than Ian. My dear, will you write to Edward now
and then for me? I don't wish to dictate letters to *him* to
a typist girl from the office.'

'Of course, Madame,' I said. 'Actually, Edward and I
have been corresponding regularly about books and things
since he went back. I must bring his letters round and r —'
I caught myself in time, 'let you read them.'

'That will be splendid, Janet. How delightful! But *you*
shall read them to me, dear. They are written to you and
for me to read them would not be proper. Edward would
not like that and he would be quite right.'

She was as cunning as an old fox, I thought but I was
forced to admire her courageous uncomplaining attitude
and when I went back to Guinea Corner, I wrote straight
away to Edward, telling him of the affliction that had overtaken his grandmother.

'Please write to her and to me as often as you can,' I said.
'Would you describe your flat in detail. She thinks about

it a lot. When I say detail, I mean things like the lavatory paper. Last spring, before this blindness came on, Ching Lee sent up some mauve bumph to the Great House and Madame gave him such a rocket it nearly carried him back to China. Now that she cannot read, she sits thinking and wondering and, today, she told me that she wondered whether you had that dreadful haircord on your floors or whether they were proper parquet floors with good rugs. When you write, see that they are parquet and Persian even if they are really linoleum.'

Now that Twice and I were to be in the island for only one more year approximately, I made up my mind that I was not, in spite of Madame's increased need of me, going to devote all my time to Paradise and the white society but that I was going to learn a little about what I called inwardly 'the real people of the island' before I had to leave it for good. Thanks very largely to Twice's coloured secretary in the office in St. Jago Bay, a pretty young widow called Freda Miller, I was successful in this resolve and achieved what few white people had achieved in being invited to the home of her family, a plantation called Ginger Grove which was presided over by a negro Madame Dulac whose name was Mrs. Lindsay, but who was known as Mama Lou. My days were very full with this new circle of acquaintance, my large correspondence and my attendance on Madame and I was grateful for the return of Marion Maclean early in December.

With the advent of my new coloured friends, my life divided itself into two parts — Paradise and the rest of the island. Formerly, I had been hemmed in socially by Paradise and the people that Paradise knew and the effect of my straying into a broader society was to make me see Paradise from outside, to some extent, as that broader society saw it, so that its customs, its views, its people and their affairs declined in importance in my eyes. In an island where millions of people were surging forward towards emancipation and a new way of life, it seemed un-important that Rob Maclean was sitting on the hill of Olympus, dreaming dreams of petty self-aggrandise-ment.

When the Macleans first came back to Paradise, Twice said that Rob was much calmer than he had been before he went on leave and put forward the idea that he had prob-ably been over-strained even before the Roddy affair, which seemed to be reasonable enough. Rob had had a complete rest and change of scene for he had gone over to Germany and Scandinavia for six weeks, as a sort of ambassador-extraordinary of Paradise, to visit buyers who normally saw only Edward. Twice said that he talked a great deal of this trip, as if he had now conquered the sugar and rum markets of Germany and Scandinavia and had become the chief power in that market, just as he was chief power in sugar and rum production in the British Caribbean.

Marion and I met at the Great House in connection with Madame's committees and charities as if the Roddy affair had never happened. Marion seemed to be deter-mined to put it entirely behind her and behaved to me as she had always done, in a cool detached way that was pleasant enough but, since that day she had come to tea with me, I had a wary eye for her. Twice might be right. She might be behaving to a pattern laid down by Rob in order to maintain her solidarity with him or, as I some-times thought, she might be hiding behind this cool de-tached façade a resentment of my invasion of the privacy of her family reserves in the Roddy affair but, however it might be, I was now conscious that Marion was not behav-ing as people normally behave. She was carrying through a plan of behaviour. She was behaving inside the frame-work of an attitude.

During the first four months of 1953, I did not realise that I was living through one of the happiest periods of my life. Twice and I seemed to have all of the world that

we wanted at our feet. We had success behind us in this
Caribbean undertaking for Twice's firm and we were look
ing forward to going home to our own country and the
bright prospect it held for us of more promotion for Twice
within Allied Plant Limited. But I was so intent on looking
forward, on chasing the bright rainbow of the future that
I did not realise that it was then that I was right inside the
rainbow itself, with its lovely light all around me.

When I look inward to my memory, I am always re
minded of a 'winter job' that my grandmother gave to
Tom and George and me to do when I was about six or
seven years old. Some old cousin or aunt had died — a
spinster, probably — who left behind, among other things,
an enormous hessian sack stuffed with bits and pieces of
wool, the left-overs from a lifetime of knitting and
crotchet work. The wool was of all colours and thicknesses
and the pieces varied from whole tangled skeins to shreds
a few inches long and my thrifty grandmother decided that
this tangle had to be sorted by 'ply' or thickness so that
the wool might be put to use and the sorting, she also
decided, was exactly the thing to keep George, Tom and
me from sinning our souls in idleness throughout the long
winter evenings.

George, my uncle, and Tom, his contemporary and
friend of both of us, have a built-in faculty for making the
most tedious task interesting and when my grandmother
had supplied us with large cardboard boxes labelled 'two
ply, three-ply, four-ply, five-ply, wheeling and Shetland'
they picked up the sack and emptied its entire contents out
into a mountain on the big kitchen table.

'We will start off with the thick stuff,' said Tom, 'chust
to get our hands in like' and he pulled out a red loop of
wheeling and handed it to me. 'You pull on that till you
get an end out and then make a ball of it,' he said, 'but
don't start till George and me is ready because we are go
ing to have a race.'

'And the winner will get a mark,' George said. 'Get a bittie paper and a pencil, Janet. Come here, Hamish,' he went on, pulling out a loop of navy blue. 'This is my horse and his name is Hamish,' he announced.

'Come, Diamond,' said Tom, pulling out a loop of grey.

'Bang! We're off!' shouted George and we began to pull, disentangle and wind, whooping and yelling and dodging round the table and one another as we pursued the course of our individual threads through the tangle. On the second evening, I broke my strand in my haste, which called down on my head a diatribe from my grandmother which ended with the words: '— and patience is a virtue which is well worth the cultivating' but George and Tom also had a built-in system for the defence of myself and an even subtler system for getting their own back against my domineering grandmother.

'It will not do at a-all to be breaking the wool,' said Tom, looking smugly at Granny. 'That is like putting your horse at a fence wrong and making him fall, poor fellow.'

'Yes, indeed,' said George 'and breaking his leg and he would have to be shot. Now, if anybody breaks their wool or if we have to cut it where there is a bad knot, that horse will have to be shot and the rider gets a mark taken off his score. Now, mind that, Janet and be more careful,' he admonished me sternly while my grandmother regarded him with profound distrust.

And well she might distrust him for, very shortly we came upon an inextricably teased knot and even she had to agree that Tom's strand would have to be cut. 'Bang-bang!' George shouted as I cut the thread and then he closed his eyes, laid his hand over his heart and began to sing: 'Abide with me! Fast falls the eventide —' which was my grandmother's least favourite hymn for she never wanted the days to end, she who had so much to do. In addition to this, our kindest friends could not claim with sincerity that either George, Tom or I could sing.

After that, at least three horses had to be shot every evening and what with the bang of the starting pistol, the whoops during the race and the obsequies for the shot, my grandmother came to regret deeply that she had ever given us the wool-winding job to do at all.

This has been a digression but, in my memory, people appear like the coloured threads that made up that long-ago tangle of wool and in my memory the many-coloured web lies, as in a sack, all the threads almost inextricably interwoven and, sometimes, in an awed fashion, I become aware that this tangle I carry within me is only an infinitesimally small part of the memory tangle that makes up the race memory of my country. In May of 1953, this awe-inspiring awareness of race memory was brought home to me very forcibly at Paradise. In the time, between 1948 and 1953, that Twice and I had been in the island, St. Jago, like the other islands of the Caribbean, was struggling towards self-determination. Politically, the island societies were growing up and were no longer willing to remain in the shadow and admonition of Britain. Growing up is a difficult process for individuals and the process is no easier for entire races or societies.

And just as every human individual carries within him his steadily increasing tangle of memory, so do races and societies carry forward with them their history, which is the remembered experience of their forefathers. The race memory of the people of St. Jago and of the West Indies generally was not long, as race memories go, for this was the memory of tribal peoples who, some two hundred years ago, had been wrenched from their roots in their native Africa and transported in chains to these islands and into slavery. This memory was as sad and ugly as any race can drag behind it, a memory of enslavement, blood and cruelty at the hands of white men. The slave ships were the Dachaus and Buchenwalds of their day and the St. Jagoans, descendants of the people who had crossed the

Atlantic in their stinking holds, still had these ships and their fetters deep in their memory.

Paradise, by virtue of a forward-looking policy, developed largely by Rob Maclean, had always been a happy estate. Madame and Sir Ian, with their attitude of benevolent despotism, were loved and respected by their people, every one of whom knew that he had direct access to the old lady or her son to present his case and he also knew that that case would be dealt with justly and with a bias towards benevolence. But in May of 1953, one of the political agitators of the island decided that it was time that the age-old peace of Paradise was disturbed and, being an experienced rabble-rouser, he caused the four thousand workers who were engaged in the harvesting and processing of the sugar cane to come out on strike after speaking to them for less than half-an-hour. This speech, to do its work so quickly and thoroughly, was, naturally, directed at the most explosive areas of the coloured workers' race experience and contained a great deal of inflammatory matter about men like Sir Ian, Rob and Twice 'bleeding the coloured worker to provide soft beds for white whores'.

At the end of a few phrases like this, Twice left the office window where he, Rob and Sir Ian had been listening to the orator and came rushing home to Guinea Corner, so shaken with rage that he was hardly able to breathe. Gasping, he told me something of what was happening, something of what the agitator had been saying and then: 'Janet,' he said, 'I ran away! If I'd stayed, I'd have died of shame!'

The next day, he went down with what, at that time, the estate doctor and all of us thought was an attack of his recurrent bronchitis with malarial complications and was confined to bed for three weeks.

I have always had an unnatural horror of illness because, I think, my attitude to it was conditioned, as all my fundamental attitudes have been, by my early years at Reachfar.

Nobody at Reachfar was ever sick, except my mother who was delicate and was a constant anxiety to my grandmother, who adored her. My grandmother, who looked upon the rest of us, especially George, Tom and me, with a hard and critical eye and spoke to us, especially to George, Tom and me, in a firm voice from a high pinnacle of authority, had a different eye and a different voice when she said to my mother: 'Have you a headache, *m'eudail*?' To me, as a child, this change that my mother could work in my grandmother endowed my mother with magical powers so that 'delicate health' was a magical mystery but, at the same time, it was also a frightening anxiety. I felt uneasy when I went down to the local village and the kindly people would say: 'So it is yourself, Janet Reachfar and how are you today?' 'Very well, thank you' I would reply and wait, with a horrid little flutter in my stomach, for the next inevitable question: 'And how is your mother keeping?' 'She is very well, thank you,' I would say defiantly. 'We are *all* very well at Reachfar.' And when I was ten years old the magic and the anxiety came together in terrible synthesis when my mother died.

During the three weeks that I nursed Twice, I was again in the grip of anxiety and of magic, an evil magic. The sudden strike, the sudden rift in the old fabric of human relations at Paradise was a shock that seemed to have been caused by almost supernatural means in that one man, by playing for a short time on the sensibilities of four thousand people, could destroy a relationship which had existed for generations. But since we are all basically selfish, this disintegration of the Paradise pattern had little importance compared with my anxiety for Twice and, in the tortuous way that the mind works, I blamed Kevin Lindsay, the agitator who caused the strike, for the illness and through Kevin Lindsay his entire race and this island which had bred him. That Kevin Lindsay was the son of Mama Lou and the brother of Freda Miller with whom I had made

94

friends merely made him more treacherously hateful. Although I knew he was a renegade from the Lindsay family, I still regarded him and even his family and his whole race as treacherous traitors who had betrayed me by causing this upheaval that had made Twice so ill.

The incident of the strike and my feeling about it along with a few other minor incidents caused a temporary strain in the flimsy fabric of my newly-formed relationship with the Lindsay family and I drew back for a short time into the enclosed world of Paradise, my attendance on Madame and my reading and writing in the Guinea Corner drawing-room. When I allowed myself to think of the month of May, I was haunted by a depressing sense of failure, for a breakdown in human relationships saddens me more than anything, but I soared out of my depression when I received a letter from Edward which told me that he would arrive for a short visit about mid-June. Here, at least, was a relationship which had not failed for, through our correspondence, Edward and I had reached an intimacy which might not have been reached by any other means.

On the first forenoon that he came to see me, the new intimacy was there between us as he said: 'Well, Janet, how are you and the Great Bear getting along? Any more dramatic scenes?'

The code name of 'Great Bear' for Rob had evolved in the course of our letters to one another.

'Never a scene,' I said. 'Everything is as smooth as silk. He was here quite a lot when Twice was sick and it was all very civil.'

'I think Roddy will be quite disappointed,' Edward said.

During these months since his last visit, he had sought Roddy out in London and a warm friendship had grown up between them in spite of the fact that the conventional Edward was in an almost perpetual state of shock at Roddy's mode of life.

'How is Roddy?' I asked.

'He sent his love, by the way. As for how he is, he is simply as he ever was only more so. At the moment, his paramour is a red-haired girl from Wales, a fashion journalist and the rows between them have to be heard to be believed.'

'Does he hear from Rob and Marion at all?'

'He had a very rude letter from Marion from Scotland last year, commanding him to come up there and he wrote an even ruder letter back saying no. Since then, all has been silence but he hears from Rob and writes to him quite often.'

'How very odd,' I said, 'and how wrong one can be. I should have thought that Marion would have healed the breach between Rob and Roddy. I should never have expected those two to make things up while Marion stood off in a huff.'

Edward was thoughtful for a moment. 'The more I see of Roddy,' he said then, 'the more of Rob I see in him. He is the young Rob, I should think, the Rob of the days before he became such a bombastic blow. But Marion — Roddy hardly ever mentions her but when he does you can feel him hating her.'

With my own childhood background of a family in which the relationships were as nearly perfect as human relationships can be, I am always appalled to hear of things such as this which seem to be as unnatural to me as some physical freak, like an animal born with two heads.

'Marion always seemed to me to be such a perfect mother,' I said, but as I spoke, I thought forward from the first four years I had known Marion to that day when she came to tea and had suddenly seemed to be so different.

'I think you saw her as a projection of yourself, as the kind of mother you would have liked to be. I think we do this quite a lot with other people. It is a sort of egotism, really. We can't really see beyond ourselves and to some extent we see other people as ourselves in a different situation.'

It was, indeed, in this way that I had seen Marion and I had derived a satisfaction from seeing her thus, a satisfaction that had prevented me from envying her those seven sons who I would so much have liked to have for my own.

'However it is,' Edward said, 'she has failed in a tragic way with Roddy. Of course, he is highly talented and people like that are not too easy to come to terms with. They create difficulties as the sparks fly upwards and they then suffer much more from the difficulties than the rest of us do. It is amusing to have Roddy for a friend but I should hate to have him as a member of my family.'

'Poor Roddy. But does his love life leave him time for any work?'

'He has a book of poems coming shortly and the next novel is nearly finished, I gather, but he talks very little about his work, never seems to want to discuss it.' This, which puzzled Edward, it seemed, I could completely understand. 'But I didn't come round here to talk about Roddy. How are *you*, Janet? You are thinner than ever.'

'But I am all right. I come of lean stock. Twice is the one who has given trouble, as you know. What do you think of Madame?'

'Except for her sight, she is in splendid form. She is furious about this business of paying the workers a cash bonus instead of giving them a slap-up party at the end of Crop but that she is furious about something means that she is well. And Dad and I can never thank you for all you do for her.'

'I don't do very much. Marion has been doing most of it lately.'

We went on to talk of the strike, of my sorties into the

coloured society of the island, of books and other things until it was time for him to go home, for lunch.

'By the way, how long are you staying?' I asked then.

'Only ten days. I love you all very much — how much you will never know until you come to understand how much I hate this island.'

On most forenoons, Edward would come round to see me and the ten days of his visit soon passed but, by the time he had gone, the shock of the strike had slipped into the past, the factory was in operation again and the breach that had opened between me and the Lindsay family had healed over. During July, I saw quite a lot of the Lindsays and other friends and hardly went at all to the Great House for, now that Marion had left Sandy at school in Scotland, she did most of the waiting upon Madame herself. More than anything, during this month, I was looking forward to spending the month of August at High Hope, a cottage four thousand feet up on the Sierra Grande, which had been lent to us by Mrs. Miller of Hope. And, this year, I prayed about our holiday in the words of my childhood: 'Please God, make everything go right so that Twice and I can go to High Hope.'

Everything went right. The fully expanded factory had processed the crop without a hitch, the machinery was run down to a standstill at the end of July and in the first days of August Twice and I, with Caleb, our yard boy, our dog Dram and Charlie our cat got into the car and set off for High Hope. It was here, on this hilltop which was, for me, a St. Jagoan Reachfar, that disaster overtook us. At the end of the first fortnight, Twice became ill and I spent a long, stark moonlit night alone, except for Caleb, on this remote hilltop, miles from anybody, with the terrible fear in my mind that Twice might die before dawn.

During that night, the enmity of the island to us white people was an almost palpable thing for me as I looked out and down at the jungle of bush and trees that rustled and whispered, malignantly and secretively under the pitiless white moon and, yet, when the next day came, it was not only Sir Ian and white Paradise that came to our aid but also the coloured Lindsay family, one of whom was the most eminent doctor in the island.

Twice was in hospital from mid-August until the end of October, critically ill for the first three weeks and then making a slow recovery and, during that time, I occupied one of the vacant rooms in the private block at the hospital and my whole life was centred there.

Often, as I sat on the veranda outside the little room where Twice slept for long parts of the day, I would trace through my memory the dark thread of his illness, examining incident by incident his various attacks of bronchitis, passing them along the thread like beads on a rosary and, always, I would find myself pausing at the incident of the political agitator's speech and Twice's garbled report of it which had ended: 'Janet, I ran away! If I'd stayed I'd have died of shame!' There was something here that was not in the character of Twice as I had known him.

The reaction to the agitator by Twice which I should have expected would have been one of raw red rage that this man was trying to come between the feudal-spirited fair-minded Sir Ian and the estate workers whom he regarded partly as his children and partly as his friends. And, in Twice, I should have expected too more rage that this agitator with his speechifying was causing a loss of the factory's time, the huge plant running empty of material while he spoke. But the final words: 'I'd have died of shame' I was at a loss to account for. Twice, in anything that he had done concerning the workers of Paradise had no cause for shame, I knew, and Twice, as I thought I had known him, would have been more inclined to roar with laughter at oratory about 'soft beds for white whores' than to be brought to shame by it.

However, I let the incident drop back into memory and be overlaid by more important considerations as Twice became convalescent, for I had to begin to wonder where and how we were to live now that we had been advised not to risk the British climate and Twice was no longer able to do the only work for which he had been trained.

It seems to me that the mind can form habits just as the body can, for I did not even think of our continuing to live at Paradise. For two years now, I had been used to the idea that we would leave Paradise at the end of 1953 and incidents such as the Roddy Maclean affair had made this idea all the more acceptable so that, when Sir Ian came to me one day, reminding me that two years ago he had offered Twice a post on the staff of Paradise and telling me that the offer was still open, I burst into tears that were partly caused by relief but partly by the shock of surprise.

'But that was when we thought he was a fit man!' I said.

'He's still fit enough for what Paradise needs,' Sir Ian said. 'The doctor says what he needs is a regular way o' life — no tearin' about in aeroplanes an' all that — an' a job that don't call for a lot o' hard physical work. All right. I ain't askin' him to climb up the cranes at Paradise or swing about from the girders by his toes the way he did before. I want him to sit at a desk an' use his brain to get the production up an' cut the costs down. Rob's not gettin' any younger an' he can't do everything. Besides, Rob don't seem to see how things are goin' in this island.'

In that moment, I was so full of gratitude to Sir Ian that there was no room in my mind for anything else and the final remark about Rob went into the tangle of memory without examination.

When Twice grew stronger, Sir Ian put his proposal to him and Twice accepted it as gratefully as I had done but it was not until we were at home at Guinea Corner and Twice was going up to the factory to take up his new appointment at the beginning of December that Sir Ian's remark was brought back to my mind.

'Remember now,' I said to Twice the night before he was to start work, 'the minute you feel tired, you are to come home.'

'I'll remember and I wish you would stop worrying.'

'I am not worrying but I don't want you to get up there and get the wind under your tail about something going well or getting into a blind rage about something going badly. Those fits of rage you went in for before, like the one the day Kevin Lindsay brought the workers out on strike, are over for good, remember. And what a thing to get in a rage about anyway! A political agitator shooting his face off! A waste of good temper, I call it. As for letting a man like that with his gabble about white whores make you ashamed, you should be ashamed of yourself for feeling ashamed.'

Twice looked at me, studying my face carefully, as if it were a drawing of a new machine which he had not seen before.

'It is as if I had forgotten what you were really like for a while and I am starting to remember again,' he said, almost shyly.

Since he had been ill, he had withdrawn from me a great deal, which hurt me in a way that I tried not to let him see and I could have cried with gratitude for this first little sortie he had made but he drew away into himself again. I think that, during his illness, he had come so close to death that he had left life and me behind for a moment — a moment of my time but it might have been a millennium in his mind and it was taking him a long time to come back, to renew contact, to believe that he was really alive again. And then, too, the paraphernalia of the sickroom was still with us — charts of temperatures, pulse beats and urine measurements had to be kept for the doctor, tablets had to be taken and a special and rigid diet maintained. All this I disliked, for my terror of illness was more morbid than ever now, after that dreadful night at High Hope. Constantly, I was struggling to conceal my dislike of the thermometer and my fear as I read what the mercury might indicate, which imposed a restraint on my entire manner. Twice and I had not the habit of restraint with one another.

Added to all this, there was the complete physical separation. When he was ready to come out of hospital, I had had his ground floor study turned into a bedroom so that he need not climb the stairs and I still occupied, alone, our old bedroom immediately above. It was a strange new way of life that we had to make and there is little wonder, I see now, that for a period of nearly a year we were like two strangers cast up on an unknown shore.

Indeed, the strongest link between us at this time, or perhaps it would be more accurate to describe it as the link between us for which we could find words, was Paradise, its people and its affairs. Paradise was something that had been in our old world and had come on with us into the new and I had noticed that, nowadays, Twice would tell me more about Paradise affairs than he would have done in the past. This may have been because he was now a member of the staff, hearing of those affairs by right instead of hearing of them incidentally as an outside consultant but, apart from this, I think that the tremendous experience of his illness had reduced such things as Paradise affairs to insignificance so that he thought of them as no more, now, than small talk.

'I wasn't ashamed about Kevin Lindsay that day,' he said now.

'No? What then?'

'It was about Rob Maclean. I thought he was going to wet his pants with fear. It made me sick to look at him.'

'Fear? Fear of what?'

'That they would start rioting, I suppose.'

'And burn out the factory like at Retreat?'

'No,' Twice said slowly. 'No, it wasn't like that. It wasn't fear for the factory. I wouldn't have minded that so much. It was fear for Rob's own skin. He was sweating with it — I could smell it. It made me want to vomit. That is why I ran away.' Very calmly, in the new controlled way which his illness had brought to him, he went on: 'To run away from that is my particular form of cowardice, I suppose, for if they had started rioting — this isn't swank, I think — I would have gone back up there. But I was so afraid that Sir Ian would turn round and see Rob or think that the stink was coming from me that I beat it. The old man was right in the open window of his office, you see, facing Lindsay across the factory yard and Rob and I were on either side of him and about a step behind. And the funny thing was that, standing there, smelling that smell, I realised that I had always known that Rob was a physical coward but I had never let myself face it.'

'Twice, in all that has happened, I am afraid that I had overlooked Rob Maclean as a facet of this new job of yours. I seem to be fated always to overlook Rob Maclean. If working with him is going to be a strain of any kind, this job at Paradise won't do, you know.'

He laughed. 'Don't worry, darling. I have gone away beyond being strained by Rob Maclean. If nothing else, being a bit sick teaches you that there are worse things than working with a bloke that you don't admire very much.'

'But isn't it possible that he resents this appointment? Remember when it was first mooted back in '52?'

Rob had been a frequent visitor throughout Twice's convalescence, spending many an hour in his room at the hospital and in the convalescent period after we were at home and I had studiously left them to themselves at these times. This was not because of any self-consciousness about the old Roddy affair but for the reason that applied at dinner parties, because Rob had no conversation for women.

Our attitudes to people can be so subtly altered by so many factors. While Twice was ill, I looked upon people entirely in the light of their effect on him so that, if a certain visitor tired him, I took a dislike to that visitor and would have disliked him, I think, even if, hitherto, he had been my best friend. When people stepped into that white room at the hospital, I saw them entirely in the light of that room. Nothing that they had been before existed. Rob, when he came to visit Twice for the first time, entered the room like a big clumsy teddy-bear who was a little scared of this clinical place, scared that he might speak too loudly or knock something over or that his big feet would mark the shining floor and some angry nurse would scold him. It made him extraordinarily likeable and what, for me, made him more likeable still was that he was the visitor who did Twice more good than any other. He talked of nothing but the factory, the distillery and engineering generally; quite often he did not even greet Twice by asking how he felt. He merely sat down carefully by the bed, looked uneasily about him and then, as if to comfort himself, began to talk about the only things he knew and when he was going away he would say: 'I wish you'd think about those filter screens and let me know tomorrow if you have any ideas', whereupon he would tiptoe out and, once on the veranda and out of danger of being clumsy or getting in the way, he would heave a great sigh of relief. In those days at the hospital, I did not think of him as Rob Maclean who had wanted to throttle me at the time of the Roddy affair or as Maclean, the manager of Paradise and sugar power of the British Caribbean. I thought of him as this big bumbling teddy-bear who did Twice so much good.

It was only now that I began to think of him again as a possible megalomaniac who had always been difficult to work with and who might have a reaction anything but friendly to Twice's appointment to the Paradise staff.

'Did he say anything after Sir Ian appointed you?' I asked now.

'He said he was pleased.'

'Oh?'

'I think he meant it too.'

'Twice,' I said with some idea that I had to give credit where it was due, as if I were paying off some of the debt of gratitude that I felt that Twice was still alive, 'Rob was most terribly good when you were sick.'

'I know. He never missed a day.'

'He helped you.'

'I know. It is queer about Rob. There is so much in him that I like, if one can only get him away from this Paradise thing. Oh, I know he talked about the factory all the time when he came to see me but that wasn't specifically Paradise. It was just the job itself — engineers talking, you know.'

It seemed that just as my attitude had been altered by the white hospital room so had Rob's attitude been altered.

'It is when — when he has fed on honey dew and drunk the milk of Paradise — ' Twice smiled faintly ' — that it goes to his head and you get all the blow and bombast.'

'I hope he is not drunk on the milk of Paradise when you go up there tomorrow and starts thinking that you are out to steal any of his honey dew.'

'No. I don't think he will think along these lines any more.'

'Sir Ian suggested to me at the hospital that Rob was losing his grip,' I said, remembering.

'He is certainly different from what he used to be, less inclined to write people off in an imperious sort of way. I noticed it after being so out of things for a bit. I seem to be rediscovering everybody and they are all a little different from what they were before. I suppose the change is in myself really, except for Rob. He really has changed.'

'As long as he doesn't get any funny ideas about you — ' I began again.

'He won't. The position is very different now from what it was in '52,' Twice said. 'You see, I am safe now. My teeth have been drawn. A man in my physical condition could never compete with Rob although he is a good bit older. No. He is manager and my title is assistant-manager and so it will be until the end.'

I did not pursue the matter further for I knew that this dead-end to his career at the age of forty-three had been a cruel blow to Twice but a blow which he was trying hard to withstand without complaint and which he could not easily talk about as yet.

After our five months beleaguered by illness, the siege was raised and we emerged on to the road of life again but while the main army of the living marched apace down the broad highway, Twice and I came along at our own slower speed on a quieter less busy side-track. We no longer gave parties or went to parties and we no longer worked ourselves into fevers of indignation as we and especially I had been wont to do at the time of the Roddy affair and before. Marion Maclean was more socially active than ever, carrying the main burden of the Paradise entertaining now that Madame was no longer able to do it and Rob remained very much in the broad highway of life and was more than ever the sugar and rum power of the British Caribbean, flying here, there and everywhere in the aeroplane that was chartered for him but never staying away for long enough to relax his grip on the estate. Indeed, in this year of 1954, I thought that Rob was probably more sure of himself than he had ever been. Edward had not been seen at Paradise since June of 1953, Twice was, through illness, no longer to be regarded as a menace and Sir Ian, devoted to his blind old mother, seldom set foot within the factory precincts.

I F, during 1954, Rob Maclean was secure in his power as a petty king. I, during that year, was afraid, lonely and bitterly unhappy with what had been my world in ruins all about me.

Reachfar, my home in Scotland which I had loved so much, had been sold at the end of 1953 because my father and my uncle were too old now to farm it and, as I sat at Guinea Corner during the long days of 1954, I would think with bitter self-scorn of how I had despised Rob Maclean for what I called his 'pipe dream' of himself as lord of Paradise. With regard to Reachfar, I saw now, I myself had been dreaming a similar dream, dreaming that, one day, I would go back there to wander over its fields and moors as I had done as a child, ignoring the economic factor that Reachfar had to be made to pay as a farm, for my family could not afford to keep it as a luxury. I was no person, I saw now, to hold Rob Maclean and his dreams in scorn.

During that year, I had plenty of time to despise myself. Ill health is an isolating thing and Twice's sickness, as well as putting distance between him and me, had put distance between us and all our friends. An illness of limited duration is something that people can stomach and over which their sympathy can stretch but nothing wears out more quickly than sympathy stretched out over a long period of time and humanity's stomach soon sickens at the sight of permanent ill-health, so that, gradually, most of our acquaintance dropped away with the notable exception of Sashie de Marnay, who called on us whenever he could snatch a moment away from the Peak Hotel in which he was a partner.

I was lonely but I did not blame people for not coming to see us because Twice's routine made entertaining, especially in the St. Jagoan fashion, difficult. His diet and his time-table were rigid to the extent that the liquids he drank were measured in fluid ounces and his evening meal was served as the clock struck seven. In a country where people were accustomed to drinking continuously — be it lemonade, whisky, cocktails or beer — from six o'clock until eight-thirty or later before having a meal, our routine at Guinea Corner was outlandish. People could not be blamed for leaving us within that routine as in a prison but although I told myself this, it did nothing to abate my feeling of isolation which was increased by the feeling that I was now not only an exile, but an exile without hope of return, a 'displaced person', one of the many such in this twentieth century.

It was during this year of 1954 that I discovered that, for me, it is not possible to live by the will. It was I who, by my will, had turned Guinea Corner into a convalescent home with all its facilities revolving round Twice, where every smallest instruction given by the doctor was carried out meticulously to the letter and it was my will to live myself within this framework, devoting all my energies, mental and physical, to Twice and his well-being. This was what, intellectually and emotionally, I wanted to do but there is some factor that is independent of the intellect and the emotions, some driving force rising out of a deeper individuality which would not let me devote all of myself in this way to Twice whom I loved and wanted to serve wholeheartedly but which insisted on the expression of itself through channels utterly apart from Twice and my relationship with him.

And, with his post at the factory and his routine at home, Twice no longer seemed to need me as he had done when

he was well. Then, he was always enthusiastically embroiled in something, requiring one to come and see or
come and listen or to hold this or that for him but now he
lay in his long wicker chair for hours, wrapped inside himself, neither speaking nor moving. He still liked to listen
to music and in the evenings and on Saturdays and Sundays he would lie on the veranda, his eyes fixed on the
green hilltops that surrounded the Paradise valley, never
moving except to put a new selection of records on the
turntable of the player. He seemed to live in some far
place beyond those green hills, somewhere in that brilliant
sky which was filled with the sound of the choral movement of Beethoven's Ninth Symphony, while I remained
alone, anchored to the earth, where the sight of the paraphernalia of the sickroom gnawed at my mind like a
canker worm.

With a feeling of guilt that I was neglecting him, despite
the fact that he did not seem to need my presence, I would
leave the veranda and retire to my writing-table in the
drawing-room and there I would sit, staring at the wall,
hating myself for hating the sickroom paraphernalia that
was keeping Twice alive and ashamed of myself for being
unhappy when I had so much to be grateful for until,
unable to face my situation any longer, I would seize my
pen and write letters.

Ever since I left Reachfar at the age of twenty-one to
earn my living, I had written home to my father every
week that I was not at home on holiday and, down the
years, a fairly large correspondence had developed round
this nucleus of the weekly letter home. This was increased
still more since I had come to St. Jago and had gone on
increasing down the years so that, before Twice became
ill, I used to spend hours of every day in letter-writing. In
those days, when I picked up my pen and wrote 'My dear
Dad' or 'My dear Monica' or 'My dear Hugh' or 'My dear
Edward', I used to escape from the heat of St. Jago and the

atmosphere of Paradise into the ambience of the person to whom I wrote but in this year of 1954, this was no longer possible. I could not get away from Guinea Corner, I did not want to get away from Guinea Corner but Twice and this house no longer seemed to want me in any essential sense. And there was nothing I wanted to say in any letter except the one thing that could not be said: 'Since he was ill, Twice has become different and I don't think he wants or needs me any more. I know that he is very unhappy but when I try to reach him, he just looks away from me and out of the window.' And so I stopped writing letters except to my father, because to write to him weekly was something I had done all my life, the one thing he had ever asked me to do for him after I had grown away from childhood and I used to begin these letters: 'My dear Dad, Twice is very well now and the doctors are very pleased with him —' and, while I wrote this, I would cry because it was so terrible to tell lies to my father for, although it was true that Twice was physically very well and that the doctors were pleased with him, these words that I wrote constituted a lie, a false communication from me to my father. And then, one day, when I had begun my letter in this way and had gone on to say how much Twice was enjoying his new job at the factory, I thought: 'All this I am writing may be lies but they are white lies, as people call them. I am writing them so that my father will not be worried. I am writing them out of love. If I deceive out of love, the love nullifies the deceit, surely.' And the other person I wrote to, putting a good face on things, was Edward. I did not write to him as often as before because, during this year, I was going to the Great House very seldom but I wrote to Edward frequently enough to have a recent letter from him, every time I went, to read to Madame. My attitude to Madame in these days was one of casting bread upon the waters. I had little affection for her, had always been critical of her, but I admired her courage and I was grateful to her for all that she and Sir Ian had done for Twice and me. But I did what little I could for Madame chiefly because she was old, in the hope that somebody would be kind to my father, should he need kindness, for he was seventy-six now and deep in my mind lurked the thought that, since Twice and I could not go back to Britain, I might never see him again.

This invisible but impenetrable screen that dropped between Twice and me was made up of many factors but, many times, it seemed to me to be composed of nothing but a web of my own guilt. I remembered how frequently I had said: 'I hate this bloody island! I wish it was a year hence and we were back in Britain!' and, while Twice listened to his music and looked away to the hills, I would feel that he was remembering these things I had said. But I could not approach him and tell him that they were no longer true, for his doctor had warned me that any scenes of intense emotion must be avoided at all costs. And, indeed, it was no longer true that I hated the island. I felt now that the worst had happened, that I had nothing more to fear from the dark gods that presided here, for the dark gods had been not of the island but of my own imagination and when the crisis of the worst was visited on Twice and me, it was Freda Miller, her brother Josh, her other brother Doctor Mark Lindsay and her sister Florence who was a nurse, who had done most to turn the tide of death away from us. I was grateful to Madame and Sir Ian for what they had done for us but I was immeasurably more grateful to the Lindsay family, people of the island, who had submerged their race memory to come to the aid of two whites, out of a friendship that, in the light of history, these two whites did not deserve. But none of this, during that year, could be discussed with Twice. It was all too emotional and lay too deep.

Once, when speaking of a woman called Muriel

Thornton who I knew long ago, I described her as the 'creaking rusty hinge' on which, yet, the direction of another life could turn. It was through this colourless woman that I met Twice, a meeting which altered the entire course of my life and, now, when I had begun to think that Twice and I must go on to the end with this invisible impenetrable screen between us, a woman as colourless and uninteresting as Muriel Thornton appeared in our lives and took on in my mind the character of the creaking rusty hinge.

She was a friend of my friend Hugh Reid, her name was Helen Hallinzeil and she was coming out from London to St. Jago for a holiday. Hugh's letter which told me about her arrived at Guinea Corner late in November, almost exactly a year after Twice came home from hospital into this long period of non-communication. The letter was a simple request that I should visit this woman at her hotel but I had no intention of complying — a failure in communication at the most important level renders an attempt at communication on a shallower plane unthinkable — until, in a strange groping way, like someone feeling his way blindly across unfamiliar territory, Twice came out of his lethargy and said that he thought I ought to do what Hugh was asking of me. This was the first time in that long year that he had expressed any opinion of what I should or should not do. I am aware, of course, that on this day at the end of November, 1954, Twice had reached the point in his recovery when he would have made some such sortie out of his withdrawn silence but, because I do most of my thinking in terms of people, Lady Hallinzeil in my mind became a force to be propitiated, a talisman to be guarded from all harm and, although in a rational sense she was merely a wealthy unintelligent bore, this was my attitude to her. She spent about four and a half months in the island, during which time she visited me nearly every day and would have driven me distracted except that, during every day that she was in the island, Twice and I came nearer and nearer to one another until, by the time she went away, the invisible impenetrable screen had completely disappeared. And although my reason tells me that Twice would have made this mental recovery from the shock of his illness whether Helen Hallinzeil had visited St. Jago or not, she still has, in my mind, the mysterious aura which hangs around the creaking rusty hinge.

In April of 1955, her husband Lord Hallinzeil, who had been on a world business tour, landed in the island to spend a few days before taking her back to England and earlier in the same week, Edward came out from London. On the day after Edward arrived, I remember, he came round to see me and our visit was interrupted by the sudden entrance of my friend Sashie de Marnay. If Sashie crawled into a room on his hands and knees and as slowly as a worm, his entrance would still have the effect of a sudden interruption for this is the sort of person that Sashie is, but there is nothing of the slow-moving worm about him. He was shot down in his fighter aircraft during the 1939-1945 war, losing both legs and, on his artificial legs, he can walk only with a dancing gait, which looks like an extreme affectation. On the principle that, if you have a disability you cannot conceal, exaggerate it and make a feature of it, Sashie has fenced himself about with a cactus hedge of other affectations, affectations so exaggerated that the gait that has been forced on him goes almost unremarked.

'Edward,' I said, 'you know Sashie, don't you?'

'But of *course* we know one another,' said Sashie. 'Janet, *don't* be affected. Edward and I have known one another for a hundred years, ever since that night you made me act in your shocking varlet play and that misguided youth burst my balloon, as you know perfectly well.'

It was not very long before Edward, looking bemused,

went away, leaving Sashie and me alone and I said: 'Sashie you were beastly to Edward. The poor fellow is green with embarrassment.'

But although I tried to keep my tone light, there was an edge of irritation in it because I knew that Edward had gone because Sashie intended that he should go. Sashie, in an obscure and extraordinary way, could always make people obey the dictates of his will. He now struck one of his silly attitudes, one hand on his hip, one small foot poised on its toe, while he looked at me keenly out of his bright dark eyes. Then he clasped his hands in front of him, rolled his eyes at the ceiling and intoned: 'Oh Edward, my Edward!'

'Sashie, stop being stupid,' I said. 'I suppose you are indicating that people are gossiping about Edward and me?'

He stopped being affected and sat down. 'Naturally, darling. They always gossip. And it doesn't matter as long as you know and it doesn't matter to me as long as Edward doesn't matter to *you*. As you know, I will *not* have Twice upset. How is he?'

'He is very well. And Edward doesn't matter. He is a very good friend —'

'And a Dulac and you are so grateful to the Dulacs for all they have done for you,' he interrupted. '*I* know.'

'Oh, shut up, Sashie!'

'I am quite shut on the subject of Edward, darling. What I came to say was, really, that it being Twice's birthday on the seventeenth do you think it would be in order for Don and me to present you with a tiny turkey? Twice is allowed to have poultry, isn't he?'

'Sashie, you are very kind. Thank you.'

We chatted to and fro for a little before I said: 'Sashie, do you think Edward is homosexual?'

'Of course not! Janet, what *is* going on in that tortuous mind of yours?'

116

'Edward is about thirty now and he doesn't seem ever to have an affaire. You would think that at his age he would be beginning to think about such things, wouldn't you?'

Sashie stared at me for a long moment before he said very quietly and distinctly: 'Are you suggesting that there is the slightest connection between taking thought and having affaires? If anybody stopped to think, sex would be at a total discount and the human race would die out tomorrow. Darling, Edward is a very dull young man and you would do better to leave him in his comfortable dullness, poor thing. He is a very *balanced* young man and balanced people are always dull, like those little bubbles in spirit levels. Now Twice is very balanced in most ways and would be unconscionably dull were he not so gloriously unbalanced about *you* and engineering. And I am so pleased that he is well enough again to have a party although I do think that you might have chosen more inspired guests, my sweet.' Sashie paused now and his slanting satyr's eyes flickered over the papers on my writing-table before he said: 'Edward and I, with our ill-timed visits, have interrupted your writing, I see.'

Defensively, I went to the table, gathered up the few sheets of paper and pushed them into a drawer.

'It was nothing important,' I said. 'Only a letter.'

'When people come a-visiting uninvited,' he glanced at the table, 'and you are writing, you should be quite single-minded and bloody-minded and send them away, darling.'

Since the age of about twenty, I had always wanted to write, but all the other incidents of life had come between me and this ambition. Mine had not been the strong urge that had actuated Roddy Maclean who had achieved his ambition in the teeth of all opposition. The opposition to Roddy's urge had been an extreme case, located as it were in the bosom of his family for my own father, to whom long ago I had once confided my ambition, had taken the opposite view to the Macleans and had said and continued to say at intervals down the years: 'I would dearly like to see your name on the cover of a book'. But the world in general does indubitably set up resistances to the practice of any of the arts, curious subtle resistances that are all the more difficult to overcome and even Twice, in a mood of self-revelation following his illness, had told me categorically that he was glad that I no longer tried to write because he did not want to share me with anything.

In thinking that I no longer tried to write, Twice was mistaken, just as he was mistaken when he spoke of 'sharing'. I still tried to write, in secret, but the part of me that was given to this activity was a part that could not be given to Twice in any case for, except in relation to the writing itself, this part of me did not exist. Twice could have of me what he created in me and what of me writing created belonged to the writing. I do not know how I came to know this but I knew it with certainty and without any feeling of guilt that I was deceiving Twice I continued my secret attempts to write.

Now, however, I was aware that these attempts were not secret from Sashie, as he said: '— you should be quite single-minded and bloody-minded' but I did not want to take him overtly into my confidence about what I was doing.

'I can be interrupted any time,' I said. 'These letters I write all the time are not important but I have a lot of spare time and I love letter-writing.'

'Of course, darling. And to love doing a thing is the only valid reason for doing anything, ever. But never, never let anyone be a nuisance.'

'You are never a nuisance, Sashie.'

'But yes, I am,' he said defiantly. 'I was a nuisance to Edward this morning, poor dear, when he was settling down to have a nice long heart-to-heart.'

I became angry. 'Sashie, you are being quite bloody! I believe you actually suspect me of having a carry-on with Edward!'

He shuddered. 'A carry-on. Darling, what language!' Suddenly his affectation fell away and his glance sharpened again. 'I have been suspecting not you but Edward — suspecting him of lighting a tiny torch for you, you know.'

'Sashie de Marnay, you are out of your mind. Why should a young man like Edward fall for an old hen like me?'

He gathered his affectation about him like a cloak, examined his immaculate finger-nails and then said : 'Because he is ripe to fall, my sweet. People, like apples, fall when they are ripe for it. If an old hen happens to be around at the right moment, she gets the apple. You will forgive me for not wanting this rather embarrassing apple to fall between Twice and you.'

'You can be perfectly easy in your mind, Sashie. Edward, as far as I know and certainly in so far as I am concerned, is still firmly on his twig. But I don't go along with your theory that people fall in love when they are ripe for it. Something about somebody must induce them to fall.'

'Not at all. How very romantic you are, darling, to hold such a view. When Edward is ripe for the fall, he will endow the nearest old hen with the body of Aphrodite, the intelligence of Einstein and the spirituality of an archangel and abase himself at her feet.'

'I have never heard such rubbish. Why, you don't even *know* Edward.'

Sashie shrugged his shoulders. 'If Edward were any sort of artist, had any creative ability — ' his eyes glanced at the writing-table and returned to my face ' — it would be different. The creative ability would be enough. All true bachelors are artists *au fond*. They may never produce anything but the spark of ability is there and they live with it on the mental and spiritual plane as a husband lives with a wife.'

'Rubbish,' I said. 'Old Andy Beaton is a bachelor but if he is an artist *au fond* or any other way, I'll eat my Sunday boots as Tom says.'

'Andy Beaton is not a *true* bachelor, darling. He is an unmarried man which is quite a different thing. He would have been married long ago had he not been victimised by his mother and then by his sister. True bachelors are very very rare.'

'Like you, I suppose?'

'Do you know I believe I *am* one, my sweet. Even if I didn't have tin legs, I don't think I should ever want to marry anybody.'

At this point, I began to feel that Sashie's argument carried a little weight, for Sashie certainly had creative ability. He played the piano better than most amateurs, he painted better than many recognised artists and he had certainly created a famous luxury hotel out of a derelict plantation in a remarkably short time.

'You have a way of turning accepted beliefs inside-out and upside-down, Sashie,' I said now. 'Most people connect artists with lots and lots of sex and things. And look at Roddy Maclean!'

'When I look upon Roddy Maclean, I look upon a competent enough young craftsman in words who has caught the public ear for the moment, but let us not speak of him as an artist yet. And an artist may have what you call lots of sex and things but his ultimate love is his art and he finds his ultimate satisfaction in it. Those who are not artists have to love some person. An occasional freak gets along by loving himself or something like money and there are those who devote themselves to religion, of course, but all non-artists have to love something and it is usually some*body*.'

'Are you an artist, Sashie? Or do you have to love some-body?'

'Darling,' he said, 'I am the apotheosis of freaks. As you so well know, I love simply *every*body.'

What I knew so well was that Sashie liked very few people and loved none and I felt it to be our good fortune that he seemed to be fond of Twice and even, a little, of myself.

'Tell me,' he said next, 'has Papa Maclean forgiven his erring son as yet?'

'Sashie, I wouldn't know. I hardly ever see Rob and Marion now. But I believe Rob and Roddy write to one another.'

'It is really just as well that they quarrelled with you, darling. They are not your sort at all, especially Rob — such a timid little man behind all that bombast and noise.'

'Rob timid?'

'Darling, he *must* be timid when he feels impelled to make such a *fuss* all the time, so tiresome.'

When Sashie had gone away, I sat for a long time staring at the floor and thinking about this gossip that had begun about Edward and me. I had treated it lightly in Sashie's presence but it was not a light matter in my mind because, if Twice heard of it, it might worry him. Malicious gossip is a feature of most small communities but in the white society of St. Jago it was a growth more virulent than I have ever encountered anywhere else, but it was a growth natural enough, I suppose, when one considered the white way of life that predominated in the island, especially the way of life pursued by most of the women. They got up late and when they did get up they had nothing to do but visit the verandas of one another, drink coffee or gin and gossip. Most of them, myself included in this respect, had found a leisurely way of life in this island to which they had not been born but, where I had not the ability to give myself up to leisure — like my grandmother, I always had to be 'at something' — most of these importee women gave themselves up to it with éclat and enjoyment. They did not seem to write, read, sew, garden or do any of the things I did. They lay in long chairs and gossiped or quarrelled the long hot days away. And I seemed to have a built-in faculty for giving them subjects for gossip, in that I made friends with seemingly eccentric people like Sashie — for Sashie's disability was a closely guarded secret — in that Edward came to call on me largely because of his grandmother, in that I made friends among the coloured people of the island. I think, too, that there was some resentment that I had never given or gone to forenoon, all-female coffee parties and I had never given them or gone to them for the good reason that they bored me and I had other things which I liked better to do. It was to be expected that they would gossip about Edward and me but it was also irritating and worrying.

When Twice came home for lunch, it was as if the devil were inspiring him when he said: 'And has your boyfriend been round to see you as yet? He has been in the island for quite fifteen hours.'

'Twice,' I said, trying to keep the anger out of my voice, 'I think I find that a vulgar thing you have said.'

He gave me the mischievous grin which was daily becoming more frequent. 'Yes, isn't it? That is exactly what I think but that is what Rob calls Edward. Rob has been trying very hard to get me to forbid him this house or something.'

'And have you felt like doing it?'

'No. I am grateful to Edward. I am grateful to anybody who entertains or amuses you. In fact, nowadays, I feel gratitude more than any other one thing.'

'I think it is devilish of Rob Maclean to be saying things

to you about Edward and me,' I said, 'trying deliberately to worry you when he knows it is so bad for you. I don't understand him. He was so good and genuinely helpful when you were ill.'

'But you have the wrong end of the stick, Janet. Rob doesn't mean to worry me. It is *you* he is trying to harm, not me.'

'When we were in hospital he was kind and good towards me too. I could feel it. He was well disposed towards both of us. It seems to me that it is Paradise here that has this corrupting influence over him.'

'It seems to me that he has changed a lot just lately,' Twice said quietly and thoughtfully, 'or maybe it is that I have changed but I don't think so. He is far less bombastic than he used to be and sometimes, when he doesn't know one is watching him, he has a lost look, as if he were staring into emptiness, almost as if his great pipe dream were disintegrating before his eyes. I feel sorry for him when I see him like that.'

I felt a spurt of anger at this, felt that in confessing to pity for Rob Maclean Twice was in some way being disloyal to myself. 'Sorry for him?' I asked. 'You have always been generous, Twice, but I think this is over-generous. I don't see why someone in your position should feel sorry for Rob. And if he is finding his life empty, it seems to me, if all I have heard about him is true, to be the logical outcome that any man in his senses would have expected.'

'I think the key phrase is those words "in his senses". I think Rob has been out of his senses for years, living in his dream and that he is now coming into them again and it is all very painful. If I could help him in any way I would, but I can't see any way of doing it. Men form such habits of behaviour. If you were to see him and listen to him today, I believe you would find him no different from what he was five years ago. The florid bombastic style is still there but it is only a style now and quite often, with me, he doesn't bother to put up this front. There was a time when he had a jealousy and a fear of me just as great as his jealousy and fear of Edward. I was younger than he was and there was a danger that I might dislodge him from Paradise but a kindly Providence made me ill and removed me from his path. This has made him even like me a bit. He exudes a sort of patronising affection for me.'

'To needle you about Edward being my boy-friend doesn't strike me as a gesture of affection,' I said obdurately.

'But it was. People have different ways of expressing affection. You see, Rob thought that I didn't know that Edward wrote to you when he was away and came round here most mornings when he is at home. Rob thinks because I can't climb the crane any more that I am totally blind to most that goes on. He is a bit like you in that way. He expects people to be all of a piece.'

'How does he know that Edward writes to me anyway?' I asked angrily.

Twice sighed almost wearily. 'All the mail that goes off or comes on to Paradise crosses Rob's desk. I thought you knew that.'

Here it was again, this supposition that this was something I must know. I drew a sharp breath of exasperation but said quietly: 'No. I didn't know. It seems to be an extraordinary procedure.'

'I suppose it is, when one thinks of it but it has always been like that in the Paradise office. The mail bag comes in in the morning, Rob has a look through it and then his secretary sorts the letters out. The same thing happens in reverse with the out-going stuff in the afternoon.' Twice smiled. 'So, one day, shortly after I became his assistant, Rob came to me looking very grave and yet pleased as people often do when they are bringing you what they think is bad news and told me that you had had six letters from Edward in the last three months. And even when I was at death's door in the hospital, he said, you were getting letters from Edward every week.'

Twice's grave face and conspiratorial voice made me laugh. 'What in the world did you say?'

'I looked surprised first, then I said I didn't believe it and then when he assured me it was true, I gave a deep sigh and walked sadly away.'

'But Twice!' I was horrified. 'You gave him the impression that I was carrying on a furtive affair with Edward?'

'Not exactly. That is the impression he had already and I merely let him retain it.'

'But why?'

'For a variety of reasons. For one, if I told him I knew about the letters and had read a lot of them, he wouldn't have believed me. In Rob's book, a woman can't write to a man anything except love letters which she hides from her husband. For a second reason, Rob likes people he can be a bit sorry for, who have things happen to them, like being cuckolded, which could never happen to a big strong man like Rob and it makes life simpler if Rob likes me and is a bit sorry for me. For a third reason, Rob hates both you and Edward and it pleases him that you are headed for a bad end. I think he hopes that Sir Ian will find you out in your illicit pleasures, disinherit Edward forthwith and send you packing and then we could all live happily ever after.'

'I have never heard anything so absurd in my life.'

'It sounds absurd when you put it into words but did you ever know the wishful dream that didn't sound so?' Twice asked. 'It is just that words are too concrete a medium for the expression of a dream but in Rob's mind I think there is some idea like that.'

'You should know. You have made a very detailed study of him but I think it is a little off-beat to go along with his idea about Edward and me.'

'There is no point in doing anything else. I couldn't alter his idea you know and I am not going to have prolonged discussions about you with him, which is what he would like. This way, there is nothing to discuss. And what do his dreams and nightmares matter to us anyway?'

'That is true enough. They matter not at all. And I don't know whether this matters or not but not only Rob has comic delusions about Edward and me. Sashie was here this morning and it seems that Edward and I are quite a topic down in the Bay.'

'I shouldn't think that matters either,' Twice said. 'There comes a time when one can't cope with everything. Having been through a year when I couldn't even cope with myself and having now reached the point where you and I understand one another, I am not going to undertake a campaign to teach the verandas of the Bay where illusion or delusion begins and ends. Let them talk, darling. They will soon tire of it and something new will come up. As long as you don't mind, I don't. Janet, you are not worrying about it?'

'Not me.'

He looked at me anxiously. 'Life in this island is difficult enough for you without this sort of thing.'

'On the contrary, life in this island is not difficult for me any more, Twice,' I said. 'I know I used to go on and on about hating it but that is no longer true. This is something I have wanted to say to you for a long time and I am glad it has come up. I can't explain this properly, darling but I have established a better relationship with this place. Before, I spent most of my time waiting to get away from it, after I got over my first enchantment with it, that was. But now I don't want to get away because it is here that *you* can work and be well and happy. And I am happy here too, now that I know a bit about the real people who belong here. They have made me feel welcome and I am grateful to them and to their island. Some echo of something Sashie had said earlier sounded in my mind. 'In fact, nowadays, I am living here for the right reason — not for ambition on your behalf with Allied Plant or any of these things. Nowadays, I am living here simply for love.'

PART THREE

'— and worms have eaten them —'

IN the time before Twice's illness, Guinea Corner had had the reputation of being a gay and hospitable house but for close on two years now we had had few visitors and we had never had any kind of formal party or social occasion. During that year when Twice had been so withdrawn and lost in lethargy, I had now and then suggested that we have Rob and Marion Maclean over in the evening for a quiet meal, for I remembered how helpful Rob had been in the hospital days, but Twice had never wanted this.

In April of 1955, however, the lethargy was gone, Twice was back in the everyday world and he confessed that he would much like to meet the much publicised financier, Lord Hallinzeil, so we decided to have a small dinner-party on the sixteenth, the Saturday before Twice's birthday on the seventeenth. When we began to make our plans for this, we decided to invite the Hallinzeils, Sir Ian and Edward and Dee Andrews and Isobel Denholm to balance the female side and then I said. 'And Rob and Marion, do you think?'

'Must we?' Twice asked. 'Rob would only spend the evening sucking up to Hallinzeil and not letting me get a word with him and it is my birthday after all and Rob sees plenty of tycoons and I never see any. And there is nothing between you and Marion any more, is there?'

'No, but I would have her if you wanted Rob. Twice, are *you* going to suck up to Hallinzeil?'

'No, but I'd like to have a look at him without Rob in between.'

'Pity. I should have liked to see you sucking up. I am

131

always interested in something new. All right, no Macleans. We shall just be eight.'

'Unless you think it would be politic to have them?' Twice asked uncertainly.

'To hell with politics!' I said with no uncertainty whatsoever.

In the event, Twice had no eyes for Lord Hallinzeil at the party for, on the day that it took place, two friends of my childhood arrived in the island to spend a holiday at Mount Melody Hotel and one of them was Kathleen Malone, the singer, who Twice had, for years, longed to meet. With Kathleen and my other friend Violetta Antonelli invited, we went on to invite two of the young engineers from the factory at short notice so that, in the end, twelve of us sat round the oval table. The party, from the point of view of Twice and myself, was a splendid success, although something of a contretemps which was entirely of their own making marred the end of the evening for the Hallinzeils but, as I pointed out to Twice the next day, success or failure is entirely a matter of point of view and, Lord Hallinzeil being every inch the bore that Sashie had prognosticated — a man that my grandmother would have described as being all brains and no sense — I felt that their marred evening was of little importance, especially as they were leaving the island that day. What was important to Twice and me was that Kathleen and Violetta, charmed with the island, decided to extend their holiday from two weeks to two months, after it had been arranged that Kathleen could maintain her singing practice at the piano, played for her by Violetta, in the drawing-room of the Great House.

Sir Ian knew of Twice's passion for music, knew that he possessed nearly every recording that Kathleen had ever made and, in his kindly way, said: 'While Miss Kathleen is here, me boy, don't you bother about that office. Take a little time off an' come round to the house an' listen to the singin' with the rest of us. You too, Missis Janet. Never heard a voice like that in me life before an' that's a fact.'

And so, every afternoon, Twice and I would join Madame, Sir Ian, Edward, Kathleen and Violetta for tea, by which time Kathleen would have done her exercises and when tea was over she would sing to us for a little while.

Madame was now completely blind but she was as sturdy in health as she had ever been and if her eyesight had dimmed, no like dimness had overtaken the sight of her mind.

'I don't know, Janet,' she said to me one afternoon while we sat in the library waiting for Kathleen and Violetta to come down from the drawing-room and for the men to come in to join us for tea, 'what has come over Marion these days. I have invited her to the singing several times but she will not come. After all, Rob is not sick. She is not tied to her house as you have been, dear. She hasn't been round here except to do my letters in the forenoons since Edward came home.' I said nothing because I could think of nothing to say. 'I didn't invite Rob because he would not wish to come in any case but I should have thought Marion would enjoy it.'

I still said nothing. It was a long time since I had given any real thought to the Macleans, having had other more personal and difficult things to occupy my mind and in this last month when Kathleen and Violetta had been visiting us every day, I had been too happy about the brightness of Twice to think of anything else.

'Well?' Madame said impatiently. 'Have *you* seen anything of Marion?'

'No, Madame. I haven't seen her for about five weeks.'

'Really they are a most trying couple,' she said irritably, bumping the arm of her chair with a plump beringed little fist.

'It is high time Rob Maclean retired, went back to Scotland and took Marion with him.'

I was blankly astonished at this outburst and Madame became aware of the effect of her words on me.

'The other day,' she went on in an apologetic tone, 'Edward used a slang expression when I asked him if he had been to call on Cousin Emmie in London since she married. Edward said he had not and added: "Life is too short." It is an expression that I should never have dreamed of using at his age but there does indeed come a time when life is too short for some things and I have decided that what may remain of my life is too short to go on making efforts for people after I am tired of them.' She paused as if expecting me to make some comment but I said nothing because, again, I could think of nothing to say whereupon she continued: 'Oh, take no notice of me, my dear. I am just an irritable old woman with what my father used to call a viper for a tongue. Here come Miss Kathleen and Miss Violetta.'

I think Madame felt ashamed of her outburst, as well she might, I thought. That she should be tired of the Macleans after their years of service to her was a poor reward for them but we often 'tire' of the people to whom we are most indebted. Deeply as I was indebted to Madame for all she had done for Twice and myself, that did not stop me in the privacy of my own mind from thinking that she could be an extremely tiresome old woman and, indeed, had often been so since the first moment I had met her. She had always been arrogant and dictatorial and like most people of this kind she was indelicate and insensitive but, in the old days, I had never analysed her. It had been pleasanter to look on her outward appearance of Victorian survival and near-eccentricity and laugh at this in a gentle way behind her back. When one is happy, one sees only the happy, pleasant and amusing things but when one has passed through the shadow of unhappiness, one learns the nature of shadows and begins to notice them everywhere beyond all ignoring.

Edward continued his practice of coming round to Guinea Corner in the forenoons largely, I believed, because he was always bored at Paradise and partly because, in the late forenoons, Madame was having her letters written and the newspaper read to her by Marion and did not need him.

'What an odd creature de Marnay is,' he said one day.

'He is a very good friend of mine,' I said repressively. 'He was wonderfully helpful all the time Twice was ill. But, that apart, Sashie is very much my type of person.'

'What type of person is that?'

'I can't tell you except by opposites. He is the sort of person that Lord Hallinzeil isn't. Goodness, wasn't Lord H. one crasher of a bore the other night?'

'You found him a bore? I was rather impressed by him and he is something of a public figure, after all.'

'Maybe, but not the sort of figure I find impressive. And he seemed to me to suffer from a basic mental weakness in that he believes that truth and accuracy are the same thing. They are not. But I noticed that you had a long talk with him after dinner. Did you find him interesting?'

'Yes. Interesting enough,' Edward said, 'but even if I hadn't he is an acquaintance I am very glad to have made and I intend to follow it up back in London. I ought to thank you for introducing me to him, Janet.'

'You are entirely welcome,' I said, a little bored with the conversation and rather wishing that Edward would go away that I might go back to my writing-table.

'When Granny goes,' he was saying, 'Dad and I intend to sell this place. It is worth a lot of money and the sale will be the sort of deal that is in Hallinzeil's sphere.'

As these words entered my mind, it was as if I were coming out of a bright warm room into the bitter frost of a dark night and I felt giddy for a moment as I thought how ironic it was that this should be the outcome of my small effort to provide a pleasant evening for Twice and my

135

friends. What was to happen to Twice and me if Paradise were sold? No other employer in this island would take on Twice, in his state of health and at the age of forty-five and if we went back to Britain, Twice would get sick again, Twice would — I shied away from the thought and was invaded by a sense of the terrible interconnectedness of life, the awe-inspiring inter-relation that Donne perceived when he wrote: 'No man is an Island, intire of itselfe; every man is a peece of the Continent, a part of the maine — ' Here was the creaking rusty hinge again in the form of Lord Hallinzeil and here too was something that brought with it a degradation in that, since Edward had spoken, the life of Madame, this old woman who, seven years ago, Twice and I had not known to exist and for whom I had little real liking, became one of the conditions of our survival. It was degrading to recognise inwardly that this frail old life suddenly mattered to me in a way that it had never mattered before because Twice and I were dependent on it and it was humiliating to realise that this self-degradation was inherent in life, a condition of the will to survive.

Perhaps something of the mental chaos I was experiencing showed in my face for Edward quickly continued: 'Dad and I don't plan to sell the house, of course.'

'The Great House?' I asked stupidly because I had to say something, if only to assure myself that I could still speak.

'We would like to keep it and come out for a month or two in the winter.'

'I see.'

I had never had any respect for wealth and was now overcome by the indignity of the human situation as personalised in myself, the indignity of being entirely at the mercy of something that I could not respect. If Twice and I only had money, the future of Paradise, the life of Madame, even, would not matter to us.

'Janet, Dad asked me to talk to you about this but it isn't easy. I don't want to hurt your feelings.'

'My feelings?' I stared at him. 'I don't think it is possible for Sir Ian, even through you as proxy — ' I tried to smile at him ' — to hurt my feelings. He has been so good to Twice and me that — that — sorry, there is nothing I can say.' I clenched my teeth for a second. This was something to be faced here and now. 'What did Sir Ian want you to tell me?'

'Not tell you — ask you. It is if we sold the estate, everything except the house and garden, would you and Twice live in the house and look after it for us while we are away?' he asked with a rush. My relief was so intense that I sobbed out the words: 'Yes, Edward, oh yes!' then burst into tears and ran out of the room.

When I came back, I apologised and he merely stared at me uncomprehendingly and then turned away to look out of the window so that after a few moments the silence became so tense that I had to say: 'I am sorry, Edward. It is difficult for you to understand the situation that traps Twice and me. We don't want to be dependent on anybody but we are very dependent on Paradise. Still, we cannot be hangers-on and there is no need for your future plans to contain us. I have no doubt we will find ways and means ourselves if need be.'

'But the plan of keeping the house turns very much on you and Twice,' he said. 'As a house, it is something of a monster in my opinion but it is an historic and valuable monster and we must have people we can trust to look after it. For myself, I would sell it tomorrow but Dad wants to keep it and so keep it we will for as long as he wants it.'

'You don't like it?'

'No. I hate it. I have hated it since I was a child.'

'Yet it is your family home. I can't understand that, Edward.' I was thinking of Reachfar. In the way of anybody or anything that is much loved, Reachfar was part of myself and although, now, it no longer belonged physically to

137

my family and me, it belonged to me in a fashion far deeper and truer than it would ever belong to anybody else for nobody, ever again, could be a child at Reachfar in the golden time when I had been a child there. Reachfar in this sense was mine only and mine for ever.

As I spoke to Edward, the warmth of the sun on the Reachfar hayfields, the warmth of the fire in the Reachfar kitchen and the warmth of the love of my family were all about me as they had been in my childhood and out of this warmth I said: 'You must have been very unhappy here if you hate this place in that way, Edward.'

'I was,' he said shortly and turned away as if to dismiss the subject but, suddenly, he changed his mind and, with an obvious effort, he said: 'It was here that my mother, my two older sisters and my newly born brother died of typhoid. I was six at the time.'

'Edward, I didn't know. I thought you were an only child.'

'No. There were four of us. Dad wasn't here at the time. Only Granny.'

'And your grandfather?'

'I hardly remember him. He was a lot older than Granny and one saw very little of him. No. There was only Granny and Rob Maclean, of course and his wife but she had young children of her own to look after.' He smiled at me wryly. 'I took against Paradise and most of the people here because there was a horrible thing. One of my sisters had a teddy-bear and she had left it in that summer house at the north-east corner of the garden. I found it there after she was dead but some sort of moth had got into it and it was crawling with big, fat, blind white worms.' He pulled his elbows close to his sides as if to repress a shudder. 'Why do you suppose I have told you this?' he asked. 'I have never told it to anybody else.'

I seemed to hear Sashie say: 'He was ripe to tell this to somebody.'

'Perhaps because the time has come when you had to tell somebody and I happen to be handy,' I said.

'Not quite that, Janet—' he paused, frowned and with determination continued: 'I find it very difficult to talk to people about private things. I find it difficult to trust people but I trust you and Twice. I have never written regularly to anybody as I have to you, I have never got to know anybody so well. I don't even know why I began to write. Yes, I do. I began to write because it was through you and Twice that I really began to believe that there could be genuine bonds between people. I had never believed before that anybody could — could love anybody,' he ended in a near-whisper while a painful flush mounted over his cheekbones and forehead.

To me, in this moment, he was no longer the debonair self-assured Edward Dulac, the thirty-year-old heir to Paradise and I should have been embarrassed had he not suddenly lost stature and years to the degree where he appeared to me as a boy of about fifteen. But, at the same time, I wanted to help him back to the self-assurance he had lost and, while he looked as if he wanted to rush out of the house and hide, I put my hand on his light grey sleeve and said lightly: 'Edward, people love people all the time. Life would be much simpler, probably, if they didn't.' I withdrew my hand, took a cigarette and sat down before I went on: 'And people love places too and something has struck me about your proposal that Twice and I should look after the Great House for you and your father.'

As I had hoped, this return to a non-emotional plane was a relief to him after what seemed to be his first sortie into deeply personal communication and he said: 'Yes?'

'Rob and Marion Maclean have a prior claim to that caretaking job over Twice and me if they want to do it.'

'Rob and Marion Maclean have no claims of any kind on Dad or me,' he said harshly. 'They are amply provided for on a pension basis.'

'I see. I am sorry, Edward. I did not mean to interfere in what is not my affair.'

'And I am sorry that I snapped at you, Janet. I know you did not mean to interfere but I find the subject of the Macleans an irritating bore. Rob is furious, of course, about not meeting Hallinzeil.'

'And that is my fault. Twice forecast that Rob would be annoyed but I —'

' — said let him *be* annoyed!' he finished for me. 'And quite right too. As Granny says: Why should one be bullied in one's own house?'

'When did you last see Roddy?' I asked to change the subject.

'About a month ago. We had dinner together. He is an interesting fellow but I don't understand him in the least.'

'In what way not?'

'He is so much the opposite of myself, I suppose. He is constantly embroiled and enmeshed with people, quarrelling with publishers, raving with enthusiasm about plays, blaspheming with disgust about other plays, having violent rows with women. I find him fascinating in a way but very wearing. Every time we meet, I swear I shall never spend another minute in his company.'

I laughed. 'At least, he isn't a bore.'

'And how he can talk! About anything, even about himself! He seems to be able to get right outside himself and talk out loud about himself as if he were somebody else.'

'I should think he is very good for *you*,' I said. 'You should take a leaf from his book, Edward. Roddy is the most carefree person I know.'

He shook his head. 'I couldn't live like that, in the centre of that web of relationships, all pulling different ways.'

'Roddy is an extremist in that and most other ways but I have often thought that I myself have no existence except in the relationships between myself and other people. If my relationships were removed, I fear I would amount to what Sashie de Marnay once described as a little bit of nothing in a skin only.'

'What an extraordinary idea! I should have said you were a very definite personality in your own right. You must be, to attract — to be friends with,' he amended awkwardly, 'so many different people.'

I began to grow uncomfortable because it was obvious that Edward was making a new departure, beginning to think in a new way and of things that he had never considered before and, in an embarrassing way, he seemed to be treating me as some sort of mentor. His amendment of the verb 'attract' into 'to be friends with' seemed to me to indicate that he thought of the first verb in only a sexual application and that, clumsily, he was making clear to me that he himself was not 'attracted' to me in this way but, by his amendment, he seemed also to be begging me, as a child might say it, 'to be friends' with him. I have in me nothing of the teacher, mentor or leader and I felt that I had difficulty enough in living my own life without undertaking the position of guide, philosopher and friend to a wealthy man fifteen years my junior but, because of this web of inter-relationship which Edward did not begin to understand, whereby Twice and I were so dependent on the Dulacs and Paradise, I felt that I was being trapped. I seemed, too, to be hearing the sardonic laughter of Sashie de Marnay somewhere just off-stage.

'If I attract people,' I said, laying slight emphasis on the word of doubtful meaning to Edward, 'I think it is because I need them, not because I am a strong personality. I attract them out of my instinct to survive, because without them I would be that little bit of nothing in a skin. I think we do by instinct what we have to do in order to go on living. We will do anything and everything to cheat the grave and the worms for as long as we can.' He was looking at me uncomprehendingly so that I added impatiently: 'There is a grave, complete with worms, of the mind or personality, as well as the physical one where: — through the eyes, the nose, the mouth, the worms creep in and the worms creep out, you know.'

'I see,' he said blankly, using the words that I myself use when I do not 'see' in the least and want more than anything to be left alone to think things out and I was relieved but not surprised when he got up and said he had to go back to the Great House.

After he had gone, I regretted my impatience with him, recalling that when I myself was thirty, I had not known either of that grave of the mind which is the dominion of the worms. I had discovered it only about two years ago when Twice and, along with him, all of life seemed to be ebbing away from me, leaving me at the mercy of those worms.

'My boy-friend was round here this morning. Joke,' I said when Twice came home for lunch and I went on to tell him of what Edward had said of the future of Paradise.

'Let's not think of it at all,' Twice said in the end. 'Let's not think of it because I *can't* think of it. When I try to visualise myself as host of the Great House for ten months of the year, I can only think of the little man who went looking for a lavatory in a theatre and eventually the curtain went up to disclose him peeing into the fountain on the stage set.'

'I will say' I told him, 'that I find you a robust and healthy change from Edward. I think he is discovering that he has a soul or something and it is all very painful.'

'He has had things fairly smooth up to the present,' Twice said. 'What's eating him? A woman? Or just the worms of time? I remember I got rather morbid about the worms of time when I was his age but then the war broke out and I forgot about them.'

When, earlier, I had spoken about graves and worms to Edward, I had not connected my words with what he had told me about finding his dead sister's teddy-bear, but now, in the devious way that the mind works, what Edward had told me rose to the surface.

'I don't think it is a woman,' I answered Twice. 'I suppose the worms of time is as good a definition of his trouble as any. But I wonder if everything has been all that smooth for him? Is it for anybody?'

'I have no doubt he will tell you about it,' Twice said, 'whether you want to hear it or not. As the Preacher said: "There is a time to keep silence and a time to speak" and when a man's time comes, he does whatever it is.'

It struck me that Twice and Sashie seemed to think along similar lines but I did not remark upon this aloud. I merely hoped that Twice, in thinking that Edward would confide in me, would be as wrong as Sashie had been in thinking that Edward might fall in love with me. I had suddenly come to the awareness that the worms had eaten forty-five of my own years and that there were things other than Edward in which I wished to interest myself in the time that remained to me.

When Twice went back to the office, I went up to the linen cupboard. It would be two hours before I had to go round to the Great House to tea and, much as I enjoyed these visits and Kathleen's singing, I was wishing that I did not have to go on this day.

Although we referred to this room as the linen cupboard, all the linen we possessed was stored on one of its long broad shelves and the rest of it was more of a lumber-room. There were all sorts of odds and ends waiting for the next jumble sale for some worthy cause, there were the air-weight suitcases which we used when travelling and which were unlikely to be used again in any foreseeable future.

There were large cardboard dress boxes full of letters from friends which I could never bring myself to throw away and there were two piles of diaries, one set kept meticulously by Twice which dealt mostly with his work and another set kept sporadically by myself and which dealt with anything that happened to come into my head. They ran from 1945 when Twice and I met at the end of the war to 1954 and our diaries for the present year were down in the veranda bookcase. Time in concrete form, I thought, as I looked at the two piles and two more bricks of time down on the veranda, waiting to be eaten up and come up here among the darkness and the dust. But it was in protest against this steady destructive progress of time that I had come up here and I looked away from the diaries to the piles and piles of manuscript that filled another long shelf, slightly camouflaged by a worn-out sheet. This represented seven years of my attempts at writing and it was to this

144

that my attention was directed. I stripped away the sheet and stood staring at the foot-high piles of paper, covered thick on both sides with my handwriting. The task looked mountainous, not something to be undertaken in two short hours on a hot afternoon or it may be that Ecclesiastes, whom Twice had quoted, might also have said, had it occurred to him: 'There is a time to organise and destroy and a time that is not for organising and destroying'. Staring at the piled shelf, I picked up in an automatic way two of the diaries and banged the volumes together, watching them bang for evidence of book worms. These destructive pests made a library of any kind an anxiety in St. Jago and I never took a book from a shelf without banging it against another and watching for the sinister particles of bitten paper to fly out, the indication that, once again, the books had to be treated with worm deterrent. On this occasion, there was no evidence of worm but I had been clumsy and the top volume left on the pile slipped from the shelf and fell open on the floor. Between its pages there was a slip of paper which, when I picked it up, showed, in a handwriting I did not know, the name 'Mrs. Iris de Souza' and an address in Port of Spain, Trinidad.

As I replaced the slip, I read a page of the diary itself. It was the volume for the year 1952 and on the page headed 'Saturday' was written: 'A slack sort of day. Planned that condenser lay-out in the forenoon and went down to the Bay office later. Somerset had made a mess of that Trinidad estimate but caught it before he mailed it. Must arrange to get over there before the end of the year.' There was a space and then a few words had been added, probably on the following day: 'The devil's own row here this evening about Roddy Maclean. Janet helped him to get away off the island and Rob literally fit to be tied. Wish we were home in Scotland. Janet and this island are constantly in collision.' I shut the diary, put it back in its place on the shelf, replaced the sheet over the piles of manuscript, feeling that the day when that diary entry was made was not some two and a half years ago but two and a half centuries ago.

Time had worked its strange alchemy upon people and events. The Roddy affair which, when that entry was made, had been important enough to thrust itself into Twice's engineering diary, had now faded into insignificance and the final sentence 'Janet and this island are constantly in collision' was quite simply no longer true. But when I thought of that short sentence, written in the truth and immediacy of its time, it was like looking at a photograph of myself as a child and wondering how it was that that child had grown into the woman that I was now.

My mind went back to December of 1949, to London air terminal. Remembering that place, the piles of luggage, the clean efficient-looking officials, I remembered my own child-like feeling of being about to be transported, literally on wings, to the fabled islands of the west, where grew the golden apples of the Hesperides and I remembered too that it was in this place that I first met Sir Ian and little Sandy Maclean and how I bought for Sandy, from the bookstall, the copy of *Through the Looking-Glass* which he wanted. Now, some six years later, it was as if, in that moment, I myself had stepped through a looking-glass into the distorted world of enchantment on the other side and as if all my time in the island until now had been spent in struggle to return to the world I had known before.

I was aware now that, from the first moment I had set foot on the earth of St. Jago, I had known that this was not one of the legendary golden islands of the west but a real part of this modern-day world and a part that had a sadder history than most others. It was a history of bloodshed, cruelty and slavery, of the total destruction of the indigenous race by the Spaniards and then of the enslavement of African tribesmen by the British and these coloured people who were all around me at the airport were the descendants of these slaves whom my race had brought here in the stinking holds of the slave ships. Standing on the hot tarmac, meeting Rob and Marion Maclean for the first time, the inimical strangeness of it all hit me like a blow, but I did not recognise at that time — or would not let myself recognise — that the strangeness and the feeling of enmity were my own race-guilt which rose like a miasma, a poisonous vapour drawn out of this blood-clotted earth by the heat of the sun.

On that first day, I turned my back on this feeling of what I described mentally as 'wrongness' in the island, refusing to recognise that the wrongness was in myself, rooted deep in this guilt of what my race had done in this place in past centuries, but the guilt and the wrongness were there and they insisted on declaring their presence in a multitude of subtle ways, using even myself, I saw now, to make this declaration. Coming forward through time, I remembered the play *Varlets in Paradise* which I had written at Christmas of 1950. In all good faith, I had written this melodrama in the first instance to amuse Sir Ian and Sandy Maclean but, in retrospect, it was interesting to note that it was set in a historic time that had never been and furnished with characters who could never be and yet, when it was played, it demanded no acting power from the players, it merely called upon them all to behave as they always did in my eyes, to behave like characters who could never be in a place and time that never were. At that time, I was in full flight of escape from the reality of the island but I had recorded, with unintentional irony, my chosen never-never-land vision of it in a farce called *Varlets in Paradise*.

Coming forward through time again, I remembered when my friend Martha's aunt visited the island, a visit which had culminated in the murder of a beautiful island woman called Linda Lee and the suicide of her lover. Linda Lee had taken a great hold on my imagination and her beauty had seemed to me to be the very spirit of the island, of the island when it was first created. But Linda was of mixed blood, her grandfather had been a white man and her beautiful body encased a mind that was, to me, clever, complex and corrupt beyond all understanding but, in spite of this, she had become the victim in a curiously innocent way of the selfish malice of Martha's aunt, a white woman spending a short holiday in the island.

Immediately after Linda Lee's death, Twice and I had left the island to spend an eventful leave at home and, in this way, the edge of the tragedy was blunted in my mind. Had I had to go on living in the island at that time, I thought now, I would have had to face this tragedy and what I felt about it, which might have caused this unrecognised race-guilt which I was harbouring to rise to the surface but this did not happen. I was enabled by the flow of life to turn my back on the tragedy, forget it and slough off any race responsibility for it but this did not mean that I had freed myself of the guilt for, when we returned to the island, it rose again to confront me more strongly than ever until, in the spring of 1952, I escaped from it by Twice's and my decision to ask his firm for a post that would domicile us in Britain.

But now, this guilt which had risen from the dark of my race-consciousness and had eaten at my mind like a canker worm for all those years, assuming a dozen disguises and expressing itself in a dozen ways, had disappeared. Through my friendships with the island people, frank friendships in which I spoke of the guilt of my race, I had, by admitting the guilt, freed myself from it, and my island friends, by the help and comfort they had extended to Twice and me in our time of dire need, had proved to me that, in their eyes, the guilt of my white forebears had not descended to me.

Thinking of these things, I had come downstairs and was looking at, without seeing, the books in the case that stood

148

opposite my chair but as I came out of the past and into the present, my eye was caught by a little red book with black lettering on its spine. It was the copy of Shakespeare's *The Tempest* which I had had since I first read it at the age of twelve at Cairnton Academy. Since then, I had read it and had seen it performed many times but only now did I appreciate the vision of the poet who gave to Prospero, marooned on a strange island far from his home, a magic cloak, a magic wand and a magic book.

In the days before I came to St. Jago, the white men who came here had come provided with the panoply of magic cloak, wand and book; the cloak being the Union Jack, the symbol of a power on which the sun could never set, the wand being the field marshal's baton that commanded from afar the military garrison at St. Jago Bay and the book being a combination of the Bible and the British legal code, in either of which lay the answer to everything. But by the time I arrived in the island, the Union Jack was a piece of tri-coloured cotton that was fading in the setting sun, woodworm had attacked the field marshal's baton when St. Jago had indicated that if a garrison were needed, it could be manned by the island's own regiment and the Bible and the British legal code lost their magic when St. Jago made the claim that the former was not British but the inheritance of all men and that a legal code beaten out in Britain down the years since she struggled free of oppressors was no more than a jumping-off place for a new country struggling free of oppressors in a different zone of the earth in the mid-twentieth century.

In addition to this panoply of imperial magic of the earlier days, individuals evolved their own minor magics to act as opiates on this canker worm of guilt. They did not do this consciously any more than I, consciously, ran away from the guilt or called it the enmity of the island or by any name other than its real one. But, none the less, they evolved the opiates in the form of the charities and good works in which Madame immersed herself, while people like Twice came to the island with their magic cloaks and opiates readymade out of whole cloth in the form of their skills which they placed, in all sincerity, at the disposal of the islands and their peoples. I, however, had come to St. Jago without this equipment, with nothing to stand between me and reality and, unlike Madame and Sir Ian, I had been unable to fabricate for myself a magic cloak or an opiate in the form of good works for, brought up as I had been, close to mere subsistence level in the Highlands of Scotland, I had never relished the unmistakable stink of smugness that emanated from those who did good works among people whom they regarded as their inferiors.

If Madame, Sir Ian or Twice looked into the dark glass of the island — this they did not do, I think, because Madame and Sir Ian were too confident of their appearance, Twice too busy — they no doubt would have seen themselves becomingly arrayed in their cloaks but had I dared to look into this dark glass, I would have seen myself enshrouded in my guilt and this was why, rather than look, I had run away. It was Twice's illness that had forced me to stand still, look straight at the island and myself and had forced me to come to terms with both. It had been painful to achieve these terms but now that they were achieved it was good to know that the canker worm had been killed for good and was not merely dormant in my mind under an opiate.

But that evening, when Twice and I came home from the Great House, I did not speak of these things. At one time, I had wished to apprise Twice of every thought that crossed my mind but, painfully, I had learned that, in the words Edward had used, life is too short for two people, even people as close as Twice and myself, to establish total communication. Where, before, I had talked to Twice in order to clarify my own mind, which frequently led to loud quarrels as at the time of the Roddy affair, I did not now talk to him of anything that might lead to excitement or contention.

Since our party to celebrate his birthday, we had dropped back into our regular routine of quiet regular meals and few visitors, the only variation being our afternoons at the Great House when Kathleen sang and I was always in need of light topics of conversation that could not lead to dispute but which, yet, would prevent Twice from withdrawing again into that uncanny silence which, since his illness, seemed always to lie in wait for him. It was to make trivial conversation that, on this evening, I said over the dinner-table: 'Look here, my lad, who is Mrs. Iris de Souza?'

'Mrs. Who?' he asked and I repeated the name. 'I have never heard of her,' he said, looking at me with just the degree of interest that I liked to see. 'Who is she?'

'I am asking *you*. She is in your diary for 1952.'

'But I have never heard of her in my life. 1952? What does it say?'

I laughed and told him of how the slip of paper had fallen out. 'She will be some woman who owns a bakery or something,' I said then. 'Somebody who made an enquiry at Allied Plant. It is a pity that someone with such an exotic name is probably a yellow-skinned Portuguese half-caste.'

'No.' Twice frowned. 'She wasn't an enquirer about plant. If she had been, the name would ring a bell.'

I felt this to be true for his memory for anything connected with his work was prodigious.

'In my diary, you say?' he asked.

'Not in your handwriting though.'

'Mysteriouser and mysteriouser. Janet, could you bother to go up and get that slip of paper?'

'If you like but I really have no suspicions of you and the lady.'

'I know that, you idiot, but I am interested. One ought to remember a name like that.'

I fetched the diary, found the slip and handed it to him. 'That's Rob's writing,' he said at once and then suddenly began to laugh. 'You have a sort of instinct for things, Janet. The lady is either extremely exotic or she is a sinister old witch. She is either a high-class tart or a procuress.'

'What in the world do you mean?'

'It would be that time I went to Trinidad in '52 that Rob gave me this. He was always very helpful when I used to go off to the other islands — glad to see the back of me, I suppose. He was always giving me addresses where I could get what he calls a bit of comfort after working hours.'

'Twice!'

'What?' He gazed blankly at my astonished face. 'Why are you gaping like a hooked cod?'

'Rob *Maclean* gave you the addresses of these brothels and places?'

'Yes. He knows every high-class pimp and procuress in the Caribbean, I think. You — you didn't —'

'If you tell me you thought I knew Rob Maclean was a womaniser, I'll break all the doctor's rules and go off into screaming hysterics!'

'But I thought everybody knew — but that's silly. They probably don't. How could they? He doesn't do any of it here in St. Jago — he is too canny a customer to shit on his own doorstep as old Mattha would say.'

'No. I didn't know. I seem to be fated never to know anything about Rob unless somebody feeds the knowledge to me from a spoon.' I took thought for a moment. 'I shouldn't have thought that Marion would care for that sort of thing.'

'She probably doesn't know about it.'

'How dim-witted can you get?'

'I don't think that is particularly dim. You imagine Marion is as nosey as you are, snooping through her husband's diaries when his back is turned.'

'Diaries! If your husband rakes round brothels, you don't have to read about it in a diary!' I exploded.

'*You* wouldn't have to,' Twice said, 'but you are back at that old thing of thinking that everyone is like yourself. Look at Lady Hallinzeil then! His lordship had a mistress for about thirty years before *she* rumbled it and even then her best friend had to feed it to her from a spoon.'

This was true. Marion might be unaware of Rob's specialised knowledge of the brothels of the Caribbean but it did not matter to me one way or the other. I merely wished I had never mentioned Mrs. Iris de Souza.

TOWARDS the end of May, Marion left for Scotland as she was now doing every summer and I understood that she rented a house there and established a holiday home for her sons. The year before, she had been away for about three months in all but Rob did not go with her. He remained alone at Olympus when not on his business trips to the other islands and Madame was inviting him less and less frequently to dine at the Great House as she used to do in former times if Marion was away.

'Granny is in a much better mood this morning now that Marion Maclean is away,' Edward told me on the forenoon after Marion left.

'You may think me very naïve but I thought for a long time that Marion and Madame were the closest of friends,' I said.

'Granny doesn't have friends much. She is not a friendly person. Granny likes to use people and manipulate them and interfere in their lives but she doesn't *like* them much, except her own family that is. I think I am a bit like her. I like looking at people and watching them wriggle like cheese mites under a microscope but I very seldom think of any of them in terms of liking them. Dad is the one of us who truly likes people, but even Dad is a bit tired of the Macleans now.'

'Edward, does it ever strike you as ridiculous that you and Sir Ian and Madame should have the Macleans here at all when they irritate you so much?'

'Frequently,' he said, smiling his wry smile. 'But having them here is just another of these things that we do but not for love, to use your own phrase. Life is cluttered with things that have been imposed on one, don't you find that?'

'Yes but—'

'You see, it suited Dad that Rob should manage here for Granny when Grandfather died because Dad liked the Army and he didn't like sugar-planting. The idea was that when Dad retired, Rob would retire from here but it didn't work out like that. Rob liked being here and didn't want to leave and one can't sack a man out of hand when he has worked for one for over thirty years. At least one can but one doesn't. That is the point where one allows life to impose on one. Then, one resents the imposition and one can't direct resentment satisfactorily at what we loosely call life and one can't get any fun out of resenting one's own weakness in being imposed on so, quite unjustifiably, one begins to resent the personificaton of the imposition— in this case Rob and Marion Maclean. And then, of course, one feels guilty about resenting them when they have managed the place for thirty years and that makes one resent them more than ever. But the root is in the fact that they were brought here in the first place for a complex of reasons but not for love and they have stayed here for a complex of reasons but not for love of us Dulacs.' He emphasised the last words and then went on: 'I have thought a lot about that phrase since you and Roddy drew my attention to it. And no love has developed between us and the Macleans. They are not very lovable people. And a relationship that is based on anything other than some degree of love is bound to turn sour, I think.'

'Perhaps,' I said but I was thinking less of what Edward was saying than of the fact that he seemed to have come a long way from that day about two weeks ago when he had told me that he found it difficult to talk about 'private things'. But this is how relationships develop. The growth of intimacy does not take place during the time when two people are together but, more often, when they are apart.

F

Edward, having confided to me that early experience of his when he found the teddy-bear in the summer house, had gone away and had projected an image of me in his mind, probably, to which he addressed his private thoughts and now that he was again in my presence, he took up the relationship not from the point we had formerly reached when together but from the point he had reached in his own mind.

'I am not entirely convinced by this theory of yours that it is the lack of love that causes a relationship to go sour,' I said after a short silence. 'I think there comes a point when one knows people not wisely but too well. When I first met Marion, I liked her and went on liking her until that row about Roddy when she broke through the image I had formed of her and exposed what I regarded as feet of clay. I doubt sometimes if we like or love people for what they really are. I think that we like or love the images of people that we ourselves project so that what we are liking or loving is really an aspect of ourselves. The human ego is a terrifying and monstrous thing.'

'But you said the other day that if it weren't for other people you would be only so much nothing in a skin!' he protested.

'That is true too. This is the anomaly. I am simply not sure whether I with my monstrous ego am the reality or whether all the other people are the reality and I am only a reflection of them.'

'Apart from our not seeing people as they really are, perhaps, a lot of people don't present themselves as they really are. But some of the poses are too obvious, like the one Marion Maclean works with Dad of heroic helpmeet of unappreciative husband, devoted mother and faithful wife of cruel philanderer. I find that tedious.'

I was growing tired of indulging in what my grand-mother would have called 'scandalising about the Macleans' and I said in a bored way: 'I am as dumb as they come. I didn't know that Rob philandered until the other day when Twice told me in an accidental way. Oh well, it takes all sorts to make a world, as they say.'

But Edward was not to be deflected from the subject of the Macleans until he had said his say.

'One of the things I resent about Rob is that he thinks that people like Dad, who is in a position to know about his nonsense, can be gulled. You, stuck here at Paradise couldn't know how Rob amused himself when he is away from home but Dad hadn't been home here for a week when somebody at the Club told him about Rob's little piece in Barbados. From there it was only a step to hearing about all the other little pieces in the other islands. It is not the little pieces that one minds, although Granny would take a different view if she knew about them, what one minds is his pose here as the good family man with nothing in his head but the Dulac fortunes.' He shrugged his shoulders. 'But having put up with him and Marion for so long, I suppose I can put up with them until the end.' He suddenly moved to a new subject that I did not expect. 'Does Twice mind my writing to you and coming round here so much when I am in the island?' he asked.

I felt my face grow hot. 'Don't be silly.'

Edward was very cool. 'I didn't think he did but I thought I would confirm it. Some people might suspect us of some clandestine nonsense and gossip and I thought Twice might mind for that reason.'

'No. Twice and I don't mind what is said on the verandas.'

'The malicious gossip is another of the less likeable features of St. Jago.'

'Gossip is a feature of every small community. I think it is born out of repression of some kind. Among the whites here, I think their malice is an aspect of the colour problem.' He was looking at me uncomprehendingly and I went on: 'Most whites who are here know that they don't belong here but they will not admit it. They feel guilty about being here, about their way of life here and they repress this too. These repressions work in their minds like a poison, distorting everything and the poison comes out in the form of anything from gossip to good works.'

'Anyway, give me London or Paris where one is anonymous and left in peace.'

'You and I differ there,' I told him. 'I would rather be gossiped about than be altogether anonymous. My ego again, I suppose. Of course the gossip is partly your own fault. All bachelors of thirty are fair game.'

He was thoughtful for a moment before he said: 'In a way, I should like very much to get married. It would please Granny and Dad so much.'

'Have you ever met a woman you wanted to marry?'

'No.'

'Then Madame and Sir Ian don't form an adequate reason. No matter how much you wish to please them, it has nothing to do with whether you marry or not. Marriage is between you and some woman and no other person in the world is relevant. Besides, I have found that all the unreasoned and unplanned things I have done have turned out best. All the planned and reasoned things have a way of turning to dust and ashes or getting eaten by the worms of time, like Twice's and my plans for our future at home in Britain. Plans for the future are a mistake. There may be no future.'

'But surely one must look ahead? Try to plan —'

'Small material things, yes, like where the next meal is coming from but it is wrong to plan your future life, to marry for social reasons. When you meet the woman you want to marry, you won't need any plans and any plans you have made will go overboard anyway. And that is how it should be. When I was your age, I rushed out to meet every day without a plan in my head and I had a wonderful

158

time. And I am getting back to something of that attitude nowadays but in a more conscious way. I think the thing to do is to take each day as it comes, be grateful for it and meet it with love.'

I had not meant to arrive on this serious plane or to reveal so much of my private philosophy and I was suddenly overtaken by a shyness that caught the breath in my throat and would not let me speak.

'Meet it with love,' Edward repeated my last four words after a moment. 'Go on, Janet.'

The shyness left me and it was a relief to continue, to say things I could not say to Twice, regretful things.

'You see, since Twice has been ill, I have often thought that I was never grateful enough for the time before, when he was well and the whole world was going right for us. I have felt that I did not love my days enough. I was always looking forward, being greedy for the next thing, next week when we would go on leave to the hills, next year when we would go home to Britain. I let my days get eaten away without gratitude and without love. That was wrong, Edward.' I smiled at him that I might not weep. 'I often think of those days now and love them in memory but one should love and honour one's days as they come along.— But to go back to marriage, I should be chary of entering into it as a social duty. It is a terribly complex relationship even if one enters into it for *your* reason, entirely for love,' I teased him.

'You and Twice seem to have made a tremendous success of it,' he said.

I do not know what complex of reasons made me say what I said next. It was comforting to talk to Edward of these things that were too emotional to discuss with Twice and this was part of the reason. Also, I was so very conscious of how deeply Twice and I were indebted to this Dulac family that I wanted this youngest member, at least, to know the truth about us but whatever the reasons, impulsively, the words came out: 'Sometimes I think we have made a success of it because we are not really married — legally married, I mean.' I smiled at him and went on: 'I don't know why I have told you this but there it is. Twice was married when he was very young to a Roman Catholic who won't divorce him.'

'So that story is true?' he astounded me by saying.

'Story? You have heard of this? Where?'

'Yes. From Dad.'

'Sir Ian? Oh, God!'

'My dear Janet, don't look so horrified. Dad isn't Mrs. Grundy even if he is Granny's son.'

'But where did Sir Ian hear it?'

'Do you remember a lot of the staff went on leave in 1952 and then Rob and I went over together? You remember the Cranstons went to Ireland for their leave instead of to their home in England?'

'Yes.' I was beginning to see the sinuous thread. Twice's wife lived in Belfast.

'In some extraordinary way, among all the stories in Ireland, Mrs. Cranston got hold of this story about you and Twice and when she came back here she came hot foot to Rob with it. And, of course, Rob came even hotter of foot with it to Dad. Rob Maclean makes frightful mistakes about people — he made the mistake of his life with Dad that day. Dad gave him a real cursing, what he calls a "proper tellin'-off, me boy" and then sent for the Cranstons and gave them a cursing too and finished up by telling Cranston to look for another job because he couldn't stand his wife's malicious tongue around Paradise any longer. That is why the Cranstons went to South America.' I was staring at him speechlessly. 'With Dad, I suppose it was what you said a little while ago. He had his own image of Twice and you and he refused to listen to the story because he did not want that image destroyed. And then he could never abide Mrs. Cranston but Cranston was quite a good man at his job and he had never had the heart to get rid of him. But Dad hates intrigue and malice and hypocrisy more than any other things and he knew that Rob was out to get rid of Twice and he knew that Rob himself whored all around the islands and thought that Rob was the last man to come with tales of another man's sins and he knew Mrs. Cranston was malice personified and the whole combination made him lose his temper so that Rob bought a proper hatful and Cranston got the sack. Dad doesn't often remember that he is the boss of this place but when he does, he makes other people remember it too. Of course, the fact that he is fond of you and Twice came into it and probably a lot of other things as well that I don't know about. The older people get, the more things they have in them to influence their actions in any given situation.'

'That is true,' I said, 'but all the same, I could be knocked down with a feather.'

'Poor Janet. Then Dad told *me* the story and gave me orders how to behave if Rob said anything.'

'And did he?'

'Oh, yes.'

'And you carried out your orders?'

'Certainly,' Edward said, very much as his father would have said it. It was only when he used some of his father's turns of speech or mimicked his Poona-parody language that I could see any resemblance between them.

'I added a little bit of my own, though,' he went on 'just to annoy Rob. After all, he annoys me and I feel it to be just that I should annoy him in return occasionally. I said the story was a lot of absurd lies and added that I admired you enormously and that Twice was a brilliant engineer.'

'Edward!'

'I know. It is childish to a degree and quite shaming but Rob brings out the lowest in me. As a rule, I don't like to embarrass anybody or make people look scared of me but in a vicious way I enjoy making Rob writhe. I think it is because he is such a coward under all that bombast.'

'I suppose we are all cowards about something.'

'I don't think we are all as abject as Rob. But we are not really talking about Rob Maclean. You were saying that you thought you and Twice had made a success of your marriage because it wasn't legal.'

I laughed. 'It sounds so silly when you put it like that. It isn't as simple as that. But I have sometimes thought, since Twice has been ill, that if I had been legally his wife I might have lapsed even more deeply into self-pity than I actually did. The fact that there was no legal bulwark seemed to call out one's greatest effort to maintain the relationship. Married, one might have lain back against the legal bulwark and have thrown one's hand in emotionally but if I had lain back like that last year, there would have been nothing left. If the relationship between Twice and me fails, there are no vows, no children, nothing to keep us together. But I don't know. The whole marriage relationship is so complicated that if I had my time over again, I doubt if I would undertake it at all.'

Edward smiled. 'If you had your time over again, you would do precisely what you have done in this time you have had. We all would!'

'You are sure? Life takes a turn on such a rusty creaking hinge sometimes. But when one thinks of having one's time over again, one is hoping that certain hinges would be better oiled and turn in a slightly different direction, I suppose.'

EDWARD had never spent such a long period in the island before. Formerly, when he came out, he had worn a transitory air throughout his short visits, as if he were looking forward to the day when he would once again board the aeroplane for London but, this time, he was more settled and expressed less frequently his dislike of the island and Paradise. It is probable that he was feeling more strongly his responsibility to Madame and Sir Ian and I knew that both he and Sir Ian were worried about Rob Maclean who, Twice told me, had begun to drink very heavily, by himself, on the hill of Olympus every evening. He would not come to us and he would not go to the Great House but spent all his evenings alone and I used to look across the dark valley to the lights on the hilltop and wonder what strange dreams were peopling his fuddled mind.

Since the time of the Roddy affair three years ago, Roddy's name had been under taboo. Twice and I had spoken of him occasionally and Edward and I mentioned him but his name was never spoken by his parents or Madame. There was an absurdity — what I referred to privately as a 'Paradise distortion' — in the entire Roddy affair. Madame had never been told the true reason for the breaking of the engagement between Roddy and Dee Andrews, a reason which she would have refused to countenance even if it had been told to her and she took the pleasing romantic view, typical of her Victorian attitude, that Dee was nursing a broken heart when it was obvious to all the rest of us that Dee was running, with great satisfaction, a most successful tourist hotel at Mount Melody, the

F*   163

former home of her mannish partner, Isobel Denholm.

Quite apart from the fact that Roddy had jilted Dee in Madame's eyes, nothing would convince her that Lucy Freeman, his coloured paramour, was a prostitute. Obstinately, Madame regarded Lucy as a little innocent who had been victimised, one of 'my people' whom she insisted on regarding as mentally retarded children for whose well-being she was responsible. This was the magic cloak and I often felt that, even after I had recognised its false nature, that I might yet be stifled in its cloying folds.

However, nothing succeeds like success and Madame was Victorian enough to have an overweening respect for success, especially success of a financial nature and when Edward had a letter from Roddy announcing that he had brought out his second novel and had also sold the film rights of the first for a considerable sum of money, Madame began to veer round in the gold-scented breeze. She held the belief, I think, that success of any kind was a reward meted out by God for virtue, as expressed in the Victorian hymn:

> 'The rich man in his castle,
> The poor man at his gate,
> God made them, high or lowly,
> And ordered their estate,'

and now that God had seen fit to reward Roddy, Madame was magnanimously prepared to admit that Roddy might have virtues that were visible to the eyes of God although not to hers and she was prepared to forgive him as, apparently, God had done, for his past sins.

While Marion was away, Sir Ian or Edward attended to Madame's letters with her in the forenoons and, after lunch, they would read the daily newspaper to her but, after Kathleen Malone and Violetta Antonelli went back to London towards the end of June, Madame asked if I would come round each day at three o'clock, when she arose after her post-lunch nap and under this arrangement, the reading of the newspaper fell to me.

'Ian and Edward cannot read the newspaper intelligently, Janet,' she informed me. 'They begin with the leader and all that political nonsense in the House of Representatives. What I wish to know is what is going *on* in the island. Just glance at the deaths for me, dear. I am sure old Julie Shaw must go any day now. She is well over eighty.'

One day, she became bored with the newspaper after I had read the deaths, marriages and births to her and said: 'Ian saw Julie Shaw in St. Jago Bay yesterday. Why she should be having herself driven about at her age, I cannot think. Janet, I am hearing splendid accounts from Edward of the Maclean boy, the one who behaved so shockingly to little Miss Dee, you know. He seems to have quite come to his senses and is doing very well.'

'Yes, Madame.'

'I have always understood that writers and people like that are inclined to be different from the rest of us although I cannot see why. Perhaps, though, if one had known he was a writer when he was here, one would have been less shocked by his behaviour. So odd of him to be so secretive about his writing, don't you think?'

'Yes, Madame,' I agreed insincerely and resenting the insincerity that was imposed by the fact that I knew it would be impossible to explain to Madame the sensitivity that made Roddy secretive.

'I have never known any writers except an American man who came down here and then wrote a book about the pirates and buccaneers who used to sail about the Caribbean long ago. He was a very odd sort of man too, when I think of it. Not like Roddy Maclean, of course, but he travelled with a large medicine chest and was always taking pills and things and trying to persuade other people to take them too. He sent me a copy of the book after he went back to the United States but I did not care for it.'

'No, Madame?'

'No. It was all about these pirates roystering about with loose women and all that kind of thing. They were people quite unlike any I have ever known. I prefer to read — or *did* prefer, in the days when I could see — about people like myself and people I have met. I used to enjoy Trollope very much and, later on, John Galsworthy.'

'And Hardy, perhaps, Madame?'

'No, not Hardy, dear. Nobody I have ever known would behave in the way that woman Tess did — so loose and undignified. That is more like Shakespeare. I know that Shakespeare is highly respected as a poet and dramatist. My father had us read the play about Cleopatra in the schoolroom, when we were older, of course, just before my elder sister came out and I thought it quite dreadful how Cleopatra behaved, talking about her disgusting love affair to her servants. If my sister or I had behaved in that way, my father would have been the first to be displeased. Of course, Cleopatra was a queen, an Egyptian queen and it was all a long time ago but I found it difficult to believe that royalty would ever have behaved in that way.'

This was my first experience of Madame as a literary critic and I could have listened to her for ever but she now left the subject of Shakespeare's works as if she had pronounced the final word upon them and said: 'Have you read either of these books that Roddy has written, my dear?'

'Yes, Madame. I have read the first one.'

'And do you think it is as good as people are saying?'

'I think it is a remarkable first novel, Madame.'

'You have a copy of it?'

'Yes, Madame.'

'If it wouldn't bore you, dear, having read it already, I should like if you would read a little of it to me one afternoon.'

'I should like to do that.'

'You are very kind and patient, Janet.'

I did not like this proud, dictatorial old lady to have to feel gratitude to me. 'Not at all, Madame. You know how I like to read and I would rather read Roddy's book than the *Island Sun* to be quite frank.'

'Yes, it is a trashy newspaper but I like to know what is going on. So Connie Travers is gone, poor thing. She couldn't have been a day over seventy-five but she always had poor health. I would have asked Rob about Roddy's book, dear, but I think he still feels badly about how he behaved when he came out here. I feel it better not to mention him.'

The next day, I went round to the Great House with my copy of *But Not For Love* and, having dealt with the deaths, marriages and births in the newspaper was instructed by Madame to read from the book. The fact that the story was set in Scotland interested her and, at first, she listened with all her attention but when I saw her nod off to sleep, I stopped reading aloud, waited for her to awaken and went on from the point in the book that I had now reached. In this way, we finished the novel at the end of about a week and Madame's knowledge of it, I knew, must be very sketchy indeed, for she had been awake only at the more critical turns in the plot but, to me, that did not matter, as long as the hot afternoons had been beguiled for her. She remained awake, however, and at full attention throughout the short last chapter when the weak vacillating young hero made his choice between the strong-minded Fanny and the gentler sister whom he had been engaged to marry and when I closed the book I waited with some inner excitement to hear whether the characters in Roddy's book had behaved according to Madame's lights and were therefore credible.

'Very clever,' she said, 'a very clever young man indeed, Janet and thank you for reading his book to me. But I am not surprised that Marion and Rob do not mention him.

How very naughty of him to drag up that discreditable incident when Marion interfered between her sister and Rob.'

I was dumbstruck and sat rigid with the book between my hands, waiting for what might come next.

'It is probably a coincidence that he used that theme, of course. It must be. He was not even born when the thing happened. When you have lived as long as I have, dear, you will find that you become a little muddled about time now and then. No. Of course Roddy could not have known about his father being engaged to Anne, Marion's sister. I had the greatest difficulty in calling Marion Marion when Rob first brought her out — I had become so accustomed to thinking of his young lady as Anne, you see. But Janet,' she continued sternly, 'I am surprised that you should consider that a nice book. I find it quite disgusting in parts and not in the least like life. People simply do not behave like that.'

It was pointless to say that I had not referred to the book as 'nice' or to say that this was an adjective which I would never apply to any book.

'You think not, Madame?'

'Certainly not. The book is a lot of rubbish and very objectionable rubbish too. It simply bears out what I was saying to you the other day. Most writers are very peculiar people and they distort everything in the most peculiar way. And artists too. Look at that portrait of me as a young woman that hangs in the drawing-room!' Madame was growing quite heated. 'My husband had it done but I have never liked it and have never seen the slightest resemblance to myself in it. I certainly did not have these great wrinkles at the sides of my mouth when I was only twenty-five. I do not have them *now*,' she said with emphasis, passing a hand over her cheeks, quite unaware as she laid down the law in her typical fashion that the great wrinkles were deeply etched on either side of her tightly-pursed,

168

obstinate little mouth. She waited for me to agree with what she said but when I merely swatted a mosquito that was attacking my ankle, she returned to the subject of the book. 'I could wish that he had not called the horrid woman in his book Fanny. It is a favourite name of mine. My elder sister was called Fanny and she was a dear sweet girl.' She sighed. 'Well, dear, I am glad to know a little of this young man's writing but I don't think we shall read the new one. I do not care for all that coarse language and these descriptions of passion and houses of ill fame, but then, I am old-fashioned. There is no doubt that he is very clever to have written something which has been such a success, very clever indeed, but one can understand that Marion and Rob must be embarrassed that their son is publicly displaying so much knowledge of the low side of life. It is very trying for them. But I like you to read to me, dear, if it doesn't bore you and I am missing your charming friends and Miss Kathleen's singing. Tomorrow, you must find Trollope's *Doctor Thorne* in the library. I have always liked that story *very* much.'

From what I had read and from my own small experience of trying to write, I had come to know a very little about the fictional imagination and its ability to seize upon a small germ of truth and develop from it a large network of plot and character. The process is a little similar to what can happen in life, when what seems to be a minor incident can have a very far-reaching effect. In my own life, such an incident happened when I was nine years old. It was prize-day at our village school at Achcraggan and, ever since the age of five when I first went to school, the highlight for me of prize-day had been the arrival for the ceremony of Sir Torquil Daviot and his wife Lady Lydia. They used to drive along the road and into the playground in a graceful wagonette, drawn by a pair of beautifully-matched greys but in June of 1919, by way of giving us children a treat, they arrived in their first newly-acquired motor car. Standing by the gate to see them arrive, I was, unlike the other children, disappointed, frightened and horrified by this stinking clanking monster that seemed to throb with a terrible, mechanical uncontrollable life of its own, a life without intelligence that would respond to speech or to a gentle pull on the reins as did the greys that I had loved so much. I have not the slightest doubt that this trifling incident was the germ that produced the far-reaching result that, in all the years between 1919 and 1955, I had steadfastly refused to learn to drive a car.

Thinking in this way, I was, naturally, very interested in the fact that Roddy's book had had its genesis, probably, in an incident in the lives of his parents and, although I had just re-read the book at the Great House, I now began to read it again. There was no doubt that the fictional imagination had Roddy in its grip. The book was set in Glasgow mercantile circles and he had made a beautiful evocation of the Glasgow weather, the fog swirling up from the river, muffling even the clang and squeal of the tram-cars that loomed through it like great charging beasts, but the extraordinary thing was that, in the light of that one small fact that Madame had innocently let drop, I now had a picture, as I read, not of Fanny and John in the grey fog of Glasgow but of Marion and Rob in the brilliant sunlight of Paradise. John and Rob identified with one another in an uncanny and subtle way, in little things like John using the phrase 'all that rot' when faced with something he did not understand and in his panic terror when he and Fanny were involved in a mob incident in the street, but it was the identification of Marion and Fanny that I found frightening. Fanny was the leading character in the book and John was little but a foil for the display of her as a monster. She was a passionate virago, inflamed by an insensate ambition for wealth and social power, all this encased in a slight frail body crowned with wispy golden hair, a woman who, physically, would be the exact antithesis of Marion, but her most repellent feature was her bland public face, her complete control of herself when she was in society. Alone with her husband, Fanny gave way to her passionate rages and her hideous cruelties while her children huddled together in terror upstairs around their nurse but when in society, Fanny spoke hardly at all but sat, with an appearance of placidity, avidly watching people display themselves and revealing their weaknesses while she, revealing nothing of herself, took note of everything that could be turned to her own advantage. It was this picture of Fanny at an important dinner-party that caused the click of identification in my mind, for I had seen Marion behave in just this outward way countless times.

Ironically enough, there was even a picture of what might have been myself in the book, but for the fact that Roddy had written it before he met me. But this merely proved that Roddy knew so well the nature of Fanny that he supplied her with an obedient and admiring cousin called Molly. Just as every Fanny has a Molly, I thought, every Marion has — or had — a Janet for, unlike Molly. I had not continued to be obedient and admiring to the end.

'How is Rob these days?' I asked Twice one night after my detailed study of the book.

'Odd that you should ask. It must be your Second Sight. Janet, I am sort of worried about that poor devil. He seems to be going to bits.'

'With drink, you mean?'

'It isn't the drink so much. Physically, he is terribly strong and the drink hasn't much effect on him. I don't think the drink is affecting his mind either. It is something else. He wanders about up there at the factory as if he were looking for something he can't find. Do you suppose Sir Ian or Edward has said anything to him about selling this place? You will say this is absurd but it is as if his heart were breaking.' He frowned at me. 'Janet, we were all wrong about Rob, in a fundamental way, I mean. All that blow and bombast isn't the real man at all.'

'I have been uneasy about him ever since you were in hospital,' I confessed. 'He was so very good then, Twice. I can't think of any other word except just plain *good*.' My voice grew shaky and I came near to tears as I spoke. 'I used to be so grateful to him and it was so difficult to believe that this was the man who was so awful about Roddy and had a stupid power complex. He was just like a big, awkward, rather frightened teddy-bear who was yet determined to help you if he could out of sheer goodness of heart.'

Twice smiled with a curious gentleness. 'I am beginning to feel that that is exactly what he is. He has changed a lot even in this last week since Roddy's new book came out. He asked me if I had read the first one and he looked as if he might burst with pride when I told him how good you thought it was but when I offered to lend him your copy, he shied like a horse and said: "Not now, thanks. Later, maybe. But I'm not much of a reader. Probably I wouldn't understand it anyway." I have never heard Rob being humble like that before. Then, yesterday, he suddenly started asking me about the war. I told him how I spent the first part of it being chased out of everywhere I set foot like France and Norway and the second part of it in heavy workshops in India so that I hardly saw a shot fired and he gave a sort of sheepish grin and said: "That would have suited me. I don't think I am what they call a brave man." I said I didn't think I was either. He was a bit like a teddy-bear, as you said. I felt I wanted to comfort him.'

Although, since Twice had been ill, I had eschewed conversation of this kind that might disturb his peace in the evenings, he was so obviously disturbed already about Rob that I thought it best to disclose what I was thinking after re-reading Roddy's book. 'Twice,' I began, 'Madame wanted me to read Roddy's *But Not For Love* to her after Edward told her about the new book coming out.'

'I hope you had your blue pencil handy. I only skimmed through that thing but — ' He said no more but raised his eyebrows and shook his head, contriving to look like a comic parody of Madame.

'I know. But when I had read it, expurgated, she said an odd thing.' I told him of Madame's remark, of how I had re-read the book and of the turn my thoughts had taken about the Macleans while he listened to me with that concentrated attention which made him stare hard at me as I made a point, blink and stare again, that 'twice-ness' of attention that made his nickname so fortuitously apt.

'It fits,' he said at last. 'It fits in a queer way but it can't be like that. Roddy would never have dared!'

'Twice, it is possible that the boy didn't know what was actuating him to create Fanny and John. I think that book is born out of two things — the fact that Rob married Marion and not Anne and the fact that, when he was a small child at Olympus, Roddy probably overheard Rob and Marion having a row and was frightened.'

'Oh, come now!' said Twice of the factual logical mind.

'I'll tell you something. Only lately have I discovered the probable reason why I cannot bring myself to learn to drive the car in spite of the inconvenience to you, everybody else and myself.'

I told him of that long-ago prize day and at last he said: 'You could be right, I suppose. You know more about these things than I do but the thing about the book theory that I find most convincing is the man — John, isn't it? — and the brothel in Byres Road. Rob is not really a brothel type like Somerset or Harry Lockyer, any more than John in the book is a brothel type. Sex is what you might call, to coin a phrase, the last bastion of a man who feels dominated. That is why so many small weedy men are so terribly randy and marry wives that are twice their size. The bed is the one place where they can get the upper hand. Rob hasn't been off the island since Marion went away this time. He has been here all the time. If he were the real brothel type we would have missed his company now and then.'

'Reading that book after what Madame said was like turning over a stone in the garden and finding a clutch of those ghastly white hawk-moth grubs wriggling about,' I said. 'And anyway, I may be all wrong. The important thing is, is there anything we can do for Rob?'

'That's the trouble. I can't think of anything.'

'I wish we could get him to come over here in the evenings.' I looked across the park and up to the distant lights of Olympus. 'Whether we are right or wrong, it isn't good for him to be sitting up there alone, boozing his nights away.'

'I have asked him to come often enough,' Twice said, 'and I am beginning to think he would like to come but that night of the Roddy affair is sticking in his gullet. I think he is ashamed of that now but can't get past it.'

'Would it help if I wrote a note asking him to come?'

'It might. Leave it for a day or two till we see how things go.'

W E said no more about the invitation to Rob for three days but, at breakfast on the fourth day, Twice asked me if I would write the note as planned and send Caleb over to Olympus with it. I was putting it into an envelope when our recently installed telephone rang and I heard Twice's voice speaking very over-casually from the factory office: 'Janet, I have changed my mind about that book I asked you to write for. Don't mail the letter till I come home. And can you take two guests for lunch — oil men? Rob was to have had them at Olympus but he has to go down to meet Marion. She is arriving on the noon 'plane.'

I put the telephone down, went back to my table and stared at the white envelope that lay there. There was a clump of bamboos outside the window and its shadow lay across the white blotter and the envelope, a shadow of little ghostly flickering fingers as the bamboo fronds fluttered in the morning breeze but, although I knew with my reason that the pattern was a combination of sunshine and bamboo, what Twice calls my Celtic Twilight gripped me for a second, constricting my lungs and throat. It was as if these ghostly fingers, which played over the envelope as if they were trying to pick it up, were at the same time warning me. With a jerk, I seized the envelope, tore it and the note inside it into shreds, threw them in the waste-basket and went out into the garden.

After a little while, I recognised this moment of panic as one of the effects that the island had always been able to work upon me. I believe firmly that expatriation affects people in a multitude of ways not as yet identified and that no person is so truly himself as when treading the earth that bore him. In my own case, I had frequently experienced in St. Jago these occasions when the climate seemed to exaggerate in a dramatic way some minor coincidence, such as Marion's sudden decision to come back coinciding with my own decision to write to Rob, so that a minor thing was momentarily magnified into uncanny and frightening significance. But I was aware now that there was no magic in this. It was merely the effect of strong sun and tropical vegetation on a mind reared in Highland Scotland. I had never seen bamboos until I was nearly forty and I had never become accustomed to their ghostly finger-like leaves, one of which always seemed to be flickering as if beckoning to something invisible even when the air was dead still.

And there were no thunder-claps or meteors rushing across the heavens when Marion arrived. She merely arrived, sent me a note thanking me for my attendance on Madame, informing me that she herself would now go to the Great House in the forenoons but that she would be pleased if I would continue to read to the old lady in the afternoons. Also, a week after Marion's arrival, Edward left for London and my days slid back into the old routine of gardening, letter-writing and going round to the Great House for reading and tea.

About the same time Marion came back, however, I had a parcel in the mail which, when opened, was a novel by S. T. Bennett, entitled, horribly enough: *And Worms Have Eaten Them* and on its title page was written: 'To Janet, a copy for free as promised, with love, S. T. Bennett.' Its title was apt. It was a well-written tale of the degeneration of a man and his mind which, conscious as I was of Rob, I found almost unreadable and I hid it from Twice altogether, saying that Edward had promised to send me a copy of Roddy's second novel but that he must have forgotten. But Rob, since Marion returned, had come back to something of his former self, Twice reported.

'We got away into the air over that bloody book of Roddy's,' he said. 'It is difficult to keep one's feet on the ground in these parts and you are always ready to take off into the twilight anyway. Rob was just missing his wife and unbuttoned himself to me a bit, that's all.'

And I did not argue about the matter. I was glad to forget it and busy myself with my own affairs.

When December came, I had more than enough to be busy with. An epidemic of measles struck the island, an infection brought in, it was thought, by some tourist and the native population, with no resistance to the disease, began to die by the hundreds. Caleb my yard boy to whom I was very attached, became a victim and, since all the hospitals were over-crowded and he was one of a large family, I had no alternative but to nurse him myself in his little room behind the house. For days and nights, I never left the boy but lived with him behind the disinfectant-soaked curtain that hung over the door, pitting all that was in me against this new scourge that the white race had brought upon these island people.

During this time, I saw nobody, had contact with nobody except the sick boy. I spoke to Twice only from the garden while he stood indoors behind the mosquito screen and Twice wrote to my father for me, in case further infection might be disseminated by an envelope that I had handled. During the long dark nights, while Caleb grew more and more weak, I thought a great deal about my father and my home, as if I were drawing strength from them and when the boy had lapsed into a coma, I would drip watery orange juice between his lips and speak to him, although he could not hear me: 'Come, Caleb, you are going to get better and in the morning I want to write and tell my father you are better. He is so sure you are going to get better, Caleb.' But when the bright day dawned when I knew with certainty that Caleb was going to get better, I received a cablegram from my people which told me that my father was dead.

Death always finds us alone, whether it be at our own death or at the death of someone we love. Twice loved me dearly, I had many friends and Sir Ian and Madame were very kind to me but at this time, there was nothing that any of them could do to help me. Sitting alone, looking out over the brilliant tropical garden, I uncoiled the long pure golden thread that was my memory of my father and which stretched from this hour in December of 1955 back to the first golden gleam which must have been an evening late in 1911 or early in 1912, for I could not have been two years old. I was lying in my wicker cradle which, I have been told, I outgrew before I was two and in the light of the oil lamp, this big tall man with the dark hair was looking down at me. I knew that his name was 'Dada', that he was the most splendid person in the world and that he belonged entirely to me and I to him.

During the long days, as the calendar of time turned round towards Christmas, I passed the golden thread through my mind, examining the long strand inch by inch but, always when I came to the picture of the last time I had seen my father, on a frosty night on the hill above Achcraggan with the jewelled lights of the town behind and below him, there would come the bang that stunned my mind when I read the cable, there would be a faraway echo of my own child's voice singing 'Abide with me' and my mind would swing back until I was looking up at him from my cradle again and begin once more its progression down the memories of the years. I could not allow myself to feel that he was dead. I could not accept the knowledge that I would never see him again.

The immediate world of Guinea Corner and Paradise became unreal. I was vaguely aware that I was worrying Twice whose blue eyes showed the strain I was imposing on him and I would try to simulate some appearance of normality when he was in the house but, as soon as he had gone out, my body would lapse into listlessness and my mind would begin to tell over again its memory pictures of my father.

'Darling,' Twice said to me one day before lunch, 'you haven't even opened your letters this morning! Oh, God,' he then burst out, 'I have been selfish. I should have sent you home for a bit. Even if I couldn't go myself, I should have sent you home to see him!'

I did not want to be shaken out of my numbness into feeling and I said impatiently: 'Twice, don't go on like that. You know I wouldn't have gone and Dad would never have wanted me to leave you.'

When he had gone back to the office, the numbness gave way for a moment to shame at how I had spoken and in a listless vague attempt to make amends, I took up the four letters that had come in and opened first an envelope addressed in the handwriting of Marion Maclean. It contained only a folded card of a heavy expensive kind, a white card edged with silver on which, in black and grey and more silver, were depicted an open book with, lying across its pages, a spray of lilies. Inside it was written: 'With deepest sympathy, Marion.' I felt myself come out of the listlessness into rigidity. My fingers straightened so that the card and envelope fell to the table top and there rose in my mind a picture of my father that had not been among the long succession of pictures that had told themselves over and over down the days. I now saw one clearly defined picture of him on the moor at Reachfar, his pipe in his hand, his ruddy face smiling at me under the strong-growing silver hair.

'I would like fine to see your name on the cover of a book,' I heard the soft Highland voice say.

It was as if something exploded inside my head, as if my brain could not contain the hideous insincerity of the cardboard lilies and, at the same time, the memory of my father, that image of the greatest sincerity, sympathy and love that I had ever known. I became possessed by blind rage and the need to fight, to make some desperate gesture against all the insincerities, all the failures of sympathy, all the lack of love in the world.

The next thing I knew, I was upstairs in the linen cupboard, picking up a great sheaf from the heap of discarded manuscript that filled the long shelf and carrying it to the spare bedroom. I was going to begin the fight by destroying all my own insincerity, my failure in sympathy, my lack of love for my father which had stopped me making the effort to write the book he had so much wanted me to write. In no time at all, I had the waste-basket full of torn paper and had gone back to the cupboard for another lot of manuscript to destroy while Caleb took the first basketful down to the yard to burn it. Like a maniac and sweating in the afternoon heat, I ripped the paper asunder, rushed down to the garden and threw it on the fire and then rushed upstairs for more. When there was nothing left to destroy, I sent Caleb indoors and whirled the ashes about with a stick until every scrap of white paper was blackened. As the last small flame died away, sickly grey in the brilliant sunlight, I realised that Sashie de Marnay was standing beside me. I felt hollow, light-headed, more remote than ever from reality, as if the smoke from the fire had clouded my mind and that Sashie should be here made this sense of unreality more acute for, in his brilliant clothes among the grey ashes, he looked like some gay incongruous harlequin who had popped through a trap-door on a pantomime stage.

'What are *you* doing here?' I snapped at him.

'*Always* the gracious hostess. You have been spring-cleaning? A little early, don't you think?'

'Only burning a lot of old papers.'

He looked down at the heap of ash. 'Let us go indoors. You are, to say the least of it, disgustingly overheated.'

He wrinkled his nose at my dusty dress and sweaty skin and his voice was level and toneless as I walked ahead of him through from the back of the house to the veranda. I felt myself begin to droop with self-pity.

'Sashie,' I said with my back to him, 'my father is dead.'

'I know. That is why I am here.' The voice was still level, cold, measured.

I turned round to face him. 'Why?'

'I saw Twice when he was in the Bay yesterday. He told me about your father. He said you were taking it very badly — his precise words.' He paused, narrowed his eyes to slits as he looked straight at me before he continued: 'If Twice says that *you* are doing anything badly, something is very far amiss.' He looked down at the table between us as he said: 'So I thought I would — ' He broke off short and then exploded: 'Good God, what *can* that be?'

I looked down at the white card that lay there, its silver embossing shining in the sunlight. 'It's a card, a card of sympathy from the Macleans.'

Sashie gave a jangling peal of harsh laughter. 'Sympathy! Lilies! Bibles! How far away from reality can people get?'

'You are being horrible. It was meant to be kind.'

'Kind? You can't be kind about death. You can't do anything about it except face the fact that it has happened. Your father is dead, Janet. You will never see him again.'

'Sashie!' I said, staring at him, horrified, while he looked sternly back at me from piercing eyes under slanting brows but as I stared into those eyes, the desolation of a truth that I could no longer escape began to fill me with a terrible finality and I wailed: 'Sashie, oh, Sashie!' and, dropping on to a chair I put my dirty arms over the white card with the lilies, my dirty face down on my arms and began to cry tears that seemed to be gouged out of my very heart.

After a little, I was aware of Sashie's hand on the back of my shoulder and, sobbing, I looked up at him. 'There, my sweet,' he said, 'that's better. I have always said that Twice was far too gentle a man for you.' He picked up the stiff expensive card which was now soiled with ashes and tears and tore it venomously into minute pieces, his delicate little hands showing amazing strength. 'Realists like you and me need nasty people like each other to bring us to our nasty real senses. Now, you will go upstairs and wash and I shall order tea.'

When I came downstairs, I felt physically feeble but mentally more stable than I had felt since my family's cable arrived and, as I came forward to the tea table where Sashie sat, I said: 'You are a very good friend to Twice and me, Sashie.'

'Don't be insulting, darling. You make me sound like the Friends of the Poor, all holy and sympathetic, sending cards with silver lilies on them. Did you have a card from Edward too?'

'Sashie, I do wish you didn't dislike Edward so much.'

He shrugged his shoulders. 'I don't *dislike* him, my sweet. I merely think he is an unrealistic slobbery sentimentalist like his old grandma and I would rather not discuss him.'

'There is nothing unrealistic, slobbery or sentimental about his taste in pictures,' I defended Edward.

'*That* is not taste, Janet. *That* is the mercantile mind that would not baulk, even, at putting a price upon a sunrise over Hurricane Point. But don't let's talk about Edward. It only points up the fact that I am a member of the Awkward Squad which does not believe in a world where everybody loves everybody and death can be concealed under a bible and some lilies painted on pasteboard.'

I did not argue with him any further. I recognised the fact that, by this last reference to the card, he was inviting me to talk of my father if I wished to and that Sashie would not mention the subject again unless I did. I wanted him to know with certainty that he had helped me, however, so I said: 'You have something of a gift for helping me out of my mental nonsense, Sashie. I feel much better now that I have faced the fact that my father is dead. I always feel better when I face up to things but I always try to avoid doing it. Why is one so stupid?'

'It isn't stupid, my sweet. It is a little built-in thing we all have for avoiding the unpleasant, for avoiding *feeling* anything, because most of the things that we humans are given to feel are quite extraordinarily nasty. Quite a lot of people get through life without ever feeling anything at all — the cardboard lilies, you know — but when someone like you stops feeling, you stop living, really. I think there are three basic groups of people, those who live by feeling, those who live by knowing and those who escape into the forest of cardboard lilies. I like the feelers, myself. The knowers I find tiresome with their pursuit of the Bomb and wanting to know the backside of the moon at first hand and the cardboard lilies lot are merely sickening. You did not merely *know* your father, darling. He is something that you felt in your blood and your bones and the knowledge of his death will soon disappear and you will feel him again as you have always felt him. We have talked of this before. For you, *knowledge* is an evil. You are not a clever knower and you often get things wrong. Here endeth today's lesson. I must get back.' He laid his teacup aside and rose to his feet.

'So soon? You haven't even told me how New York was. When did you get back?'

'The other day. It was as depressing as ever. The tourist agency side of New York must be its nastiest side and that was all I saw. But one thing. That young man Maclean's new book was the talk of the town which is very gratifying. Are his extraordinary parents as disapproving as ever?'

'No. At least, Twice says his father is coming round and Madame has come round completely.'

'Ah, yes, because of the money,' said Sashie with his acid acuteness.

Although Sashie and I never stopped talking when we were together and there were few things I did not discuss with him, the ramifications of the Maclean affair was one of these because of some inhibition that dictated that Twice and I could not discuss the peculiarities of our 'bosses' except with one another. I therefore made no comment on Sashie's last remark about Madame and, very shortly, he went away.

The next morning, after Twice had gone to the office, I remembered with a shock that blind destructive debauch of a bonfire the afternoon before and, with horror, I began to wonder whether my destruction had been confined to my own manuscripts and notebooks of various kinds. I sat trying to assure myself that I had torn up nothing but my own writings but I was haunted by the idea that I might have laid crazy hands on some of Twice's stored papers or drawings and, in the end, I went up with trepidation to the cupboard to make sure.

After a little time I knew, with tremendous relief, that I had not destroyed anything of importance but I had made the place very untidy so I began to set it to rights, putting back on the shelves various things which I had thrown on the floor the more readily to get at the papers for which I had felt such a sudden violent hatred. When I had finished, I sat down on a trunk on the floor and, flicking idly at the leather strap of a suitcase which hung down from the top shelf, I faced the truth that the debauch of the day before had been an attempt to expiate my guilt that I had never really tried to do the one thing my father had ever wanted me to do for him, to write a book. I had let the worms of time eat away his life and now it was too late. This sadness was away beyond tears. This was a grief of the blood and

184

bones and I sat in the dusty place beneath the glaring unshaded light bulb in the arid irreclaimable desert that was of my own making.

After what seemed to be a long time that was yet out of time altogether, I rose heavily to my feet, pulling unthinkingly on the down-hanging strap. A very old leather suitcase that belonged to Twice and which had not been used since 1949 came crashing to the floor with an unexpectedly metallic noise. Unable to account for the nature of the noise, I opened the case to find that, inside it, there was the helmet of one of those bogus suits of armour with which some people decorate the halls of their houses. I picked it up, held it in front of me, raised the visor and let it drop again with a hollow 'clonk' as I remembered the moment when I first saw this thing.

It was a forenoon in July of 1931 and I was twenty-one years old. In those days, all the great world belonged to me, a world in which anything was possible and I roamed about this world with reckless abandon. On this forenoon, I had arrived at the front door of a house in Kent to which I had roamed from Devonshire, having left precipitately the job I was doing there and hoping to find a new job that would be more to my liking here in Kent. In those days, I seldom paused to consider the wisdom of my actions but, when the front door of this house was opened by a man-servant, I had a sudden moment of horrid panic, of wondering if this time, perhaps, I had gone what my grandmother would have called 'a bit past myself' for in the hall, just beside the door, there stood a suit of armour, hideously bogus, even to my untutored eye and for some inexplicable reason it made me want to turn and run as fast as my long strong legs would carry me. It may be that the suit of armour had no relation to the panic for this was the testing moment, the end of my present journey and the panic might have overtaken me in any case but, be that as it may, I disliked the suit of armour ever afterwards and, in a vengeful way, always referred to it in my mind as 'the Two-Handed Engine', from the Miltonic couplet:

'But that two-handed engine at the door,
Stands ready to smite once and smite no more.'

Now, as I listened to the 'clonk' from the severed head of the 'Engine', a head that had come into the possession of Twice and myself after many vicissitudes and some discreditable behaviour on my own part, I remembered that moment of panic at the first sight of it and I could hear again in my mind the voice of my grandmother as I hesitated on that doorstep.

'Janet Sandison, you started this and you will finish it. Don't you dare to turn and run like a rabbit from a weasel!'

And I could hear again in my mind the voice of my father: 'Do the best you can with anything you undertake, Janet and try to carry it through to the end. Always mind that.'

And I could hear the scornful voice of my Aunt Kate: 'Go on and run, herring guts!' and once again I seemed to be stepping across the threshold of that house and following the manservant round the suit of armour towards the door of the drawing-room.

Looking back to that faraway time, I carried the helmet downstairs and set it on my writing-table, staring at it while I lit a cigarette. The Two-handed Engine. Two hands. Two ways to go. Always in life there are two ways, the element of choice, Swann's Way or the Guermantes Way. What would have happened after that moment of panic if I had turned about and run?

The first consequence to leap to my mind was that, had I run, I would never have met Twice and next I thought: 'But I could not have run away anyhow, of course, not with my father and my grandmother and my sort of family behind me. They had made me so that to run away from that situation was not in my character. To have run away I

186

would have had to be a different person from a different background. What sort of person? A person like—what? She could be a tall girl of twenty-one, as I was, but without my father or grandmother or any of my family. She would have to be a Scot, with a country upbringing because this is the only upbringing that I know about. Her name? Something ordinarily Scottish without being too heathery and hooch-aye. Jean. Jean is the thing, finely Scottish and short to write too. Write? Well, why not? I pushed the helmet to one side of the table, sat down and at once began: 'I rang the bell, the door opened and then I ran away.'

I wrote on impatiently, at tremendous speed, for the story of Jean, Jean Robertson, seemed to be coiled up inside the helmet and to be flowing out through the visor and down through the barrel of my pen to the paper but, at last, the ink in the pen ran out so that the point made no mark and as I reached out in an exasperated way for the ink bottle, the clock struck four.

As if coming out of sleep, I stared round me, feeling as an animal in danger must feel and realised that Twice would come in at any moment and catch me with this heap of closely written paper on the blotter and this absurd helmet on the table. I scooped up the paper and the helmet into my arms and fled upstairs to the spare bedroom and pushed the entire heap into a drawer, the helmet giving another 'clonk' as I slammed the drawer shut. As I came downstairs, Twice's car pulled up at the door and he came up on to the veranda.

'Well, what sort of afternoon?' he asked. 'Still feeling all right, darling?'

'I am really all right now, Twice. A very lazy afternoon. I have been amusing myself doing a great deal of nothing at all.'

'Then come and amuse me for a change.'

If I have nothing else that real writers like Roddy

Maclean have, I thought, I have most certainly got the secrecy and the cowardice and I went on being secretive and cowardly. In the spare bedroom, the heap of written paper mounted hour by hour and day by day until, at the end of three weeks, the first instalment of the life and times of Jean Robertson was spun out line by parallel line on some two hundred sheets of paper.

It was not a good piece of writing I knew. It was a formless spill of words that no publisher would look at but when I had wrapped it in brown paper and had stowed it away on a shelf of the linen cupboard, I thought that one day, perhaps, my young niece Elizabeth might read it. If it was nothing else, the story of Jean Robertson was true to the period in which she and I had lived and the brown parcel took on the appearance of a little bulwark against those destructive worms that live in the heart of time.

PART FOUR

'But these are all lies. Men have died from time to time and worms have eaten them, but not for love.'

Shakespeare. *As You Like It* Act IV, Sc. I.

B u s y in the spare bedroom with my pen, I became irritatedly aware that Christmas of 1955 was all but upon us, for I viewed the break in the routine and the festivities of the season as a mere untimely interruption of this new activity I was engaged upon. Although, in the past, I had covered reams of paper with script, this writing I was now doing was new in that, never before, had I had such a feeling of being in complete control, a control so complete that I could afford to write as if in an uncontrolled spontaneous outburst.

When, a few days before Christmas, Edward landed in the island and there was the prospect of his daily visits, I had a foretaste of frustration. I did not want to see anybody except Twice. I did not want to do anything except write and, in the evening, when I had written myself out and the hand that held the pen was aching, I wanted nothing but to sit with Twice and listen to music or talk trivialities. When, therefore, a day or two before Christmas, Clorinda came to the spare bedroom and told me that Sir Ian was downstairs, it was with irritation that I stopped in mid-sentence and came down to join him. To be called away like this was like stepping from one world into another, not only out of the past and into the present, for I was now writing of Jean's childhood during the Great War, but out of a world which operated by different rules from the world of every day so that, in the first second of meeting, it was as if I were seeing Sir Ian for the first time, but not through the eyes that first saw him in 1948. I saw him now, as if for the first time, through the eyes of Janet Alexander of 1955. He was a fine-looking man of about seventy, very erect of carriage and he had the ruddy-fresh skin and strong-growing silver hair which had been characteristic of my father.

'But, of course,' I thought with a little shock of astonishment, 'I would naturally form an affection for a man who looked like this!'

I also became aware now for the first time that Sir Ian had much of the simplicity that my father had had. He was a much better educated, more travelled man than my father had been but they had a similar simple and direct approach to life and brought to its problems a similar simple code of a few rules which they had discovered to be serviceable. They both believed in a few simple human things like personal integrity and fair dealing and were both predisposed to love their neighbours rather than hate them.

'Mornin' me dear,' he said. 'Hope you weren't busy?'

'Goodness, no. I wasn't doing a thing. Sit down. I'll get Clorinda to bring you a beer.'

In the style of a St. Jagoan planter of half a century ago, he was dressed as usual in a suit of immaculate white drill, the trousers sharply creased above his highly polished black shoes and he had a look of what I can only describe as a shining physical and mental cleanliness but he was obviously worried about something. For a moment, he sat half turned away from me, frowning out over the garden but, suddenly, he turned in his chair, placed a hand on each knee, drew down his eyebrows and, looking at me sharply, he said: 'Look here, Missis Janet, you been seein' anythin' o' Missis Marion lately?'

'No, Sir Ian. I never see her except very seldom at the Great House. She doesn't come here and I don't go to Olympus. We haven't quarrelled or anything. It is just something that happened after that row about Roddy back in '52.'

'Are ye still holdin' that against Rob? He apologised, ye know.'

'I know and I am not holding it against him. It is simply that Marion and I sort of decided that we were different sorts of people with not much in common and then Twice was ill and we just drifted to the point where we never meet except at the Great House. There is no quarrel or anybody holding anything against anybody.'

'I see. Pity. Was hopin' maybe you could help me. There's somethin' goin' on up at Olympus. Don't know what it is but I don't like it.' He paused, frowning. 'Rob's drinkin' too much. Fact is, Rob's been goin' steadily down hill the last few years, ever since the time o' that damn' silly carry-on about Roddy, now that I think o' it. Rob has his faults — I'm not sayin' he hasn't but I don't like to see a man — dammit, he looks as if he's tryin' to destroy himself!'

I sat looking back at him as he frowned at me but I could say nothing because my mind was churning heavily in a way that made me think of the big mud-filter drum that turned slowly over and over in the factory and through which the sugar cane juice was sieved and the mud extracted. Great slimy black gobbets of thought were dropping and slopping about in my mind, memories of discussions with Twice and Edward about Rob and thoughts engendered by the terrible world that Roddy had created in his two novels.

Our relationships with different people do not all exist on the same plane. In each friendship, we ourselves undergo some mutation of personality to meet the demands of the relationship so that although, with Twice, I could talk of Roddy's fictional character Fanny having been born out of Marion, I could not talk of such things with Sir Ian. This was not merely because of the variation in intimacy between myself and Twice and myself and Sir Ian. It was that the pressure of Sir Ian's personality — his strong practical approach to life—on my own weaker, less practical and, I think, more thoughtful personality tended to dominate me, except in cases where I was personally involved very deeply. In the Roddy affair of long ago, I had been prepared to defy Sir Ian to the bitter end because the boy had written what I thought to be a worthwhile book but, now, presumably because neither Rob nor Marion meant as much to me as that book had done, I sank under Sir Ian's domination. Although he had said that he did not know what was going on up at Olympus, the conviction that Rob's drinking too much was in some way connected with Marion leaked from his every pore but that Marion could be at fault seemed to him to be unreasonable and impossible. My quandary was that I thought that Marion was indubitably at fault but my conviction of this was too nebulous to be put into words of the kind that were current on the plane where Sir Ian and I were related. When he began to speak again, his tone was coaxing.

'Look, Missis Janet, you've got your head screwed on when it comes to people. Don't you go bearin' a grudge about the night Rob lost his temper about the boy whorin' about an' then writin' books instead o' engineerin'. The Macleans have forgotten about that long ago an' Rob's as proud as Punch about the boy now. You take yourself up to Olympus an' have a chat with Missis Marion an' see what —'

'I am sorry, Sir Ian,' I interrupted him. 'I would try to do anything you asked of me but I cannot do this.'

'But you an' Missis Marion were *friends*, dammit, havin' tea-parties an managin' Ho Varlet an' everything!' he protested and then: 'Look here, what are you hidin'? Tell me that!' I felt that this was my father who was looking at me. 'Don't ye see I want to help Rob, me dear?'

'Sir Ian, you have often said that I could never keep out of trouble —'

'Oh, bless me, me dear, you don't have to go draggin''

that up! An' anyway, I never meant that what you did was trouble, not really *trouble*. Besides, since Twice was sick you've stopped all that — sometimes I wish ye hadn't. The place is damnable dull sometimes an' I'd enjoy hearin' you goin' for Don Candlesham like a fishwife or goin' on like that night ye had the row wi' Beattie Denholm when you were all covered with that blue stuff after you got stung. By Jove, those were the — '

'Sir Ian,' I broke through this barrage of reminiscence, 'what I wanted to say was that those times when I got into what you called trouble, I always gave something of myself away. I gave you a chance to find out what sort of person I was.' I had his full attention now and he was watching me keenly with wise bright eyes. 'The night I had the row with Mrs. Denholm, you found out that I was the sort of person who didn't like old grandmothers who bullied their grandchildren. The night I went for Don Candlesham, you found out I was the sort of person who didn't like handsome lady-killers trying their arts on me. The night I had the row with Rob Maclean, you found out I was the sort of person who likes books and would try to help the people who write them. Isn't this so?'

'Certainly. Until that night you went for Candlesham, I thought you were havin' a bit of a carry-on with him, to tell the truth. But what are you gettin' at?'

'This,' I said. 'Have you ever seen Marion Maclean in what you call trouble?'

'Missis Marion? Good God, no!' He looked at me as if I had propounded some theory that was contrary to the laws of nature. 'I've seen her a bit grumpy now an' again if Mother told her she was havin' a party for fifty an' then invited a hundred by mistake so that the sandwiches were short but I've never seen Missis Marion leadin' off the way you used to do in the old days. 'Smatter o' fact, I've never seen anybody, man or woman, that could go it like you could when you were on the top o' your form.'

'Never mind that now, Sir Ian. The point is, how much do you know about the sort of person Marion Maclean is?'

'The sort o' person?' He frowned at me. 'She is a nice quiet sort o' woman. Between ourselves, I've always found her a bit dull an' stoopid, not interested to have a chat about anythin' much, ye know.' He was still frowning at me and, suddenly, as if a coin had dropped through a slot in his mind, tearing the fabric of his accepted picture of Marion, he burst out with: 'Dammit, I always thought she was an ordinary sort o' woman like anybody else! But I see what you're at, me dear. I don't know what she's really like at all.' He looked out over the garden for a moment, took a drink from his beer glass, then turned upon me quickly. 'What do *you* think she's like?' he said with a pounce.

'Sir Ian, I simply don't know. Like you, I thought until the time of the row about Roddy that she was very much like myself and then I found out just one thing — that she wasn't a person like me about Roddy and his book. If I had been his mother, I should have been pleased about the book. Marion wasn't. The truth is that I think now that it was Marion who made Rob go tearing off that day to catch Roddy and punish him. I think she felt that Roddy, doing the things he did, was getting out of her power — sort of —' My voice trailed away into uncertainty as the words were swallowed up by the nebulous thing I was trying to express and dragged down into silence.

'Bless me soul!' Sir Ian said, frowning at me, but I could see that I had started a new train of thought in his mind. After a long time he said: 'I've always known Rob was a queer fellow — a bit too ambitious an' a bit fond o' the sound o' his own voice. But mind you, he did a lot for us here at Paradise an' I don't want anybody to forget that. He was just inclined to get a bit big for his boots now an' again with me bein' away an' Mother fiddlin' about with her charities an' nonsense an' him gettin' all his own way. But this last year or so, he's quite different, as if all the ambitiousness an' bumptiousness had gone out of him. 'Smatter o' fact, he started changin' a long time ago. Around that time Twice was so sick in hospital, it was. I noticed then he was drinkin' a bit more than was good for him an' sort o' losin' his grip.' He took thought for another long moment and then said sharply: 'So ye think Missis Marion's at the root o' the trouble?'

There is no doubt that thought can be communicated without the medium of words.

'Now, Sir Ian, I did not say that. All I said was that Marion did not react to Roddy and his book as I should have reacted,' I defended myself. 'And Twice will tell you that I am hopelessly hipped on books anyway so I may be biased. The facts are that I know nothing about Rob and Marion at all and I can't help you about them.'

'You've helped to the extent o' makin' me aware that I know damn' little meself. But things can't go on like this. Rob's makin' a fool o' himself an' that won't do. Dammit, *there's* a thing I never thought of. It's always when *she's* here that he gets queer since he started gettin' queer. He's always all right when she's away in the summer.'

I began to feel an ugly unhappiness, as I wondered whether my own dislike of Marion, which had been born at the time of the Roddy affair and which, since reading Roddy's novels had grown monstrously in the depths of my mind like some poisonous fungus, had led me, out of malice, to set Sir Ian questing along this new track. I wished that he would go away, that I could go back upstairs to my pen and be free of all these pressures which seemed to originate among the Macleans and flow, unwanted, towards myself.

'Sir Ian,' I said, 'you should discuss all this with Edward instead of with me.'

'Edward?' His glance was startled for a moment. 'Oh,

Edward wouldn't know anythin', me dear. He's never spent much time here an', between ourselves, he an' Rob have never got on since Edward was a youngster.'

'Edward is extremely clever about people,' I said and there was something pathetic in the light that showed in the old man's eyes at these scant words in praise of his son. With a stab at the heart, I knew that this is how my own father would have reacted to a few words in praise of myself.

'You think so, me dear?'

'Yes, I do and I know that during these last few years Edward has been seeing something of Roddy in London. Roddy knows more about his parents than any of us and young men like Roddy and Edward talk to one another as they might not talk to you and me.'

'I'll have a word with Edward. It's all very worryin'. And, me dear, with all we've been sayin', I forgot what I came round here for in the first place. Mother is goin' on about Christmas. She says it's two Christmasses since you an' Twice had dinner with us but Twice is a lot better now and I am to arrange a party. Mother may be blind but she still knows Christmas from August Bank Holiday an' she's dead set on this party but it will be only you an' Twice an' one or two others an' the Macleans, of course. You two will come, me dear?'

'Thank you, Sir Ian.' I had not any inclination to share a Christmas dinner with the Macleans but I had to allow life to take control. 'We shall probably have to leave early, of course.'

'We wouldn't be late anyway. I wouldn't bother if it wasn't for Mother. Things are pretty dull for her, ye know. Sometimes I feel it would be better if she were really in her dotage — livin' in an imaginary world, ye know. People are happier that way than havin' all their faculties except their sight like Mother.'

When he went away, I did not return to the spare bedroom that forenoon. I continued to sit on the veranda where he had left me with my thoughts milling round the Macleans and, at the same time, resenting their intrusion into my mind. When Twice came home for lunch, I told him that we were required to dine at the Great House on Christmas evening with the Macleans among others.

'Don't look as if you were haunted,' he said at once. 'It will be like a hundred other dinners at the Great House.'

'For me it won't. What really brought Sir Ian round here this morning was the Macleans. He wanted me to go up to Olympus and find out what was goin' on, as he put it. He is on to the fact that something is wrong with Rob. Have you noticed anything lately?'

'I have hardly seen him for the last two months but admittedly I have hardly been out of the drawing-office up there but lately I have felt he was avoiding me.'

'But why should he?'

Twice shrugged his shoulders. 'You know how people are. I suppose he feels he gave himself away a bit to me, like the time when he said he wasn't what they call a brave man and now he is sorry he did it and wants to forget about it or something like that. What did you say to Sir Ian about going to Olympus?'

'Simply that it was something that I was not going to do. I told him he should talk to Edward about the Macleans. The fewer people who are mixed up in this, the better.'

Twice frowned at me. 'You are still under the influence of these damned books of Roddy's,' he said accusingly.

'What if I am?' I asked crossly. 'Does it matter? If I keep quiet, nobody else around here is going to be influenced by a book, God knows.' I at once regretted my spurt of irritation. 'Sorry, darling. But I find the Maclean subject too hard on the temper. Let's forget it.'

Twice, less personally involved than I was and, of course, uninfluenced by Roddy's novels, forgot the subject at once,

199

for which I was thankful but the impending dinner at the Great House hung between me and my sheet of paper in the spare bedroom like a black impenetrable curtain, but when the evening came, the dinner was, as Twice had said it would be, exactly like other Christmas dinners at the Great House except that the guests were fewer in number but, throughout the evening, I found it difficult to keep my eyes away from Marion Maclean.

In the first moment that she and Rob came into the drawing-room, I could see that Rob had been drinking hard that evening and that he had probably been drinking for some days. His square teddy-bear face was now puffy in outline, there were heavy brownish bags under his eyes and there was a tremor in the hand that held his sherry glass. There was no tremor of any kind in Marion. Cool, calm and with that detachment which had always been in her and which, formerly, I had taken for a shy dignity, she moved about the room but I noticed now that, periodically, she cast a curiously penetrating and even hostile glance in the direction of Edward. I suppose that to the some dozen guests from beyond the boundaries of Paradise, this looked like any other Paradise party, with Madame upright in her throne-like chair with the high carved mahogany back, Marion as chief lady-in-waiting by her side, while I, as second in waiting. did little things like seeing that glasses were kept filled at Marion's instructions in the way that I had always done. It was only on this evening that it occurred to me that, all the time I had been at Paradise, I had taken instructions from Marion. It was the most natural thing in the world that I should have done this, for I had been brought up in a strict code of obedience to my 'elders and betters' and from the day of my arrival in the island, I had looked to Marion as my elder and better in this new way of life I had to take up as well as my elder and better in the hierarchy of Paradise. I wondered how she would react if I were to ignore one of her behests but decided that it would not be socially politic to run the risk of finding out.

One thing was certain. With Madame blind and no longer able to assert herself to her former degree, Marion was more rocklike in her placid security than she had ever been and, that night, easily might have been taken by a stranger to be the mistress of the Great House of Paradise.

'You know,' I said to Twice the following day, 'you and everybody around here are very fond of making out that I am one of these contrary people, obstinate as mules, who can't be dominated by anybody.'

'I should say that is a fairly accurate description of you and it is indeed what most of us think of you. So?'

'It's a pack of lies. Ever since I came here I have been dominated by Marion Maclean.'

'The notions you get!' Twice laughed. 'Was it Marion that dominated you into making a boon companion of Sir Ian so that he spends more time on this veranda than in any other one place?'

'It could have been. She could have influenced me into it to leave her free for her machinations at the Great House.'

I did not, of course, believe this but to say it rendered concrete in my mind the fact that I could now suspect Marion of almost anything. Indeed, after watching her that evening in the light shed by Roddy's novels, I could scarcely get her out of my mind at all. I kept plunging into that tangled web of my memory, pulling out loops of the thread that was Marion Maclean and one part of the thread that I examined again and again was the memory of the night that her youngest son, Sandy, had found the body of the murdered Linda Lee. On that night, I had felt very closely akin with Marion.

Little Sandy had gone with Sir Ian on an expedition to the interior of the island which took them through the settlement of Siloam where, in a swamp beside the river, there was a carpet of large and lovely water lilies. On their way home, Sir Ian stopped the car that the boy might wade into the swamp to pick some lillies that he wanted to bring back to me and it was here that the child found the body. The boy arrived home in a state of severe shock, still clutching the flowers he had picked and, in the end, Rob and Marion brought him to Guinea Corner because he kept repeating 'Flowers for Missis Janet' and would say nothing more. But when he handed the flowers to me, the shock that had gripped his mind broke down, he was able to put into words the terrible thing he had seen and eventually he cried himself to sleep. And now, when I recalled that evening, I would remember Marion's grey eyes as she kneeled on the floor with the boy crying against her shoulder and I would remember how she had looked at me over his red head and said: 'God bless you, Janet! He'll be all right now —' In spite of her strange behaviour on the day she came to tea with me, in spite of all that Roddy had written, Marion Maclean emerged from the memory of that night as a woman capable of the most devoted love, a love that, for a second, had spread from her youngest son to myself because I had been able to break the spell of his shock. It was comforting to think that, although much had been destroyed down the years since then, that split second of pure love remained between Marion and me like a small gleam of survival.

A FEW days after the new year had come in, Edward paid me one of his forenoon visits, on the Tuesday morning when the factory went into the 1956 cropping period to be precise.

'It is pleasant to hear it working again,' I said to him, nodding my head in the direction of the plant. 'Is everything going all right?'

The first week of cropping time was always a little anxious until all the minor hitches in the running of the complex machinery had been ironed out.

'The factory is running like clockwork and the manager is sitting in his office as drunk as if drowned in a butt of malmsey,' Edward replied with disgust. I made some sound of protest which he brushed aside with an impatient movement of his hands before he continued. 'Oh, it doesn't matter but this is the end. The man should have retired long ago and if he stays here much longer he will kill himself. If he wasn't stronger than any ox he would be dead already. Dad and I have made up our minds that he and Marion are to go home for good at the end of Crop.'

'Have you told Rob?'

'Not yet. You can't talk business with a drunk man and he has been drunk ever since I came home.' He sat down, looked past me into the garden and it struck me that he had grown much older in the last few months. 'I am hating all this,' he said, 'but it has got to be faced. I can't have Dad worried like this. He has enough to contend with in Granny. He is devoted to her and so am I but she is not easy to live with and it is no use to pretend that she is.' He continued to frown at the garden. 'It would be easier if I disliked Rob the way I used to do but I don't any more. I am sorry for the poor devil.' He turned to look at me and smiled. 'Anyway, you will have me grisling around here until the end of Crop, Janet.'

'You are welcome to come and grisle any time you want to,' I said, not entirely sincerely for I would have preferred to spend my forenoons in the spare bedroom.

'I wrote to Roddy Maclean yesterday,' he said next.

'How is Roddy?'

'As ever, only more so. I hope you will see him for yourself soon. I have asked him to come out here.'

Until this moment, I had been refusing to interest myself in the Maclean affair, had been trying to push it aside, telling myself that Rob having a drinking bout was nothing unusual, for most of the whites in the island drank too much as a matter of course — it was one more form of the magic cloak — but that Edward should have taken the step of sending for Roddy cast a new gravity over the situation.

'What for?' I asked.

He did not answer me but asked instead: 'Janet, how much do you know of Marion Maclean?'

I felt suddenly angry. 'Nothing,' I said snappishly. 'What does anybody know of anybody, come to that?'

I wanted to run away upstairs to be by myself and away from all these complications because I did not know what I knew about Marion Maclean. On the day that she came to tea with me, at the Christmas dinner at the Great House, she could have been Fanny, the monster in Roddy's novel but on the night that Sandy brought the lilies to me, she had been a woman quite unlike Fanny.

'I am sorry, Edward,' I said after a moment. 'This entire Maclean thing is away beyond me. I simply don't know what I think about Marion. She behaved very oddly about Roddy that time three years ago but, before that, when young Sandy was in trouble, she seemed to me to be like

204

the most perfect mother I had ever known, my own mother. I can't say better of any woman than this, Edward.'

'When was that? How old was Sandy?'

'Nine or ten. Why?'

He did not answer me directly but said instead: 'I have been seeing a lot of Roddy in London during these last three months. I was worried about Rob when I was out here during the summer. As you know, I am not very good at talking about intimate things but I did manage to convey to Roddy that I thought all was not well with his father. Roddy gave me a bit of a shock. *He* doesn't find any difficulty in talking about private things. He said that the only thing that was wrong with his father was his mother,' Edward ended, looking at me with that wry smile of his.

I was outraged. 'What a disgusting thing for a son to say!' I burst forth. 'Disgusting and unnatural! Why — '

I stopped short. Unnatural. This was what I had felt in Marion that day when she came to tea with me, that her behaviour was unnatural, in the pure sense of the word. It was behaviour not in accordance with the physical nature of a person, not in accordance with the nature of a mother of a son. And now I seemed to be faced with the inexorable result, the unnatural mother drawing an unnatural response from her son.

'Edward, I don't understand any of this. Why have you asked Roddy to come out here?'

'Roddy is devoted to his father,' he said, 'but he has a strong dislike for his mother.'

'I suppose I am just old-fashioned and unsophisticated but I just don't understand. Why should Roddy dislike his mother? Whatever Marion may be, she was the most wonderful mother to these boys. Nothing will shake me out of that belief. This is something I have seen, something I know!' I said angrily.

'Roddy would agree with you,' Edward said coolly. 'He

would agree that she was a perfect mother until her sons began to grow away from her and at that point she became a devouring monster.'

'Oh, rubbish! I don't believe a word of it!' But I was shouting in the dark, shouting against the logic that what Edward was saying brought together the Marion of the night that Linda Lee was drowned and the Marion who had come to tea with me that afternoon, brought together two facets of the same person.

Edward rose from his chair, took a turn along the veranda and came back to stand looking down at me. 'I want very much to get you and Twice on my side and Roddy's over this, Janet,' he said. 'I don't want to dramatise this thing but I don't want to under-estimate it either. Roddy, probably because he is what he is, knows his mother in a way that few sons do, I think. He says that she loves passionately but that her desire for power is more passionate still and that, rather than let anyone she loves go against her will, she will destroy him — not intentionally, you know, but she will fight to the death to work her own will.'

This was Fanny, the heroine of *But Not For Love* that Edward was describing and horrified, I stared up at him, saying nothing.

'Roddy and I are not imagining things, Janet. I can prove it. I am going to tell you something that I thought I would never tell to anybody but it is something that convinced me that Roddy's view of his mother is exact. "She loves us all so much" Roddy said to me one evening, "that she wants the earth and the heavens for us, to be given to us from her own hand, but none of must try to do anything for ourselves, we must only have earth and heaven from Mother's hand."' I felt a shivery tremor pass over my shoulder-blades as Edward went on: 'And from what I am going to tell you, I think you will see that Roddy is right. Remember I told you about my mother, my sisters

and the baby dying in the typhoid epidemic? I had typhoid
at that time too. I was in the bedroom that I have round
at the house now and my old Nan — she came from Ayr-
shire — was nursing me. Marion came along the veranda
and looked at me through the open window and then she
said to Nan, she said — ' he paused and drew a breath as
if for an effort before he repeated again ' — she said: "He
will die — he is bound to".'

I felt that I was going to choke and was astonished to see
a strange tender smile relax Edward's tense face. 'Nan
went between me and the window and said: "Ye are a bad
wicked wumman, Madam an' go your ways away from my
Edward" and then I knew I wasn't going to die after all.' I
did not speak and after a moment he went on: 'During the
last months of the war, I was in bombers. I was pretty
young and pretty scared most of the time but when the
flak came up over the target area, I used to hear Nan's
voice saying to it "Go your ways away from my Edward"
and it always did.'

'Edward, you have never told Madame or Sir Ian about
this?'

'No. Kids don't tell big things, frightening things — they
can't. I was only six, you know. I couldn't have found the
words for what I felt in order to tell it and Nan was there
to protect me. And when I grew older, there was no point
in telling it so I buried it deep and did not ever dig it up
until that evening Roddy spoke to me about his mother.'

To understand someone completely, to be in full sympathy with anyone, we have to be able to translate his
experience into our own terms and with the speed of
thought I returned in my own mind to the age of eight and
remembered how, one day, I had been sent on an errand
to an unhappy house in my home district, the house of
the Miss Boyds. When I came home, I tried to tell my
family of the terrible dreary sense of misery that had communicated itself to me from those women but I could not

find words. All I could do was to weep and shout almost hysterically: 'It's the Miss Boyds! It's the Miss Boyds!'

'Yes, I can understand that,' I said to Edward. 'Children can't find the words for what they feel. Indeed, it is difficult enough when we are grown up to say exactly what we mean.'

'If I could find the words to say what I mean about Marion, I wouldn't have told you about this thing. But I can only describe her by using her own words.' He was quiet for a little time, turned in on himself, until he said: 'I wish now that I had paid more attention to Rob down the years. There is a barrier between us now which makes it difficult for me to help him.'

'Twice and I, for a long time, thought that Rob had what we called a pipe dream of himself as the great power of Paradise,' I said. 'It was Twice who told me about this of course. I hardly know Rob at all. I thought it petty and silly. I still do. I don't understand about this power thing. I cannot understand how people can give themselves up to dreams of something that cannot possibly be. Even if you, Sir Ian and Madame were wiped out tomorrow, there are a lot of other claimants to Paradise well ahead of the Macleans.'

'It seems to me that everyone who dreams of power must ignore all obstacles. Think of Lady Macbeth, Napoleon, Hitler — Marion is small compared to them but she is true to a terrifying tradition. And, of course, there were all sorts of possibilities to encourage her to dream that the obstacles might be removed. Rob didn't go to the war but Dad and I did. She probably hoped that neither of us would come back.'

'Edward!' I protested but he merely smiled coolly as if he had lived with these thoughts for some time and had grown accustomed to them.

'I really think she did hope that, Janet. In fact, the Dulac family is pretty thin on the ground and they are all pretty old. Dad and I are the youngest and the thing about the most absurd dream is that it might come true. During the war, Marion's dream only needed a pair of well-placed shots. And Granny was very fond of all the Maclean boys when they were young, after losing all her own five except Dad in the Great War. Certainly all the young Macleans are mentioned in her will.'

'Madame lost four sons?' I asked.

'You didn't know? No, I suppose you wouldn't. Granny buries her dead.'

We were both silent for a little while until I said: 'Do you think Roddy will come?'

'I am hoping so.'

'But what do you think he can do?'

'It is difficult to explain. Dad and I think Rob is drinking because he is miserably unhappy. We have never told him in so many words that we mean to sell Paradise eventually but Rob is no fool. He sees the political and economic drift as clearly as we do, probably more clearly. I think he feels he has come to a dead end with nothing left except Marion and she won't listen to reason about politics or economics or anything else. And she has alienated four of the boys from him completely. Roddy will tell you that. She tried to attach all seven to herself and to make them disregard their father. He hardly knows the boys but Roddy and two of the others are attached to him in spite of Marion. I think Rob feels now that his job is going, he has lost his sons and he is left with nothing. And Marion is not much of a joke to live with, I gather. She has the temper of a fiend.' This was Fanny again. 'So I thought that if Roddy came and Rob realised that he meant something to at least one of the boys, it might help. You see, in the same way that Roddy knows his mother, he knows his father. He is fond of him but he knows him with a terrible sort of clarity too. "Everybody thinks that Dad is a big strong man" he said "but Dad has always been a babe lost in the woods. He will do whatever a stronger person tells him to do." I am hoping that Roddy is stronger than Marion and I am inclined to think he is. I think that when he was born she endowed him with some of her own monstrous will.'

While Edward was with me, I could visualise Marion as a monster, exercising her monstrous influence on everybody around her but, as soon as he had gone, this image faded because it seemed too improbable. I also began to think it very unlikely that Roddy would return to the island because, since the time of his departure in 1952 in Dee's borrowed car, the departure had taken on the finality of a passing bell.

BUT Roddy did return to the island. He arrived about the middle of January, totally unexpected by everyone, Twice told me and the first intimation that he was in St. Jago came when he telephoned his father at the factory office one forenoon from the Peak Hotel in St. Jago Bay.

'I don't think I have ever seen anyone so pathetically pleased as Rob,' Twice told me when he came home for lunch. 'I wish you had heard the way he said: "Roddy? It's *you*, Roddy?" I couldn't bear it. I ran away through to the drawing office.'

'Has Rob gone down to fetch him?' I asked in a carefully normal voice for I could see that Twice had been much moved by Rob's reaction to his son's arrival.

'Sir Ian sent a driver with him. Rob was pretty shaky this morning but it was a queer thing that when he went out to get into the car he was quite steady, as if the sound of Roddy's voice had sobered him completely. Then he asked me to 'phone Marion and let her know about Roddy and his voice had more authority in it that I've heard since the old bombastic days.'

'And did you?'

'Did I what?' Twice's mind was entirely engaged with Rob, brooding happily over the emotion that had been communicated to him, so that he did not at once catch my meaning. 'Oh Marion?' he said after a moment and grinned. 'Not me. I got Edward to do it which was fun for him and fun for me to listen to. He called Roddy "your prodigal son" when he spoke to her. Edward hates that woman.'

I had told Twice nothing of what Edward had told me of Marion and I now let the matter of Roddy's arrival drop although I felt a horrid pricking uneasiness down my spine.

However, when Roddy arrived at Paradise, no meteor crossed the heavens as the explosive nature of the situation in my mind had made to seem likely. Rob's big car merely came in along the south approach, crossed the park and disappeared into the trees that covered the hill of Olympus and across the green valley I heard no thunder-clap but only the hum of the busy factory.

I was now intently occupied again in the spare bedroom, using the life of the imaginary Jean Robertson as an escape from present events as much as anything. Although I had stored the first parcel of manuscript about her in the linen cupboard, putting it behind me, Jean Robertson herself refused to stay behind me. She haunted my mind almost constantly, drawing me up the stairs to the spare bedroom to record yet more and more of her life and times. As soon as Twice went out in the morning, I would do my routine jobs and then run upstairs and again, as soon as lunch was over and I had seen him off to the factory, I would run up again and remain there until I had to go round to the Great House. In these hours, I was shut inside this world of Jean Robertson's which was also a world inside my own mind where I was discovering all sorts of things whose presence I had never suspected. It was as if I had discovered a hitherto unknown country where the going was sometimes perilous, where the snakes of motives for certain actions, recognised now for the first time, suddenly slithered out of the undergrowth; where, sometimes, looking into the river of time that flowed through this territory, my heart would leap at the sight of a small shimmer of gold dust that I must try to raise from the depths.

The day after he arrived, Roddy came round to see me.

Twice had told me that Rob had arrived in the office that morning completely sober for the first time in months but that otherwise he had behaved as if Roddy's home-coming were the most natural thing in the world, a pleasant social-family visit of a son to his parents and friends. And during the forenoon, Edward had called to tell me that, on the evening before, the evening of Roddy's arrival, he, Rob and Marion had called at the Great House, that Roddy might pay his respects to Madame and Sir Ian.

'We were just one big happy family,' Edward said. 'Granny told Roddy that he had been a very naughty boy — these were her exact words — when he was here last time but that we would say no more about that at this late date and after that everything was all merry and hey-nonny.'

'Perhaps we have been imagining things.'

'I haven't imagined that Rob was drunk for about six months and now he isn't and I don't think that I am imagining that Marion Maclean would like to murder that son of hers because I honestly think she would like to.'

'Oh, rubbish, Edward!'

'He has not only crossed her will,' he said as if I had not spoken, 'he has crossed it in a highly successful way with lots of éclat and, what is more and to put it coarsely, he is not at all averse to rubbing her nose in the fact.'

When Roddy walked on to the veranda that afternoon, the picture of him which had formed in my mind from what Edward had said, from the articles written about him by journalists and even the picture of him that my memory had retained were dissolved by the impact of the actual personality of Roddy Maclean. I think this process always takes place when we meet someone again after an interval of time, for, during the interval, we ourselves have changed, so that we regard the person with different eyes and the person regarded has also changed, causing some mutation in his attitude towards ourselves. Compared with these changes, the physical alteration of grey hairs and wrinkles is a very minor thing.

That afternoon in 1952, when Roddy had come to me for help, he had his inner conviction about what he wanted to do with his life but, in spite of a notable first book behind him, his confidence had been shaken by the inimical mental climate of his family and of the people in general whom he met in St. Jago. He had described himself as a fugitive on the run and about him there had been an aura of fear that he would always be a fugitive, that the world was merely a macrocosm of the microcosm that was Paradise and that he would always be, socially and in every other sense, an odd man out.

This afternoon in 1956, this fugitive air had gone. The first impression I received was that here was a visitor from another wider, more important world than Paradise and that here, too, was someone who was fully aware that he was of some consequence in that wide important world. The next thing that struck me was his extraordinary physical resemblance to his father. Although physical, it was difficult to define. The colouring was different, but Roddy had the big square bone structure of his father now, the blunt robust teddy-bear look. In 1952, he had still had a boyish air which had now disappeared and his body had set into the stocky mould of Rob's but was carried by Roddy not with Rob's heaviness but with the old easy swing of the swashbuckling buccaneer. The total impression he made on me of mental confidence and sheer physical bulk and strength had the effect of scaring me a little.

'Roddy, you have grown,' I greeted him nervously.

Smiling, he handed me a box of a hundred cigarettes and a packet containing a dozen boxes of matches. 'These are in payment of a debt. One can't send matches through the post so I didn't send the cigarettes either.'

In a way which I felt to be ridiculous, I was so proud of him that, looking down at the packages between my hands, my eyes filled with tears.

'Life has been unkind to you since we last met, Janet,' he said.

'No. It isn't that. It's — Roddy, I am so *glad* to see you!' Three years ago, he had never used my Christian name. At Paradise then, he had been one of the 'young people' who, led by Sir Ian, called me 'Missis Janet' but I felt now that in the course of these three years Roddy had outstripped and passed me in mental age and that it was fitting that he should address me in this different way. It would almost be fitting, I felt, for me to address him in the Paradise idiom as 'Mr. Roddy' now.

'Unkind but not impossible,' I replied now to his remark about my life since our last meeting, 'but don't let's waste time on that. One's bad times are one's own and one can't share them even if one wants to but one's good times can be shared with anybody without getting any less good. Tell me about everything since you went away.'

'A tallish order,' he said but he summarised his journey by lumber-boat to Belize, his journey from there to San Francisco in a cargo boat and his tramping, hitch-hiking journey across the United States to New York. I could visualise this odyssey because Roddy was so much of a piece, so much the adventurous wayfarer in appearance, that I seemed to see the wakes of the ships that carried him and the long highways of the United States trailing behind him as he made his way from west to east across the continent.

'And now tell me about you and Twice,' he said.

'We are very much as we ever were, only more so, thank you, although we have had our ups and downs and talking of those, there was quite a to-do on this very veranda that evening you ran off in Dee's car.'

He gave a chuckling laugh. 'She got the car back all right though?'

'She doesn't even know now that it was ever away, I think.'

'You were very good to me that day, Janet.'

'You were the only one who thought so. Your father nearly throttled me that evening.'

'Oh, Dad,' he said in a quietly indulgent tone and when he looked away from me across the garden I noticed that all the dark gaiety had disappeared from his eyes. Then he seemed to reach a decision. 'Dad has been drinking too much, Janet.'

'I believe so of late.'

'No. For a long time. People like Dad and me don't show it much, you know but he was drinking too hard when I was here before. He is getting older now and it shows more.'

'We all get older.'

'I want him to retire.'

'Won't he miss Paradise terribly, Roddy?'

'Oh Paradise!' He was quiet for a space and then he went off at a new angle. 'I am buying a croft in Inverness-shire. I thought I had better buy something solid before I squander all my new-made wealth. Don't you think it is a good idea?'

'A splendid idea. It won't cost much to keep even if you use it for only a month or two in the year.'

'I was thinking of only a month or two in the year when I arranged to buy it but I might use it a bit more if Dad were with me.' He paused and there was a heavy silence. 'One might as well say it out loud,' he then said suddenly. 'I think Dad should leave my mother. He has served her for long enough.'

'Served her?'

'Yes,' and his voice was as brutally savage as his words when he added: 'sexually, mentally, morally and in every

216

other way. If he waits any longer, she will have eaten all of him away.'

'I don't know what you mean, Roddy.' As so often in this Maclean affair, I had a panic urge to run away. 'Surely your father and mother must decide their own —'

'You don't understand, I think,' he interrupted me quietly but authoritatively. 'My father has never made a decision for the last forty years.' I began to protest but he brushed this aside with: 'I don't mean decisions about trifling things like labour policy on the estate here or where to sell the Paradise sugar and rum. I am talking about decisions on personal and moral issues. The last of these that Dad made was when he decided to marry Mother. And he didn't really make that decision either — *she* made it. And if you spend forty years having all your decisions made for you, you cannot decide for yourself any more. The part of your brain that can do it is atrophied — the worms have eaten it.'

Frightened, hating what he was saying, wishing he would go away and say no more, I sat staring at him until I realised that his speaking to me like this was a natural development in his mind out of that day in 1952 when I had helped him to circumvent his parents. On that day, in his eyes, I had ranged myself on his side and he would never understand, now, that I had taken up that position without realising the full nature and scope of the battle. This situation between his parents was something that Roddy had been aware of, probably subconsciously at first and later consciously, all his life. It was a part of his personality as the harmony of my childhood at Reachfar was part of mine and he felt that anyone who knew him at all must automatically know this facet of him, as I felt that all my acquaintance must know that I was born and brought up at Reachfar.

But I felt that he was dragging me from the solid earth

217

of the world that I knew into some dark quaking morass where evil of a kind I had never imagined had its lair and, desperately, I clutched at the earth I knew, the solid family earth of blood relationships.

'Roddy, have you talked with your brothers about this?'

'Yes.'

This astonished me momentarily for, since 1952, I had been thinking of Marion Maclean as a woman who had six sons and a renegade son called Roddy who had no contact with the rest of the family. 'We are three to four over it,' he said with a bitter smile. 'The line-out as in Rugby football is Number Four and me and the kid versus the rest. I haven't discussed it with the rest, of course. There is no point.'

'The kid? Meaning Sandy?' I said, remembering how the most frequent phrase Sandy had used as a little boy had been: 'My Mother says —'

'Yes. Sandy,' Roddy said with emphasis. 'Sandy is fifteen now, you know and my little carry-on here in 1952 is nothing to what he did last year. Mother wouldn't let him go to camp with some of his friends and he just disappeared overnight. He'd got himself aboard Number Four's ship — stowed away — Number Four is sailing Third Engineer in a cargo liner to New Zealand and such far parts, after tramping on Mother's neck to get to sea. Sandy got himself taken on as a bell-hop or cabin boy or something Number Four helped him of course. And Mother didn't see her darling little boy again for five months. If it comes to a fight for Dad, the kid and Number Four and I will get him,' he said confidently and then he went on in a quieter tone. 'It is odd — we three *look* like Dad, especially the kid since a lot of the redness went out of his hair. The others look like Mother, especially Number One, Donald and he is one big slob. Do you know he is divorcing Myra?'

'Is he?'

'Mother has never liked Myra.'

'Roddy,' I said, striving to be coldly matter-of-fact, 'it strikes me as very odd that a family should be split into two factions warring for the custody of their father. Doesn't this strike you?'

'I suppose it is odd. Yet, is it? I have been doing it for so long. I can't remember the time when I wasn't on Dad's side, you know, in spite of the fact that he always took Mother's side against *me*. And Number Four was the same. The kid was a bit different. He was around with Sir Ian a lot and he didn't come down on either side until after he had been at school for a year or so. But after I misbehaved here, Mother started that thing of spending about half the year in Scotland and getting in the kid's hair and there we are.'

'But your mother is a splendid mother, Roddy,' I argued. 'I have always thought so and I still think so.'

'You are welcome to think what you like, Janet, but I would point out that much depends on what you mean by a mother. Our particular mother, by the force of nature, had to release our bodies from her womb at the end of nine months but she held on to our minds and souls until three out of seven of us tore them away from her by main bloody force.' His dark eyes glowed at me as, brutally as he went on: 'And when she married my father, she gave him the right to enter her body and for about forty years she has encompassed his mind too and she has damned nearly got his soul. Three sons fighting for the custody of their father, you said? Can't you see that we are fighting for his very life?' He fell silent and when he spoke again his voice was very quiet. 'Dad has put up a good fight one way and another. He has protected himself as best he could, bolstered himself up as a commercial big shot and boss of Paradise which was something that she wanted him to be but it has provided an escape for him too. But he is getting tired and yet he is still fighting. Rather than let her swallow

H

him completely, he is trying to drown the little that remains of his free self in drink.'

'Roddy, this is your mother you are talking about, not some creation of your imagination.'

'You bet it is. My imagination doesn't run to her scale of creation — it takes God or the Thing Itself to create them on that scale!'

During the few days that followed Roddy's visit, I felt frustrated and ill-tempered, for the things he had told me seemed so monstrous compared with the events in the lives of what I called 'ordinary' people, people like my imaginary Jean Robertson whose little life journey through the troubled twentieth century I was trying to record. In one way, Marion made Jean Robertson seem too trivial to write about but, in another way, the Jean Robertsons seemed more important than the Marions because the world held more Jean Robertsons than Marions.

I had told Twice of Roddy's visit and something, although not nearly all, of what he had said and an evening or two later he said to me: 'I suppose it is Roddy and his confidences that have put you on edge. A pity. Everyone else about the place is what Edward calls hey-nonny. I think it is possible that Roddy has let his dramatic imagination run away with him a bit. After all, he is busy turning his latest book into a play, I gather. Without being aware of it, he might have been working out a scene with you as Mrs. Interlocutor or something.'

'If he was, it was very poor theatre,' I said, 'but I wish I could think he was. Is Marion all hey-nonny too?'

'She seems to be. She was in the office this morning with Madame's letters and she didn't look a bit like a female Mephistopheles with a power complex to me. She looked pretty much as she had always looked but a little older.'

As the days went by, I was almost induced to believe that Roddy's visit to me and the things he had said in the course of it were figments of my own imagination, for he did not again raise the subject of Marion and neither did Edward nor did Sir Ian say anything more to me about Rob. It seemed that a tacit agreement had been made all round to, in the words of Madame 'say no more about' the Mac-leans and my own feeling about this was to wish that the agreement had been made before anybody had mentioned the subject to me at all.

The cropping season was going well with no trouble either from the labour or the machinery and the tension of the start of Crop and the arrivals of Edward and Roddy wound down. I was able to retire again to the priv-acy of the spare bedroom and my own petty affairs, inter-rupted occasionally by visits from Sir Ian, Edward or Roddy, during which we spoke of what I termed 'normal' things, petty local news punctuated by reminiscence with Sir Ian, pictures and the like with Edward and Roddy's work with Roddy.

This last was the most interesting to me of these con-versations for, in a secretive way, I was hoping to learn from Roddy a little about the craft of writing. At this time, I had not realised that a writer, or any other artist, however minor, is what he is largely because of being greatly or slightly more of an individualist than people of other gifts and that, because of this, one writer's methods are unlikely to be of much avail when copied and used by another.

One forenoon, however, tiring of his obsessive talk about his work, I said to him: 'Tell me about your croft in Inverness-shire. Whereabouts is it?'

'On a hill above a village called Drumnadrochit. It looks out over Loch Ness.'

'A lovely countryside, a bit haunted — I don't mean the Monster — but in a pleasant way. How did you find the croft?'

'I got some addresses from a solicitor type in Inverness

and went looking at the places.' He paused thoughtfully and added: 'I had the most extraordinary experience up there in the Highlands. Looking back on it, my going up there and everything connected with it was extraordinary. It all began about the beginning of December, one morning when the girl friend and I had a row. I don't know how the row started but I think I generated it because I suddenly felt that everything was phoney—me, the girl friend, the writing racket and the London shops all full of bright lights and tinsel, getting steamed up for a really commercial Christmas. I told Deb, the girl friend, to get the hell out and not come back and then I got drunk. Then I packed a bag, went to the bank and got some money and put myself on the night train for Inverness. I was terribly pleased with myself in a drunken-logical sort of way and as happy as a lark now because I was doing something so utterly reasonable. I explained it all to a bloke in the dining-car, about how my name was Maclean and how I had never been nearer to the Highlands, my native stamping-ground, than Arbroath and how here I was going to the Highlands and didn't he see how reasonable that was? He was a commercial traveller type and he obviously thought I was mad as well as drunk but I didn't give a damn. When I landed in Inverness the next morning, though, I was cold sober but I wasn't furious with myself as I usually am when I do these daft things. It was terrific weather up there, frosty, the air crystal clear, you could see for miles. I put up at a bed-and-breakfast place and every day I went out into the street and got on a bus, any bus but a different one each time and bought a ticket for as far as it was going and then I got off if I saw anything interesting and pottered about all day and got back to Inverness somehow when it got dark.'

'You are a born tramp, Roddy,' I told him.

'I suppose so. Anyway, one day I got on a bus and it went only a few miles to a ferry and then indicated that it didn't go any further but there was a ferryboat and I could see another bus waiting at the other side, so I got on to the boat.'

I was smiling, for there was only one ferry as near to Inverness as this but Roddy was not looking at me. He was staring past my shoulder at the Paradise valley but his intense dark eyes were not seeing this either, for he was totally immersed in his memory of that day when he crossed the Highland ferry.

'The bus took me about twenty miles,' he continued, 'right out to the east coast. For the last few miles, I was the only passenger and at last we came to the terminus, a little town called Achcraggan.'

'But Roddy —' I began, with joy flowering inside me, but he did not seem to hear me.

'It was a town of the dead,' he said. 'All the shops were shut, all the blinds drawn down, not even a dog to be seen in the street and all under this bright sun that was melting the hoar frost so that it ran in black streaks down the slates of the roofs. The bus disappeared. It was like a nightmare.'

I was staring at him now, a little frightened by his intense dark gaze, by what he was saying, by the distance that lay between us, as if he were at Achcraggan and I at Paradise with all the grey Atlantic rolling between. And, on another level of thought, I was aware that he was making no connection between me and Achcraggan and it seemed to me inconceivable that he should not know that I had been born at Reachfar, four miles from the little town. Surely, at some time, I myself or Dee Andrews or Twice or Edward or *some*body must have spoken of my home in Roddy's hearing? It did not seem possible that anyone who knew me should not also know that this place was part of me. Roddy went on speaking as if out of a hypnotic trance. 'The bus stopped in the middle of the town in front of a sort of town hall building and when it had gone away round a corner, I *felt* this silence and I got into a sort of panic. It was the silence of the dead of night but in the bright sunshine. Down at the end of the street, I could see the sea and with the idea that that would be *alive*, would be moving, I began to run but my feet made too much noise and I had to slow down and creep along in the shadows of the houses with the blinds drawn down, feeling I had no right to be in this place. By the time I got down to the sea and the little harbour, I was in a crawling cold sweat and made straight for a little pub called the Plough Inn that was opposite the pier. This place was all shut up too, with all the curtains drawn but there was a bell and a knocker and I banged and rang and banged and rang. It sounded obscene but I was so frightened that I went on doing it and at last a chap came and opened the door, an ordinary looking chap of about forty with a lame leg. I was never so glad to see anybody in my life. I asked him if I could have a beer. He didn't seem too keen but remarked that I was a stranger and asked me to come in. Then he locked the door again and I began to sweat some more but in the bar I managed to ask him what was going on in this place.

"It is the day of the funeral," he said. "Reachfar's funeral." I said what did he say the man's name was and he repeated it, spelled it out even, as if I were some sort of moron and then said that the man's name was Sandison but he was always known as Reachfar, the name of his farm.'

Roddy paused, still staring away across the vast distance and I sat rigidly silent. I did not, now, want him to be aware of me. I wanted to hear of my father's funeral exactly what Roddy, the stranger within the gates of Achcraggan, could tell of it. 'He talked a bit about this man,' he went on, 'and in the end I apologised for barging in but there was no bus back to Inverness until six in the evening so I asked if I could attend the funeral. He said: "We

224

will be glad to have you with us. Reachfar can't have too many to pay their respects to him." It was the most extraordinary thing. I felt as if I had suddenly been baptised into a family, the *human* family, when he said that.'

Momentarily, Roddy became conscious of me, glanced at my stiff face, noticed nothing amiss and, still caught up in what he had seen and felt, he looked away across the valley again.

'I had a sandwich lunch with this chap and his wife and he lent me a black tie and then we went out to go to this man Sandison's house. It was along a road near the shore but the three of us could get nowhere near it. This town where, an hour before there had not been a living soul in sight, was jammed with people and cars, so we just waited at the corner of the road until the hearse came by and all the cars and then we walked with the people at the back up this hill to the little churchyard.' He paused, took thought for a moment before he went on: 'Up to now, I had been sort of mesmerised, as if all this were a dream, where things were happening to me as if I had no will of my own but when the hearse stopped at the churchyard gates, my mind began to work and I got that feeling of significance that sometimes comes to one. I felt that this was something important, something I had to *know*, so I left the crowd, hopped over a fence, ran up crouching behind the churchyard wall and then hopped inside. I saw the open grave over on my left and although I felt in one way like a sacrilegious criminal, I felt in another way that this thing was more important than anything I could feel about *myself*. I ran through among the gravestones until I was behind a great tall obelisk thing higher up the slope than the grave. I saw the coffin carried straight up the path towards me. There was a wreath made of purple heather and white chrysanthemums on top of it. Coming first, carrying the coffin, were two old boys with white hair who

225

looked like brothers — they must have been over seventy but they were as straight as ramrods and I have never seen two men look so proud and so sad. That was it. Just proud and sad, all at once. Behind them were two younger men and the last two bearers were in their thirties, I should say. One of them was a tall spare chap with red-gold hair that flashed in the sun. I kept out of sight during the service at the graveside but I looked out when the coffin was lowered. I saw the two old white-haired chaps on either side of the younger one with the red hair and then I couldn't bear it any more. There was such a pain of acceptance, such an intensity of mourning among these people that I felt it was sacrilege that I, who had never known this man they were burying, should be there at all. I dodged round behind the church and ran for it, away up to the top of a cliff that looked out to the sea and stayed there till they had all gone home and then it got dark. I didn't go back to the pub even. I posted the bloke's tie back to him from Inverness. I felt like an outsider and yet, in a queer way, I was *in*. I found the yard where the bus was parked and went and sat in it until the driver and conductress came and we drove away back to Inverness, but while I sat in that bus in the dark, with this quiet little town all around, I decided that some place where people *felt* like this about people was the place for me. The next day, I didn't go for any bus ride. I started looking about for some little place that I could buy for Dad and me.' He looked down at me, smiling, before he became grave and said: 'Janet, what is the matter? You are crying?'

The tears were of gladness but of sadness too. The sadness was because, in 1952, Roddy had depended on me to help him because he had the perception to recognise my love of books, but he had not recognised the second 'because' which was that I had been reared in the house of Reachfar which respected and loved books more than any other one thing. How could he recognise this? But that he

226

could not was the sadness, the sadness of how little we can ever know of one another. The gladness of my tears I could explain to him by saying: 'I am glad you were there, Roddy. I am glad that you attended my father's funeral.'

W H E N, later, I thought how deep had been the impression made upon Roddy by the funeral of my father, an impression so deep that he spoke of it as if it had been a vision, it struck me that what he had experienced had been an extraordinary flowing together of truth and love. Roddy, true to his impulsive, enquiring wandering nature, true to his rebellion against what he called the 'phoney', had left London for Inverness in response to some call from the country of his ancestors and, as if in response to his gesture, that country had admitted him to its very heart by letting him witness its sorrow, the sorrow that the people of Achcraggan felt at the death of my father who had loved them and whom they had so deeply loved. I felt that, just over the horizon of my mind, like a sun about to rise, there was some perception of a hidden law of life, a law based on truth and love, if only it would come over the horizon and let itself be formulated in words, but it would not come.

What was definite, however, was the comfort I derived from what Roddy had seen and told me and, naturally, it led to an ease and intimacy between us which had not been there before. I felt that I was bound to Roddy by this experience of his which touched myself so closely and I listened with more sympathy to what he had to say about his parents because I had now more confidence in his perception than I had had before.

As the spring of the year went past, there seemed to be no doubt that Roddy's arrival had improved the situation as far as his father was concerned but I gathered that Roddy and his mother had many a violent exchange. However, the social face of Paradise was smooth which was something to the good, I supposed, and everything remained smooth until the beginning of May, when the yard boy from Olympus arrived at our door one morning, bearing a note from Marion that asked me to tea that afternoon. Olympus had always had a telephone and Guinea Corner had now had a telephone for some time and this gave the white envelope a curious significance. I retired with it to my writing-table and having opened and read it, I sat staring at the wall. It was the typical Paradise invitation of two lines whose like used to fly across the park by the dozen in what Sir Ian called 'the good old days' before we had telephones, but the longer I thought about it the more did it take on the character of a stick of high explosive. But the boy was waiting and every second of delay on my part seemed to take on significance too. I did not want to accept the invitation but to refuse it would be to make a definite move and it was suddenly borne in on me that Marion had always moved by never making definite moves and, although not making a definite move was not my natural way of handling a situation, I decided that, for once, I would try the method. I sat down and wrote, in a tone as polite as the tone of the note itself, my acceptance of an invitation to tea at Olympus that afternoon at three-thirty.

It was shortly after I had sent the boy back to Olympus that Edward arrived and, after a little general chat, he said: 'Roddy and I and some of the off-duty chaps are running down to the Bay this afternoon to have a swim at the Peak. Would you like to come and have a gossip with your chum Sashie?'

'Thank you, but no. I have another engagement. I have been bidden to tea at Olympus today.'

I had meant the announcement to have dramatic effect and it could not have better satisfied my intention. The muscles of Edward's face became taut with interest.

'Now, I wonder why?' he said after a moment.

'That is what I wonder too.'

'You have said you will go?'

'Of course.'

'There is some sort of move behind this but I can't think what.'

'When you use the word "move" you make me think of politics and chess and I am no good at either.'

Edward smiled. 'But there is one move you are extremely good at. It is called stone-walling. This afternoon, simply stone-wall with a dead pan through everything, keep your eyes and ears open and tell us later on what happened. And I think I shall change my plans. Roddy and the others can go to the Bay but I'll stay here and blow into Olympus around four-thirty to drive you home.'

'There is no need for that, Edward. I don't have to be rescued.'

'It isn't that. It will be a pleasure. Don't you realise I can't wait to hear what goes on?'

Shortly after Edward went away, Twice came home for lunch and when I told him of my tea engagement, he at once said: 'Now, I wonder why?'

'I thought you might come up with something original instead of the same old question,' I said. 'Has anything happened up at the office to cause her to make a move?'

'Nothing that I know of. Rob is better than he has been for a year and everything is going as merrily as a marriage bell. Look, Janet, you don't have to go to Olympus if you don't want to. Ring her up and make an excuse.'

'No. I won't do that. If all I am being told by Edward and Roddy is true, that woman has been making a fool of me for far too long. That fool over at Guinea Corner, she calls me, I gather. Well, we'll see.'

He looked at me sternly. 'Janet, this is no time to run the red flag of that temper of yours up to the masthead.

If Marion is the virago she is painted to be, you don't want to rouse her.'

'Are you suggesting that that — that hypocrite might be too much for me in a free fight? Look here, I have done many things with much effort to maintain the shining social face of Paradise but if Marion Maclean puts one foot wrong this afternoon, don't be surprised if you see the roof of Olympus come crashing down the hill into the gully.'

'Janet — '

'Twice, I am joking. Don't be absurd. I won't start anything unless she starts it first, I promise you. And don't go worrying.'

'Actually, I am not worrying,' he told me with a smile. 'I have every confidence that Marion will get the surprise of her life. You see, if you did not see her as she really was, which is seeming to be more and more the case, she certainly has never seen *you* as you really are. If she refers to you as that fool at Guinea Corner, she is making a big mistake. She probably thinks you can be bent exactly to her will. That is how you always behaved in relation to her until the time of the Roddy affair. She probably has no idea that she can bend you just about as easily as she could bend the factory smoke-stack with her bare hands. It is all rather interesting and it is a pity that one can't spectate. What will you wear for the big fight?'

Looking at him, I began to laugh and so did he but, after a moment, I said: 'I'll wear that green linen. Marion has never been able to wear green.'

'Lord, but women are dirty fighters,' he said.

After he had gone back to the office, when I took the green dress from the cupboard, I thought of this remark. But I did not want to fight in any fashion with Marion. To me, she was not important enough to fight with now, in the sense of being important in my own life and heart, that is. I come of a race renowned as fighters, it is true, but although Scottish Highlanders have fought as mercenaries, they did not fight as such with the conviction, selflessness and savagery which they brought to battle when they fought for the lost cause of Charles Stuart whom they loved. Marion might be a monster that Roddy saw as a threat to his father but, in relation to me and mine, this monster was no threat.

As I put my cigarette case and lighter into my handbag, I heard the car on the gravel down below and I rose and went downstairs. I no longer thought I 'knew' Marion Maclean, I no longer had anyone in my life called 'my friend Marion' and I was going out, dressed in my smartest green linen, cool, self-confident and interested to meet and have tea with a stranger.

When I stepped out of the car on the flat summit of Olympus hill, I felt for a moment that there had been a slip in the time-scale, that the last four years and their events had never happened, that the Roddy affair, Twice's illness, my father's death and the things I had been told about Marion were events in the future of which I had been vouchsafed a preview and that, in reality, this moment was in May of 1952, before the Roddy affair and not in May of 1956. Marion came down the steps to greet me, elegant and matronly in a grey dress printed with pink, looking so ordinary and unlike the dark shadow in my mind that, with a feeling of something like guilt, I turned away from her and looked out across the Paradise valley which lay spread around this eminence on which we stood like a vast and fabulous setting, constructed around a central gem by some master jeweller.

From here, the factory with its hundred and fifty feet of black smoke-stack and pattern of white buildings looked like diamonds accented with a spike of jet, the Great House with its roof of red cedar shingles showing among its green trees looked like a ruby surrounded by emeralds and on every side the cane fields stretched away like square pieces of jade in different greens and, here and there, a ploughed cane piece was a deep reddish gold. To look at it all, to see Guinea Corner which contained me and my life looking like a small greyish pearl down below, made me feel infinitesimally small but then it struck me that I had come up from below, that I was one of the little people who lived down there and looked up, as a rule, to this height. If I had lived up here for about forty years, looking down all the time, might not my mental attitude be different?

'It is such a long time since we had a chat, Janet,' Marion was saying.

I turned to her. 'It is a long time but the view from Olympus hasn't changed. It is as beautiful as ever.'

As I waved my hand at the curving sweep of the hilly horizon, her eyes swept round the valley, her glance seeming to sweep through the air above the cane fields and roof-tops as the beam of a searchlight sweeps, with a cold all-seeing arrogance and I felt a little tightening of something like fear inside my chest but her glance came back to my face, became urbane and kindly and turning, she walked towards the house and I followed her.

As always at Olympus, the household seemed to run on oiled wheels which was one of the things that had aroused my admiration for Marion. Under my management and in spite of my best endeavours and intentions, my household at Guinea Corner frequently got out of hand. My four servants had, like other people, personalities and temperaments of their own so that, at one time, my cook had suffered a severe attack of a new brand of religion imported from the United States, at another time, Clorinda my housemaid had suddenly produced a baby and Caleb, my yard boy, had often to be prevented from using a shaving lotion called 'Kiss of Conquest' which had a perfume so virulent that it pervaded the house from foundations to roof tree. No such things ever seemed to occur at Olympus. Today, a butler in black trousers, immaculate white monkey-jacket and black bow tie brought in the heavy silver tea tray and behind him came a trim maid with a second tray that held the sandwiches and cake.

I thought now that it had always seemed to me down the years that there existed a special different race of people who were born to be servants to Marion, a race quite different from the laughing, careless, lovable inefficient people who had arrived at Guinea Corner and had stayed there, in the teeth of my repeated resolutions to get rid of them and find others less exasperating, for all the years that Twice and I had been in the house. During those years, it now occurred to me, there had been many changes in the servants at Olympus for Marion would not tolerate, as I did, religion that interfered with the cooking, Clorinda's baby rolling round the garden or Caleb's 'Kiss of Conquest'. No wonder, I thought, Marion refers to me as 'that fool at Guinea Corner' for I am a person who gets fond of people and fondness and folly are closely linked. I was fond of Cookie, Clorinda and Caleb, religion, illegitimate baby, 'Kiss of Conquest' and all and I was fonder still of old Minna the laundress who, sometimes for weeks, did no laundry at all because she said 'me belly cuttin' me' which was revenge upon myself, I knew, for forcing her to have her appendix removed before she died of peritonitis.

During the last few years, I had thought of Marion mostly against the background of Guinea Corner where I had last seen her. I had forgotten about this veranda off the Olympus drawing-room. I had forgotten it willingly, probably, for it had always made me uneasy. I have no head for heights and this veranda was built round a corner of the house and extended to the edge of a sheer precipice. It was shaped like the prow of a ship, with a low table that held the tea tray in the V of the angle, behind which Marion sat with her back to the tall, open sash windows. There was no need for mosquito mesh at this height and this room held none of the wicker or canvas chairs that were normal veranda furniture. It was an annexe to the drawing-room, set about with chintz-covered chairs and the windows had long curtains, of pale gold silk backed with sun-proof linen, that lifted and swayed a little in the current of air that entered from the north and went out through the windows round the corner on the east.

I sat down in a chair against the wall of the house proper, opposite Marion and as far from the open windows as I could get, for even to think of that sheer drop beyond them made me feel giddy and as I looked about this place so familiar to me in the past, I looked about it in a different light. The view from these windows was one of the most celebrated in the island and many distinguished people had been brought to this house to see it. I noted Marion's large, red morocco-bound visitor's book, which usually lay in the hall, lying on one of the broad window-sills and remembered that, when Twice and I signed it, the first time we came here, we had been amused to put our names immediately under the names of royalty. On other window-sills there were other relics that had been found about the estate from time to time, among them a valuable silver bleeding cup found on the site of the old slave hospital and another thing which I had always disliked, a rod of mahogany about eighteen inches long, bound with brass rings, which was thought to be the handle of an early overseer's whip.

While we drank tea, Marion chatted equably of Madame, the cane crop, the European staff in the bungalows of the Compound and all the things which made up the afternoon tea talk of Paradise. Accepting a second cup and lighting a cigarette — Marion did not smoke — I glanced at my watch. It was nearly four o'clock. If Marion did not get to the subject which, whatever it might be, I was now certain underlay all this froth of chat, Edward would be 'blowing in' and her opportunity would be gone, I thought. I was now thoroughly curious and interested and wished that Edward were not coming at all and as if my anxiety that the thing she wanted to say should be said had communicated itself to Marion, she suddenly leaned forward and said: 'Janet, I suppose I should be grateful to you after all for conspiring with Roddy that time in 1952. He has been very successful in this strange way of life he has chosen and I am very pleased with him.'

'I am very glad, Marion,' I said.

'Indeed, I was as much annoyed with myself that day as I was with you,' she said, smiling in an indulgent way, as if to forgive herself for a small error she had made. 'I knew that you were having one of your little whirls with Roddy and I was cross with myself for not realising that of course he would go to you when he was in trouble with his father and myself.'

Had I not come to this house with every guard I possessed clamped in place on every side of my mind like the stone wall Edward had spoken about, at that phrase 'one of your little whirls' my mouth would have dropped open with astonishment and my fine china tea-cup would have gone smashing to the floor. As it was, I said with a smile: 'One of my little whirls? Marion, what can you mean?'

'Oh, come, Janet,' she said impatiently, 'I am a woman of the world. Your attitude to sex and marriage and such things is different from mine but we are all free agents. Your love affairs are no business of mine but you are foolish to imagine that nobody knows of them. Why, since the time of your affair with Don Candlesham, we have all accepted your — your gentlemen visitors and your peculiar friends.'

'My peculiar friends?'

She made another impatient movement and at once controlled herself. 'I suppose they seem quite normal to you but to the rest of us many of the people that you know seem rather odd. The Andrews and Denholm girls up at Mount Melody — that is hardly a normal relationship, is

236

it? And then there is your predilection for that effeminate Mr. de Marnay down at the Peak Hotel. But I am not being critical, Janet,' she assured me. 'We are all made differently and your friends and your love affairs are none of my business, although I did think it was wrong of you to come between Roddy and Dee Andrews at the time the engagement was broken. However, that is for the best, peculiar as she is. No. I am not being critical. Your way of life is entirely your own affair.'

'That is true,' I agreed solemnly.

I was concurring in her statement that my way of life was my own affair but I could not have been more astonished by her conception of what that way of life was. It was true that, in my early days in the island, I had carelessly danced too often with the local Lothario, Don Candlesham and had given rise to some scandal about him and myself but when the scandal had been brought to my notice, I had mended my ways and dismissed the whole matter from my mind. To Twice and me, the Candlesham affair had been something of a comic myth, something that had been created out of the empty air in the minds of the island and, when we laughed over it as a joke and put it behind us, I had deluded myself that everyone else, Marion included, was as satisfied as Twice and I were that the affair between Don and me was a myth and nothing more.

Marion, it was now emerging, had carried in her mind a picture of me as untrue and unreal as mine of her and with fascinated attention I listened to her proclaim her broad-minded understanding of the fact that someone as highly-sexed as I was and whose favourite lover's health had failed, must obviously do something with her spare time. To listen to her was, aurally, parallel with looking into one of these distorting mirrors that are found in fun fairs where the glass, with cold certainty, sends back an image of one as a creature with an enormous head, small body, short legs and tiny feet while all the time the brain knows that one has a thirty-six inch bust, takes the longest length of stocking and requires a five and a half shoe.

After Marion had dealt with her views of my love life, she rang to have the trays removed and when they had gone, she said: 'Rob is talking of retiring.'

'Oh?' I said but there was a click of certainty in my mind of 'Ah, this is it.'

'I consider it absolute nonsense. He is only a little over sixty and remarkably fit for his age. What are two people like us going to do pottering around some little house in a Scottish suburb?' She got up with an impatient jerk and looked out over the wide valley and, with the new knowledge of her that was flowing in upon me with every second, I thought that I could see in her face a transcendent love for what she saw and a determination never to lose it. 'He says that if he retires, Edward will come home here for good and manage the place,' she said impatiently, 'but that is a lot of rubbish. Edward Dulac is not interested in Paradise and never has been and he knows less than nothing about it.' There was no doubt that she hated Edward, I now knew, for I could hear the hatred grating in her voice as she spoke his name. 'And Madame can't last much longer. When she goes, Edward will be off back to London, taking his father with him. The Great House will be closed. That is what will happen.'

Still looking out of the window, she spoke rapidly, not addressing me specifically, but as if she could see in the sky over these wide lands her dream of the future, when the Great House in the centre of the valley would be a dead heart, the life gone from it and all Paradise would be under the control of Marion on the hill of Olympus.

With a tug that was almost visible, she detached herself from her dream, turned round and concentrated her smiling attention upon me as she said: 'I am fond of this place, having been here for a lifetime and, naturally, I should hate to see it degenerate as it will if Rob leaves it. Besides, I don't think he would be happy in retirement. He is too active still.' She paused and then, with the curiously calm charm that was characteristic of her when she asked one to do something for her, she said: 'You have a great deal of influence with Edward, Janet. He is never out of your house.' She gave me a smile as if to say: 'Oh, naughty-naughty but *I* understand' before going on: 'Get him to talk to Rob, dear and make him be sensible. I am sure you can do it in such a way that everything will be all right.'

In just this way, practically in these same light words even, had she at many times in the past asked me to invite Mrs. Murphy and Mrs. Cranston to tea and patch up the latest quarrel between them but that was in what Sir Ian called 'the good old days' and in this new day of May, 1956, I was a new Janet listening to a new Marion. In a voice which I tried to make as light and urbane as her own, I said: 'I am afraid you are mistaken, Marion. I have not the slightest influence with Edward.'

'Oh, come, Janet,' she said with laughing impatience, 'It is much too late in the day to make out that there is nothing between you. He has been writing to you every week for years — one hears these things. It is foolish of you to think that you can keep secrets here at Paradise, you know,' she told me with roguish indulgence.

'I can only repeat, Marion,' I said, admiring myself for how I was controlling my temper but having to admit that there was no question of control because I did not even feel angry, 'that I have no influence with Edward and I may tell you that even if I had, I would never dream of interfering between him and his estate manager.'

'Rob isn't *Edward's* manager!' she said on a sharp burst of temper and I knew the horrid satisfaction of having drawn first blood which made me more cool and wary than ever, but she controlled herself quickly and went on in a voice as cold as blue steel: 'I suppose that if Rob retires, you think that Twice will take his place?' All the coaxing charm and smiling indulgence were gone now. I made no reply. 'If you are thinking along those lines, Janet, you are even more foolish and light-minded than I thought. Twice, in his condition, could never take the responsibility of this place. You have to face facts, you know. It would kill him. He would die within months. He would be bound to. But maybe that is what you want?'

In this moment, I saw the monster, the monster that had shadowed Edward's bed when he lay ill with typhoid, looming darkly over my very own life and I thought of Edward's old nurse and her protecting love. I rose to my feet, facing Marion where she stood with her back to the window.

'But these are all lies, Marion,' I said. 'All this that you are saying and thinking is completely false.' I myself must have looked menacing for she backed away from me into a long gold silk curtain which the breeze wrapped round her like a long royal cloak. 'Edward Dulac will do as he pleases with Paradise and his staff but not for love of me.'

There was a spurt of gravel under the tyres of a car from the square beyond the front door and Marion made a quick angry movement as she looked through from the veranda to the windows of the drawing-room to see who this intruder might be. I knew that it was Edward arriving and did not take my eyes from her face. As she moved, sliding her back along the edge of the window-sill with that angry jerk, the slave-whip handle rolled to the tiled floor and, long ago rotted with worm, it disintegrated into a little ridge of powder and a few brass rings. Then the golden curtain slipped from her shoulders as she made a wild lunge outwards through the window.

'My book!' she shouted, whirling round on me like a savage beast. 'Oh, my book!'

Far beneath, there was a diminishing rustle of vegetation as the heavy morocco-bound visitors' book made its way down through the tangle of bush to the bottom of the impenetrable jungle in the gully below.

'I am sorry about your book, Marion,' I said, 'but I have to go now. Here is Edward to take me home.'

'No hurry, Janet, if you're not ready,' said Edward in a breezy way that was very unlike him and was a very poor piece of acting.

'But I am quite ready. I saw Twice's car go home across the park a moment ago.'

When I was a child, it was impressed on me that self-control was one of the most admirable virtues but now I was appalled at the power of Marion's control. In that moment when the book fell from the window, she had been the stark embodiment of hatred and savage rage, but as Edward stepped on to the veranda, a mask dropped over her face and body, turning her into a smiling placid matron who had spent a pleasant hour with a friend. She came out to the car with us, waving as we drove away, as we left her standing there on the square of gravel with all Paradise spread around and beneath her.

'What happened?' Edward asked as we rounded the second corkscrew corner of the precipitous drive.

'Wait till we get back to Guinea Corner,' I told him. 'I am all in a muddle.'

When I was home, however, Twice recognised my state for what it was, which was shock and it was only after I had had some brandy and had walked about the familiar room that held my writing-table and my books that I could become coherent. I then recounted to them what had happened, but leaving out the horrifying moment at the end when Marion spoke of Twice, saying: 'He would die within months. He would be bound to. But maybe that is what you want?' I ended my recital on the lightly spoken words: 'She seemed to think I was trying to persuade you Edward to retire Rob and make you boss of Paradise, Twice.' But although it was possible to convey the meaning of what

Marion had said, I did not even try to describe Marion and the emanation of cold evil that came from her on that high veranda and when I had finished my account, Twice began to laugh and said: 'The woman must be mad! Edward, can you honestly see Janet as this sort of *femme fatale*?'

To laugh seemed to me to be the best way to get through this discussion, to get it over, done with and buried in the past for I did not want Twice to know, ever, the cold horror I had known that afternoon.

'You two may not see me as a Serpent of old Nile,' I said mock-huffily, 'but Marion always will. It saddens her, I think, that all men are wax in my hands and I am too stupid to profit by my powers. She probably thinks she would be an empress by now if she had been endowed with my fatal attraction in addition to the brains she's got.' I stopped fooling, shivered and said gravely: 'The frightening thing about all this is that Marion and I have known one another for about seven years now and down these years we have learned absolutely nothing about one another. We don't see people as they really are at all. We make them into reflections of ourselves in different circumstances. The egotism of it is terrifying. I saw Marion as myself, married to the manager of Paradise and the mother of seven sons. If I had been in that position, I would have wanted to be a good wife and mother, an efficient chatelaine of an important house and a general help to Madame and I saw Marion like that.'

'By that theory,' Edward pointed out, 'if Marion had been Twice's wife, she would have been having affairs right, left and centre, including with the young man who was engaged to the girl who was staying with her.'

I did, indeed, believe that Marion, in my position, would have behaved in something of this way but I did not say so and we were all silent for a little while until Twice said: 'Look here, Marion must know that Janet and you and I are sitting here giggling about all this, Edward. Mustn't she be feeling a bit of a fool?'

Edward frowned. He knew more of the real Marion than Twice did. 'I think it is possible' he said, 'that she can think that Janet hasn't said a word to you or me about what happened this afternoon any more than she, Marion, will say a word to Rob.'

Twice was frowning gravely now and, not liking this, I said, clowning again: 'You don't get the point of all this at all, Twice. Marion doesn't merely think — she *knows* — that I have come straight back here to go on with my low-down carry-on with Edward while you are in the bath, so that *you* will end up by ousting Rob from Paradise.'

'Janet!' Twice protested and we all began to laugh again.

I had not attempted to tell Twice and Edward of that moment when the whip-handle fell and disintegrated on the floor, when the cloak of curtain slipped from Marion's shoulders and the book went out of the window down into the gully but, the next day, when I recalled these things, I began to see Marion in a less horrific light. There was no doubt that she had always been an ambitious woman, it seemed, but it also seemed to me that Paradise and the island were partly responsible for what she was now. She had been only about twenty years old when she came to this place and I, who was nearly forty when I came, had fought a long hard struggle against the distorting enchantment that the island could exercise over the mind of a white woman. The seed of this overweening ambition may have been in Marion and also the seed of the lust to possess as she had tried to possess her children, as Roddy had said she wanted utterly to possess Rob, but the island had contributed the atmosphere in which this ambition and lust could grow to their present monstrous flowering. Marion was the victim not only of herself, but also of the history of her race in the island.

I said nothing of this to Twice, Edward or Roddy however. There was no point. To Roddy, I did not speak of the afternoon at Olympus at all and with Twice and Edward I tried to keep the interview on the plane of a joke, which was not difficult.

It is a matter of social history that, not very long ago, the lunatics caged in Bedlam were regarded as comic entertainment to be visited by ladies and gentlemen on Sunday afternoons and it is part of the human tragedy that all forms of mania have in them an element of the comic which offers an easy escape from darker thought for those who consider themselves sane. During the days that followed my visit to Olympus, this escape factor was operative between Twice, Edward and me so that when Edward came round in the forenoons, he would greet me with: 'Come, my love and influence me a little' while Twice, arriving home, would say: 'Well, has Edward been round for a little influence this moring?'

But when I was alone, the darker more puzzling thoughts would come crowding in and I would remember how Marion had catalogued what she called my 'peculiar friends'. When, in my early days in the island, I had made such a false estimate of the character of Marion, I had made the mistake of putting myself in her position and had made my estimate not by studying Marion as an individual but by seeing Janet Alexander in the situation of Marion Maclean. Marion, in her turn, had made as false an estimate of myself but she had arrived at her mistake by a different route. She had not studied me as an individual either but as a unit of society and she made her estimate of me in accordance with what she believed to be my behaviour in society. She saw me as the erstwhile mistress of Don Candlesham and her son Roddy, as the friend of the 'Andrews and Denholm girls up at Mount Melody — that is hardly a normal relationship, is it? And then there is your predilection for that effeminate Mr. de

244

Marnay —' And Marion now saw me as the mistress of Edward.

It occurred to me now that society was both Marion's battleground and her weapon in her pursuit of power and that it was probable that she looked upon everyone in social terms, as pawns to be moved this way or that in her pursuit of what she desired. Are any of us, I began to ask myself, capable of seeing people clearly as individuals in their own right and not as wish-fulfilments of oneself as I saw Marion or as social pawns as Marion saw me or as slightly inferior beings constantly in need of one's help and interference as Madame sees everybody? Is there no real communication between people at all? Can none of us ever see what another person is a person like?'

'Sir Ian is a person something like my father,' I thought at this point and, at once, came the confident answering thought: 'I really knew what my father was like because I loved him. And I love Sir Ian quite a bit too. Physical love may be blind but the love that really matters is very clear-sighted. I saw Marion as a projection of myself because I loved myself more than I loved Marion. Love thine enemies. Does this mean that, if I had been capable of love for Marion I would have seen right away what she was a person like? But I *have* seen *now* what she is a person like!' With my brain whirling and buzzing, I stared at the wall as the thought formed like a faint dawn on a far horizon: 'And I believe that, in spite of everything, I love her more truly than I hate her!'

On the plane of everyday life, however, there remained what I inwardly called Marion's 'addiction' to Paradise, for this place seemed to have her in a drug-like grip and, with anxiety more than anger or fear, I would wonder what she might do next to attain her ends, but May turned into June and nothing happened. I saw her car come out of and go into the Olympus drive as it had always done, she did her forenoon duty to Madame at the Great House while I did the afternoons as we had been doing for months, Rob went daily to the office and was no longer drinking and Roddy and Edward, the best of friends, went down to St. Jago Bay to play tennis or swim or dance when their short working day was over.

ON a Saturday afternoon early in June, Twice and Sir Ian drove down to St. Jago Bay. As a rule, I also went on this outing, which we called the 'hair-cut run', going to visit Sashie at the Peak Hotel while the men were in the barber-shop but this day was very hot and I decided to stay at home. Also, I was once more involved with the life and times of Jean Robertson and was looking forward to a long luxurious afternoon, for Twice had brought a message that Marion was going to the Great House that day. She had, of late, been spending more and more time with Madame and I was a little suspicious about her activities in that quarter in regard to myself but I did not worry unduly about this because I did not believe that she could do much harm.

Just after four, when Clorinda had brought a pot of tea to me in the spare bedroom, I heard her climb the stairs again.

'Boss Maclean, him downstairs, ma'am.'

'*Boss* Maclean, Clorinda?'

'Yes, ma'am.'

'All right. I'll be right down. Take this tray away, Clorinda and bring tea for two of us, please.'

As soon as I stepped on to the veranda, I saw that Rob had been drinking but he did not look angry as he had looked the last time I had seen him against this back-ground. He looked uncertain and tentative, in a strangely childlike way, like an innocent teddy-bear who was aware that people were cross with him.

'Hello, Rob,' I said. 'You are not on the hair-cut run?'

'No.' He regarded me with drunken solemnity. 'Came to apologise.' The words that he spoke were not fluffed in any way but he uttered as few as possible, as if speaking in verbal shorthand. 'Should have come long ago,' he said looking at the floor but suddenly he looked up at me from under his eyelids in a way that reminded me of his lovable youngest son, Sandy. 'Didn't like to, though.' Clorinda came with the tea tray and put it down on the table.

'Sit down, Rob,' I said. 'Tea? Or would you rather have a drink?'

He shook his head from side to side. 'No drink. Came to apologise for calling you bitch.'

'That was a long time ago and all over and done with. Sit down and have some tea and a sandwich.'

He sank into a chair like a large toy gone limp and said: 'Thanks. Soon sober up. Had one too many round at the Club. Can't drink nowadays. Too tired.'

He looked very pathetic sitting there, so very big and bulky, yet contriving to give an impression of worn-out weakness. I wondered what I was going to do with him, wishing vainly that someone, anyone, would come to help me out.

'Came to apologise,' he repeated after he had drunk a little tea. 'Very sorry about that night. Very sorry indeed.'

'That's all right, Rob. Let's say no more about it.'

'Must say more. Grateful to you for helping Roddy. All due to you Roddy is where he is.'

'Nonsense! Roddy is a brilliant boy who would have got there anyhow.'

'No.' The big head shook from side to side. 'Couldn't have got there without help. Like me. Can't get there without help.'

'Where is Roddy this afternoon?'

'Swimming gala. Been away all last two days. Haven't seen him. Home at six on Saturday. Saturday today. I'll stay here till six?' he asked pathetically.

'Of course, Rob, if you like. Shall I telephone then at Olympus to tell Roddy you are here?'

'Yes. Tell butler. Marion's at Great House. Not home till dinner.'

I went to the telephone and when I came back Rob had emptied his teacup and was munching dutifully at a sandwich, like a sad bear who was trying very hard to do what he was told. I refilled the cup and put it down beside his chair.

'You like Roddy?' he asked suddenly.

'Yes, I do very much.'

'Got seven boys. Don't know any of them. All away at school. All in the nursery. Then all at school. Know Roddy though. Know him now.' He drank some tea and took another sandwich. 'You and Roddy never had affair,' he stated suddenly and positively, then added anxiously: 'not really?' while he looked at me out of solemn round eyes.

'Certainly not, Rob,' I said firmly. 'Twice and all other considerations apart, I am old enough to be Roddy's mother.'

'So you are,' he agreed with grave satisfaction before he added mysteriously: 'Knew you could help me.' He ruminated over his sandwich for a moment. 'Nice fellow, Twice,' he said then, 'but wouldn't stand any nonsense even from Edward.'

I said nothing, my slow wits failing to catch the processes of his mind and he looked at me out of hurt eyes, as if he had asked for help which I was failing to give.

'What sort of nonsense?' I asked.

'Nonsense with wife.'

At last I understood. 'No,' I agreed. 'Twice is not the sort to stand any nonsense with his wife, even from Edward' and I had a hysterical desire to laugh but Rob nodded his head very gravely, sighed deeply and said: 'Had things wrong for a bit. Getting straighter now. Taking a lot of important decisions.' For a fleeting moment, his face had the old self-important, executive-power-in-sugar-and-rum look but it lapsed back into the look of the bewildered teddy-bear before he said: 'Want to retire. Home to Scotland. Roddy got house. Small house. No servants. *Will* retire —' His head nodded, the remains of his sandwich slipped from his fingers to the floor. The rough head with the rough sandy-silver hair fell forward on to the thick freckled forearm on the table and there was a deep snore as Rob laid down his burden and went to sleep.

After a moment or two, I put a cushion on the back of the chair and, exerting all my considerable strength, I lifted the huge sagging shoulders until the head rested against it. Then I fetched a stool and lifted the heavy legs and feet on to that. More than ever now, with the eyes closed in the dark sunken sockets in the closely freckled face, with the big hands curled into loose blunt fists and the big feet with the toes upwards in the broad brown shoes, did he look like some huge toy bear that a giant child had abandoned here in the heat of the tropical afternoon. I took the tea tray to the kitchen, fetched my needlework and came back to sit beside him while my heart cried tears of pity. Roddy, I felt, had underestimated his father's need of him and I was angry that he had abandoned him for the two days of the swimming gala.

I threw the needlework down, went to the telephone, called the Peak Hotel where the gala was being held and asked Sashie to find Roddy and in a moment I was saying: 'Roddy, come up here as soon as you can. Your father is with me. He was drunk but he is asleep now and he needs you.'

'I'll be there right away. Sorry, Janet,' Roddy said and the line went dead.

It was thirteen miles of twisting precipitous road up the gorge of a river from the Peak Hotel to Paradise but in less than half an hour, Roddy came up the steps.

'Come in here,' I said and led him into the drawing-room.

'What happened?'

I told him how Rob had suddenly arrived, but Roddy said: 'Start at the beginning and try to tell me everything he said, Janet.'

'Why?'

'Oh, please!'

'All right. Sit down.' As accurately as I could, I told him everything that Rob had said ' — and then he suddenly announced: "Want to retire . . . *Will* retire" and then he fell asleep.'

'He *said* that? He actually said "will retire"?'

'Yes, Roddy. Yes, he did.'

He jumped up, caught me by the upper arms and so much vibrant joy emanated from his grip that it made me shake.

'God, Janet, I've won!'

He let me go and began to pace up and down the room as if he were bursting with energy that had to be released.

'He kept on saying that he wished he *could* come with me to Scotland but no. He couldn't leave Mother and she wanted to stay here. Oh, Janet!'

'But Roddy, he wasn't sober when he said it. When he wakes up he may be quite different.'

'No, he won't. Not now. Before, when he was drunk he was even more adamant about staying. Got to stay. Can't have Olympus without me. Got to stay. Married to your mother, love her, can't leave her.'

As Roddy imitated the drunken shorthand, I was struck anew by his resemblance to his father.

'No. It is going to be all right and, Janet, thank you for looking after him for me.'

'Oh rot!' I said in Rob's own words. 'I didn't do anything.'

There was a window screened with mosquito mesh which

looked from the drawing-room to the veranda where Rob slept and we sat there, talking in low voices, watching him.

'He looks so completely exhausted,' I said.

Roddy nodded. 'He probably had no sleep at all last night. Her energy is devilish. I should never have gone away but I thought she was beginning to calm down. She has been different this last week, or she *was* but it was probably only a lull. She is really a bit mad.'

I was glad that Rob began to stir at that moment. 'Your father, Roddy. Go out to him. If you want me, I'll be upstairs but if he is embarrassed or anything at being here, just slip away. Do what you think best, Roddy.'

Sitting in my bedroom, I heard the murmur of their voices down below and then I heard Roddy call Clorinda and ask her if they could have coffee and sandwiches. It was about a quarter of an hour after that that I heard Roddy call my name and I went downstairs.

They were standing side by side, the tray with the coffee in front of them, looking like an older and a younger edition of the same man.

'I want to apologise, Janet,' Rob said, 'to apologise for calling you a bitch years ago and for coming here drunk today.'

'Say no more about any of it, Rob. Sit down and have your coffee, both of you.'

I sat down myself, lit a cigarette and smiled at them.

'Roddy tells me that I have already told you my plans,' Rob said with that upward look that reminded me of Sandy. 'It is time I retired. The sun is setting on the sugar barons anyway and Edward and Twice will get along nicely.' There was a touch of the old bombastic patronising manner here but I felt that I knew the real Rob now and recognised it for camouflage. It was difficult to believe that, a little more than an hour ago, he had been so drunk that he could hardly speak and that even that robust physique had such remarkable powers of recovery.

'Roddy is buying a cottage up in your part of the world,' he told me, 'a quiet place where he can get on with his writing and where I can get a bit of fishing and shooting and so on. And we will be keeping the house in St. Andrews. Marion will be there mostly to be within reach of young Sandy at school in Edinburgh and Dan and James at the university and they can all join Roddy and me in the holidays.'

'It all sounds perfect,' I said, 'provided you come out to visit us here sometimes.'

'We might do that too.'

When Twice, Sir Ian and Edward drove in, the three of us were still sitting there, drinking beer and chatting as if Rob's retirement after a lifetime at Paradise were the most ordinary event in the world.

'Hello one and all,' said Twice who, I could see, had already been apprised, along with Sir Ian, of my telephone call to Roddy.

'I have been spending the afternoon with your missis, Twice,' Rob said, entirely master of the situation. 'In fact, I have been thoroughly unbusinesslike and unorthodox altogether.' He rose to his feet and faced Sir Ian. 'I want to tell you, sir, that I intend to retire and go home to Scotland at the end of this Crop, if that is in order' and having made this formal announcement, he sat down and set about his glass of beer again.

'Gad, me boy, I'm delighted! Delighted! No, dammit, that's not what I mean. Glad to see ye end your days here if ye want, me boy, but I know you'd rather finish up in the old country. Well, this splendid news! Dammit, that's not what I mean either. Edward, why don't ye *say* somethin'?'

When Roddy and his father went home to Olympus at dinner time, I expected thunderbolts to come hurtling down but nothing of the sort happened. The peace of evening descended over the valley, unbroken except for the hum of the factory at its centre.

As day followed day, as the sudden sun came up in the morning and set as suddenly in the evening, it was difficult to believe in the reality of my encounter with Marion at Olympus or of Rob's drunken arrival at Guinea Corner. The island cast its strange light over everything, swept everything into the past with its quick tempo, so that these stark moments when Marion and Rob had appeared to me in their reality were hidden away, as the site of a settlement burned out by lightning could be overtaken and lost in the quick-growing bush in a matter of a month.

I did not see Roddy for a few days after that evening when he took his father home but when he did come round to see me, it was on a day of pouring rain and when he took off the light mackintosh he was wearing, the first thing I noticed was a long, deep red scratch that ran from the elbow to the wrist of his left arm.

'What in the world have you done to your arm?' I asked, with some horrible but unclear picture of Marion in my mind.

'Caught it on a thorn in Dead Man's Gulch,' he said.

'Dead Man's Gulch?'

'That gully to the north-east of Olympus. We always called it Dead Man's Gulch when we were kids. I was trying to hack my way in there, to see if I could find Mother's visitors' book. It went out of the veranda window.'

'What a pity,' I said. 'Did you find it?'

'No. All I found was a skeleton — a dog, I think.' He looked out at the rain. 'We have never retrieved anything that went down there and the book is hopeless now. This rain has really put paid to it.'

'I am sorry. I know your mother valued it.'

'She did but, as she said today, it wouldn't have the same interest back in Scotland. It belonged to Olympus and

Paradise, really.' He frowned at me. 'Janet, something has happened to Mother all of a sudden. She has grown old inside a few days.'

'This is a thing that happens, Roddy. I suddenly became aware one day that my grandmother had grown old and the same thing happened to Sir Ian with Madame.'

He shook his head. 'This is more than just age. Last Saturday, when Dad and I went home from here, I was ready to do battle to the death but there was no battle. When Dad said he was going home to Scotland, she just said: All right, Rob, and went away up to her room. When she came down the next day, she was like someone getting up for the first time after a long illness. There is something pathetic about her, as if she had lost everything, even herself and she doesn't care. That is why I've spent all these last days looking for that book but she doesn't care about that either any more.'

It struck me that Roddy, although he had recognised clearly Marion's possessiveness towards himself, his brothers and his father, might never have recognised how she felt about Olympus and Paradise.

'Roddy,' I said, 'It is going to be a horrible wrench for your mother to leave this place. She loves it passionately.'

'She *loved* it,' he said, 'but not any more. I think that is what is the matter with her. She loved this place as if it were all hers and now it has broken away from her like me and Number Four and the kid. But with this place it is worse. Number Four and the kid and I will always be partly hers but this place has broken away completely.' He got up, went close to the window screen and, looking across the park and up to Olympus which was hidden with the curtain of rain, he spoke with his back to me. 'This is a very untriumphant victory I have had, Janet. For nearly all my life, I have wanted to break Mother's grip. Well, it is broken but now that it is — Christ,' — his voice became violent — 'I find that I love her in a way that wrings my

255

very heart!' He made a sound like a sob and turned round to face me. 'Janet, you are a woman and you know her better than any other woman. What can I do to help her? I'll never forgive myself if —'

'Roddy,' I broke in, 'you have said some monstrous things to me about your mother and I have thought some monstrous things about her too, but there is a factor that neither of us has taken into account and that is this terrible island. This is not white man's country, Roddy and especially it isn't white woman's country. It has taken me a long time to find this out and I only found it out and faced it because I had to, because Twice and I *have* to live here.'

'Go on. Explain a bit more.'

'White people have committed dreadful sins here and this place takes a terrible and subtle revenge. To live in it as a white woman and retain some identity, you have to turn into an old phoney like Madame or assert yourself in a wild distorted way like your mother or stand still, as I was forced to do when Twice got ill and admit that these white men's sins were committed and that you bear the guilt for them. When you do this, the guilt disappears but, Roddy, it is terribly hard to do it. I think your mother is going through some process of this sort now. She doesn't know she is going through it or what is happening to her. She is lost, as you said. But when she gets back to Scotland, she will find her real self. She has begun to find it already. That is why you have discovered that you love her, I think.'

'How long have you felt like this about St. Jago, Janet?' he asked.

'It is only recently that I have been able to identify and formulate this thing but I felt from the start that the island was my enemy. But it isn't. The enmity was in myself, a by-product of my guilt about the past, about our lavish white way of life here, about a thousand other things. But with me it took a long time to get at the truth because all the lies about doing good and bearing the white man's burden were so much more palatable. For your mother, I think the truth has come as a sudden shock and she hasn't yet recognised it as the truth, even. It is something she has to accept, Roddy. The island has broken away from her. It is breaking away from all of us whites except the — ' I almost ground my teeth in the effort to speak the next words ' — the sick, like Twice, who are no longer able to govern. But this is a shock for your mother and very hard for her.'

'I believe you are right about this,' he said quietly. 'I hate this place myself. It was fine when we were kids, the riding, the swimming and everything but that time of the jamboree in 1952, God, I hated it. In fact, I think that was a large part of the reason for the jamboree. It was a fight between me and something that I couldn't even recognise.'

'That's it,' I agreed. 'It affected me very much as it affected you. I made a perfect ass of myself in my early days here. But in a practical way, I think it would help your mother if your father spoke to her about the economic drift of the island, pointed out to her these moves towards the nationalisation of the sugar industry and so on. She is not the woman to relish being here to see Paradise Factory entirely in the control of a coloured staff.'

'By Heaven, she isn't!'

'And Roddy, there is another thing,' I went on, looking at the floor while I could feel a flush spreading over my neck and face, 'I told you I made an ass of myself when I first came out here. There was an island-wide scandal about me and Don Candlesham at one time.'

'So I have heard.'

'It was all lies. I danced with him too often, that was all but I think your mother believes we had an *affaire*.'

His dark eyes gleamed at me. 'You are sure it was all lies?'

This made me angry. 'Yes. As surely as the *affaire* your mother believes I had with *you* is all lies!'

'With me?'

'Yes. Your mother believes I came between Dee and you.'

'For Pete's sweet sake! She must be —'

'Listen, Roddy, this is another aspect of the distorting light of the island. I believe it will help your mother if you make clear to her that you never had any *affaire* with any old hen like me. She is faced with this very difficult adjustment and every bit of truth that can be brought home to her will help, I think.'

I do not know by what means Marion became adjusted to her final departure from Paradise but adjusted she seemed to become. She sent me a polite note, asking me if I would take over the afternoons at the Great House again because ' — with this removal to Scotland on my hands, you will appreciate that I have a great deal to do —' and I sent back a note equally polite, informing her that I would certainly attend on Madame and ' — please let me know if there is any other way I can be of help —' They were very barren and sad, these notes, the last of hundreds that yard boys had carried across the park.

The cropping season ended on the nineteenth of June but by this time Rob had already retired and had sent in, too, his resignations to all his federations and committees. He still left Olympus at about eight in the morning as he had always done in the Out-of-Crop periods but he was now spending his time at the Great House with Madame, while Sir Ian, Edward and Twice ran the estate.

In the afternoons, when I went round, Rob would still be there and there was something very lovable in his care and gentleness with the little old blind lady who was still full of energy and wanted to walk about her garden. Once, long ago in the course of an argument, Rob had used the phrase: 'My employer right or wrong' and I saw now that this had been the real Rob, with his simple code of loyalty. Marion, in the past, might have entertained ideas worse than disloyal to the Dulac family but Rob, fundamentally, had not. And this was the real Rob who attended on Madame.

She did not like to be held by the arm or, indeed, treated in any way as if she were blind but would stump along the paths and across the grass on her firm little feet, with her big green parasol held above her head. Rob would walk behind her, his head and shoulders showing above the spread parasol, his big hands held out, one on either side of her but not touching her, like a big teddy-bear guarding one of those little fat dolls with lead bases that always seem to be in danger of falling over but never actually fall.

'Now, Rob,' Madame's voice would say, as firmly dictatorial as ever, 'this is the croton hedge, isn't it?'

'Yes, Madame.'

'Has it been properly watered?'

'Yes, Madame.'

And on they would go, the stiff, stumpy little doll and the big soft guardian bear coming behind.

Madame had always been fond of her garden, much of which she had designed and had had laid out under her own supervision in her younger days and she was still prepared to invade the adjoining parkland, fence in and cultivate a new piece of ground and plant another grove of trees. Her memory picture of her garden was so complete that, although she could no longer see, she would say things like: 'If we planted a dozen eucalyptus trees there behind the hibiscus border, their trunks would look very pretty against the bush on the hills at Riverhead from the south veranda in a year or two.' For Madame, the garden was a dimension where time and space could be welded together.

It was now our routine that Twice, on his way to the office after lunch, would drop me at the Great House where Rob, having lunched at Olympus, would join Madame and

259

me. Madame would tell me what she required me to do: 'Write to Cousin Emmie, dear and tell her I have no intention of dying as yet and to mind her own business' or 'Write to that shop in the Bay, dear and tell them to come and remove those sheets they sent me at once. I have never handled poorer linen in my life' and then she would take her parasol from the corner and go away round the garden with Rob. Then, about four o'clock, Twice, Sir Ian and Edward, having finished at the office, would come to join us for tea and, quite often at this time, Roddy would join us too.

It was an idyllic few weeks, with everyone at peace with one another, all the tensions of the past years gone and a great air of satisfaction emanated from Rob who was leaving behind him a huge monument to his own lifetime in this island in the form of the newly reconstructed factory which, as Twice said, was a gladness to the heart of any engineer.

One very hot afternoon in the middle of July, a few days before Rob, Marion and Roddy were to leave for Scotland, we were all having tea behind the creeper screen of the north veranda when Madame said: 'When you come back to visit us, Rob, you will see a change. We intend to remove that old summer house over there.' Unerringly, she pointed to the little round building in the north-east corner of the lawn. 'Edward tells me there are chi-chi worms in its woodwork and in any case he has never liked it.'

'I think it looks like a corner of a suburban garden in Morningside or somewhere and a bit silly,' Edward said, pushing some crumbs round his plate. 'You don't want summer houses here. What we need in weather like this is an igloo or two.'

'By jove, jolly good!' said Sir Ian. 'Quite right, me boy. Let's have it down an' plant a tree or two in its place. Can shove it down with the bulldozer.'

Like his mother, Sir Ian always liked to be doing some-

260

thing but, unlike his mother, he seemed to derive more pleasure from the preparatory destructive side of construction rather than from the construction itself and of all the equipment on Paradise, Sir Ian liked best the bulldozer. With Big Sammy, the negro who drove it, Sir Ian would arrange for the uprooting of an area of jungly bush, the cutting of a new road or the removal of a minor mountain at any time and then, when he, Sammy and the bulldozer had done their worst, they would move off to something else and leave someone else to finish the work of construction. 'If you're all finished eatin',' he said now, 'let's go over there an' have a look at it.'

In a body, Rob shepherding Madame under her parasol, we went over to the little building in the corner. It was circular, with a round tree trunk in the centre, supporting the shingled roof, while wooden posts supported the roof's circumference and these posts were linked together to a height of about three feet from the ground with trellis woodwork. It was a little like, on a small scale, those bandstands that are found in public parks, but its floor was rotten and when Rob banged one of the wooden posts with his fist, a shower of powdery dust flew from it.

'Chi-chi all right,' he said.

While Sir Ian and Madame argued about how they could bring the bulldozer in without damaging the lawns, while Rob tried to convince Sir Ian that the bulldozer would not be necessary at all, I stood beside Twice, Edward and Roddy, nearer to the entrance to the summer house and looked across the wide lawn at the pillared colonnade of the north veranda while I remembered that it was in this little place that Edward had found his dead sister's teddy-bear long ago. I could understand his desire to be rid of the summer house even although he knew the memory of it would always remain with him. The worms of time are not destroyed by the destruction of a structure in space.

Suddenly, I felt the rotten boards vibrate beneath my

feet as if an express train were passing underneath and at once recognised the tremor of earthquake which, felt once, can never be forgotten but, before I could move, I was thrown violently aside against Twice, Edward and Roddy, while Madame and Sir Ian were thrown equally violently the other way as Rob, breathing stertorously with terror, charged like a panic-stricken ox for the comparative safety of the open lawn.

'Outside! Quick!' barked the voice of Sir Ian as he supported his mother and propelled her forward but Twice, Edward, Roddy and I had been thrown sprawling to the rotten floor which was crazily tilted and rocking under us, so that we could not get to our feet.

'Crawl, Janet, but get out!' Twice said behind me and I began to creep on hands and knees towards the grass of the lawn. Ahead of me, I could see Rob running blindly along a path until, across the heaving distraught world, there came a voice, sharp as a pistol shot, cracking across the rumble of the tortured earth the one word: 'Rob!'

Transfixed on hands and knees on the grass, I watched Marion, who had not been with us at tea, emerge from the colonnade of the veranda. She was wearing one of the long straight dresses she always wore in the evenings, a deep crimson dress which stood out against the grey stone of the old house. She looked very tall and she seemed to dominate the whole demented world as Rob stopped dead, in obedience to the voice he had obeyed for so long. In a split second, he changed from a panic-stricken beast into a courageous man as he shouted: 'Come into the open, Marion!' and began to run towards her, his arms held out, ready to drag her to safety.

They were within three yards of one another, she radiating courage and pride in her control of herself and Rob, when the whole vast bulk of the Great House heaved against the sky, stayed tilted for what seemed to be a long moment and then settled back on its foundations amid a clamour of splitting wood, falling masonry and breaking glass and, in a settling cloud of dust, I saw Rob and Marion sprawled on the grass, he on his back, she face downwards. Across their bodies lay one of the great stone pillars of the colonnade.

The earth settled back into a dreadful stillness as Sir Ian left Madame, whom I supported while he went across the grass to the crimson dress and the pale suit under the dark grey pillar. He bent over them for a moment and then took off his white drill coat and covered the two heads with it.

'Janet,' said Madame's voice, less dictatorial than usual but still firm. 'Where has Ian gone? Are all of you all right?'

'Yes. Everybody is all right, Madame,' I said. 'Sir Ian is over there with our friends the Macleans.'

PRINTED IN GREAT BRITAIN BY
NORTHUMBERLAND PRESS LIMITED
GATESHEAD